Lemon In The Basket

CHARLOTTE ARMSTRONG

Lemon In The Basket

Coward-McCann, Inc.
New York

Lemon In The Basket

1

THE under sides of the trees were awash in light. All around the terrace fat yellow candles burned under hurricane hoods, sending off subtle fumes to charm the insects away. Within the magic circle, the summer table was daintily spread; white-webbed chairs were comfortable and cool. The eight people gathered here seemed, on the whole (one of them was thinking), very handsome and civilized, and worthy of paradise.

They were just the family. Here sat a man and his wife, their three grown sons, and the women those sons had married. All here were Tylers, and here were all the adult Tylers. Tamsen, the youngest and newest of them, who had been Mrs. Duncan Tyler for just a half a year and was not quite yet completely out from under the halo of her wedding veil, was seeing the scene and sensing the whole with an especial delight. She thought it was none the less paradise for being a private one.

When the Judge, her father-in-law, rose to his feet, down at the other end of the table, she corrected herself. *He* isn't handsome at all, she thought fondly, but he is certainly civilized. William Rufus Tyler (who was not, in fact, a judge anymore) had a tall gangly set of bones. His high sloping shoulders were silhouetted against the glimmers on the surface of the pool that lay behind him, in the dark reaches of the lawn. His white brows, raised to ask for attention, were bushy crescents on his long, tanned forehead. The candlelight was kind to the small half-moons of flesh that sagged under his steady eyes and were complemented by the double roll that made a ruff under his long chin. It's a clown face, thought Tamsen (the artist), and yet it isn't comical, nor is it pathetic. It is . . . she captured the word she wanted . . . endearing!

The Judge was going to be ceremonious. He lifted his goblet of light wine. "As you may know," he began, his deep voice easy on the quiet air, "there is being built in the new Cultural Center a theatre of some magnificence. It is my pleasure to announce its newly chosen name. Shall we toast the Maggie Mitchel Theatre? Or shall we toast Maggie?"

It was the family custom to applaud in a mere pitter-patter, not loud, and in a quick light rhythm. All, applauding, now turned their faces toward the woman at the other end of the table, who was their mother, and yet also, in her own right, "the incomparable Maggie Mitchel," and still a first lady of the American Theatre, although she had not been on a stage for years. Tamsen, pattering away with the rest, watched Maggie take her bow with her own skillful perfection. Just right, thought Tamsen approvingly. None of this phony surprise, or "Who, little me?" stuff. Nor does she look too solemn, as if she took herself awfully awfully seriously. Now, how does she do that?

Maggie Mitchel Tyler was not a large woman. Her flesh was still compact. She was not a pretty woman and never had been, but she could be beautiful, if she liked, or anything else, for that matter. It isn't a rubber face, thought Tamsen, who had long ago despaired of ever painting Maggie's portrait. Still, Maggie knew how to manage so that one saw through her face to whatever she wished to seem to be thinking. Tamsen felt close to her mother-in-law. She and Maggie were in the arts and although they were not in the same art, there was a communication.

"Good going, Maggie," said her oldest son. His wife, Phil-

* 8

lida, said gaily, "For whom else should they name a theatre of some magnificence?"

"Wonderful," said the middle son. And Lurlene, his wife, cried, "Say, Maggie, that's really something!"

Tamsen put in shy congratulations and her husband, the youngest brother, said, "Well, well, after all those fragile little old light bulbs, now they are going to carve your name in stone, eh, Maggie?"

Maggie's voice was, of course, a trained instrument. "In marble, on my gilded monument," she said with a touch of mischievous ham.

They drank. As the Judge sat down, Maggie, who was sixty-two years old, contrived to flow to her feet and Tamsen, aware that all arts have their techniques, thought to herself, Now, how does she do that?

"However," said Maggie, "since we are just the family—" (This was a code phrase and meant "don't tell.") "I think we must put a make-believe past behind and drink to something real and present. There is soon to be created a Fact Finding Committee, to which the President of the United States intends to appoint, and appoint to act as the head of it, a certain William Rufus Tyler. Your father, children, will be shooting trouble of some size." Maggie, lifting her glass, looked the very image of the proud little wife who does not really know what her husband does in his business, but is sure that he does it very well.

The pattering exploded. Duncan said, "Facts, eh? Otherwise, knocking stubborn heads together in a fatherly sort of way?" In spite of his teasing tone, his broad and boyish face was radiating pride.

What a pair they are, thought Tamsen, as proud as he. Maggie and the Judge! She thought of something and wailed, suddenly, "You'll be going away to Washington?"

"Washington!" said Lurlene with a startled look, as if the connection President-Washington had not occurred to her.

9   *

"Ah, well," said the Judge, "Maggie is being a bit premature. Shall we say that the real-and-present fact is, I seem to be considered for the job?"

"But just to be considered," said Rufus, the middle son, rather solemnly, "that's quite an honor, Dad."

"Indeed it is," said the Judge agreeably.

"And quite a chore, if P.S. he gets the job," said Phillida in her blithe way. "But speaking of honors . . ."

Now Phillida Tyler was up. She was a tall slim woman, always perfectly groomed, with a handsome face that seemed to reflect a composure in her mind. She and Maggie, Tamsen thought, are both strong, or even dominating, women, but so differently. Maggie dominates because if she speaks or even just walks into a room, you are compelled to look and listen, and there is no telling how she does that. But Phillida operates behind the scenes. People do what she wants them to do, but she doesn't especially want them to realize that. It is just that what she wants them to do is the best way to accomplish some good purpose. Tamsen and Phillida had, so far, gone their separate ways, but with great goodwill and admiration for each other, just the same.

"Shall we drink to Dr. Mitchel Tyler," said Phillida in her clear crisp voice, "for whom a new operating theatre and a whole floor of the new wing has been designated to provide a place where he is to perform and to teach a certain surgical technique already known in the trade as the 'Mitchel Tyler'?" She wound up, not even breathless.

Before the applause was over, the oldest Tyler son stood up, as Tamsen had somehow known he would. She began to squirm with the knowledge that here, at this not unusual family Sunday night supper, on the east terrace of the Tyler house in San Marino, California, on a night in August—this time, something was ballooning. An inflation was happening. Eight people on a summer evening, and among them Maggie, whom the world called "incomparable," and the Judge, whom the world trusted, and Dr. Mitchel Tyler, who had earned a clearing of his path toward an even greater contribution to the world. All these honors and more to come! More to come!

"If we are naming names," the Doctor began a little gruffly. Mitchel Tyler was not short, but burly enough to seem shorter than his five-eleven. His face, however, was thin, and his dark good looks gave a sharp effect as if he were destined to become wizened, and not too long hence. Tamsen thought he was both clever and brave and she was glad he was alive.

"In the wall of the new Free Clinic for Handicapped Children, in the Valley," Phillida's husband said, "there will be embedded a bronze plaque in praise of Phillida Tyler."

"Who worked very hard." The Judge beamed, when another spate of lively pattering was fading.

"Who scampered about, raising the money," said Phillida impudently. "Oh, it's money that counts, you know."

"My goodness," said Lurlene weakly, "everybody's names!"

Rufus said, "Well, well, well. A Tyler here and a . . ."

But Tamsen had gathered up her nerve. Was it her turn? Yes, surely it was her turn now. So she stood up, abruptly, before she should lose the nerve to do this, a small girl, small and dainty enough to seem more of a child than she was, at twenty-five. She had pinned her long dark hair up neatly for this occasion. Her brilliant eyes were looking frightened in her small face, and her voice, ordinarily soft and low, came out too shrilly, she feared, in her effort to give it volume. And too soon, because it cut off Rufus.

"Shall we toast—" she said. "Oh, excuse me, Rufus."

". . . and a Tyler there," he finished lamely and fell silent.

"Shall we toast," Tamsen began again, "Professor Duncan Tyler, who has just been appointed Vice-Chancellor of the University's newest branch, to take office in January?"

She did not feel that she had put her news as gracefully as the others had known how to do, so she sat down in a fluster. But the pitter-patter of hands rose even faster than before. This

✳

made five out of the eight of them that the world was choosing to honor.

Duncan was saying, "And don't tell me I'm too young, because that's *been* said."

"Of course you are not too young," said Maggie, making her face as fierce as a terrier's. "What has age to do with it?"

"Never fear," said Phillida. "That job will age him rapidly."

"Good going, Duncan," said the Doctor. "That is, if you want administration."

Duncan was answering that he did, and why, when Tamsen saw that Lurlene was licking her lips and looking lost. "Vice-Chancellor just means . . . well . . . sub-chief," she said because Lurlene might not know. Tamsen felt a rustling beside her. She turned. "Wouldn't you say, Rufus?" It was her impulse to defer to him, in some way.

Duncan, abandoning his own exchanges, said, "Hey, if it weren't for old Rufus, pretty soon all Chiefs, no Indians."

Tamsen winced, but to her surprise Rufus answered cheerfully. "Fewer Indians every day. How about some more firewater for us Indians, eh Tamsen?"

Tamsen dimpled at such wit. "Oh, us Indians . . ."

But there was Duncan, getting to his feet.

"Oh, gosh," said Tamsen under her breath. (More to come!) She felt Maggie's quick supporting sympathy as Maggie caught her shyness and then threw it away from them both. Even Maggie was riding above herself, as they all were. Or almost all.

"You may conclude," said Duncan in his most pompous lecturer's voice, that he didn't often use on Sundays, "that we must be, on the whole, Very Important People, with our names, one way or another, on their way into the history books. But if you would care to consider immortality, you must include the fact that *Tamsen* Tyler has been hung!"

"Oh, *ho!*" cried Maggie, as her fingers pattered.

"Is that so?" beamed the Judge, inane with pleasure.

"What do you mean, *hung?*" said Lurlene in a startled whine.

"Twenty by twenty-five inches, County Art Museum," said Duncan, losing his professorial pose and looking even younger than his chronological age of thirty-three. "One oil." He thumped down.

"Darned good going, Tamsen." That was Mitch.

Phillida leaned around to cry, "I'm hanging on to my original."

Lurlene said, "But I mean, *hung?*"

"Oh, well, that's a phrase they use in the trade. It means . . ." Duncan began to translate, kindly.

Maggie picked up her little bell to summon Hilde and the shrimp, because the balloon had gone as far as it could go.

But Tamsen, who was often painfully aware of all kinds of invisible currents, heard herself saying to Rufus Tyler, the second son, "I'm just lucky, you know. It doesn't take too many brains . . ." She caught her breath and hurtled on. "I only keep thinking how my children are going to be proud. It is a wonderful thing just to belong to this family!"

Then she felt like dying. She had sinned; she had gushed.

He didn't answer. His large eyes rolled in her direction, briefly. He was thirty-four years old and already getting bald. His round face pinched in at the bottom to a tiny pointed chin. His full lips did not move.

But Lurlene was gushing responsively, "It certainly is, Tamsen. It's like too much! I mean, how lucky can you—"

Maggie came in, stepping on that line, to say, "Oh, did I tell you? I've had another letter from Alice Foster."

The talk must turn. It was right and proper for the family to toast those of its members who had been honored by the world. Six out of eight! And to enjoy all this in concert. It was right and proper to celebrate each individual's achievement, but the Tylers were not going into a long session of group-gloating. Not if Maggie could help it, and she could. Tamsen approved.

Maggie had chosen a good subject to swing this supper party into another mood and another pattern. Tamsen knew all about it.

Duncan said quickly, "No. What's up in Alalaf?"

But Tamsen, for a moment, only half listened. She was ashamed to have been so clumsy, that her intention to be tactful had come out insultingly. She didn't look at Rufus but watched Lurlene, who had presentably fine features, a straight nose, well-shaped eyes, a good enough chin, but whose hairdo had emerged from some neighborhood beauty parlor and bore no relation to her face or personality; whose body, at not much more than thirty, was slopping into too many soft lumps, whose dress was too busy with too many printed flowers and did not flatter the body, whose basically well-cut mouth was wearing a twist on it.

Or was Tamsen imagining? When that mouth opened too wide to receive too large a portion of the shrimp cocktail, and a bright fingernail came up to push in a spot of sauce at the mouth's corner, Tamsen turned her eyes. She had never yet had what could be called a conversation with Lurlene Tyler. Tamsen sighed and began to pay attention.

"Alice, and Jaylia too, are really pushing, and it doesn't do to underestimate them, you know," Maggie was saying. She became a Sybil, with veils. "It will happen."

"What will happen?" Rufus rumbled.

Tamsen knew what Maggie expected to happen. A little boy's life was going to be saved. And the fact that this little boy was a member of the royal family in a small country all the way around at the other side of the earth would make no difference. The Tylers would save him. Tamsen couldn't help agreeing with Maggie. She felt a mystic certainty, tonight, that anything the Tylers proposed to achieve would be achieved. Oh, there were complications and impediments, but no matter.

*   14

This Alice Foster was a woman with whom Maggie had gone to school, long ago. A person, Tamsen had gathered, of some force, who, although seldom seen, had retained, as some people know how to do, her status as an old chum, forever loyal. Alice Foster's only daughter had married a young man who was a prince, and however small his country, he was not only rightfully a prince, he had been in line to become a king.

But this prince was dead; he had been killed in a spectacular accident. His little boy was now, by several strokes of fate, in line to become the King of Alalaf, when the present monarch, the child's aging grandfather, should die, or as soon thereafter as the boy himself came of age.

The question was, would he ever become of age? The little prince had a very serious physical defect. Tamsen knew it had to do, somehow, with his heart. This condition was expected to end his life fairly soon unless something drastic was done about it.

It was Duncan who had discovered all this and involved the Tylers. A year ago, Duncan the college professor had, through the channels of the old friendship between Maggie and Alice Foster, been invited to the tiny kingdom of Alalaf, to visit the new university which the fabulously wealthy old king had very recently caused to be built in his capital city. Once there, Duncan had, of course, been entertained at the Palace and he had then heard about the child's condition. So Duncan had bethought himself of his brother, Dr. Mitchel Tyler, and his brother's position as the pioneering expert in the field.

At last, at last, and only last week, the Doctor had been invited and implored to come and see. So Mitch had flown to Alalaf, where in conference with the doctors there and by what examination he was able to make on the spot, he had held out hope that if the boy could be brought to Mitch in his own hospital, where he had his batteries of instruments and aides, perhaps he could, as Mitch would put it, be patched up.

This was progress, of a sort, but evidently there were still complications and impediments. Had the Prince been a Pauper, Tamsen surmised rather sadly, he would have come long ago.

"Will it be awkward for you, Judge, if this happens?" Phillida was saying with bright devotion. She must mean politically.

"No, no," said the Judge. "Can't have that."

"Why?" said Rufus. "What's awkward?" His gaze rolled all around the table and lit on Tamsen, finally.

He seemed to have no clue to the conversation, so Tamsen said, "You all go so fast." She made herself plaintive. "Some of us can't follow. Please?"

"Well, you see, honey . . ." Duncan began to explain. He knew that Tamsen could follow well enough and was only trying to be kind. But Duncan was with her. Tamsen sent him her sparkling gratitude. "There's politics," said Duncan flatly. "The old King of Alalaf—Al Asad is the handiest of his names —is not only notoriously anti-American as well as, parenthetically, anti-everybody else, but it so happens that Americans are pretty anti-him at the moment." Duncan couldn't help this racing along. "Ever since he clonked twenty-eight American professors into the hoosegow, according to his royal whim, last week."

"Oh," said Rufus, "that's right. I heard it on TV. I see what you mean."

Tamsen thought, No, he doesn't.

And to her shock, the Doctor said, "No, you don't, Rufus, old boy. Just sit tight."

Tamsen began to rephrase what Duncan had said, in her own mind. The King of Alalaf has just arrested twenty-eight Americans on suspicion of espionage, and Americans don't like that. Therefore, Alalaf is, at the moment, in the bad graces of the news-conscious people of this country. Therefore . . .

"That does make everything a *little* awkward," said Maggie and glided smoothly on. "Did you meet those men at the University there, Duncan?"

"I met some of them, sure," Duncan said. "Just a bunch of poor-but-honest schoolteachers trying to get along. Not obviously the cloaks-and-daggers that Al Asad, may his tribe increase, is saying *he* thinks they are. Of course, who knows?"

"Our government is going to have something to say about this, eh, Dad?" said Rufus smugly. "I'll bet there's pressure on."

Rufus wants to play inside-dopester, thought Tamsen as she watched the Judge move his shoulders, refusing to state what inside dope he might really know. The Judge had long ago given up the bench, so Duncan had told her, for the exercise of his native talent, which was that of negotiation, the art of the possible, or compromise. How could he give a wise and seasoned answer to a question so . . . well . . . inept?

Phillida answered. "Now, Rufus," she chided in her gay and somewhat mocking manner, "you've seen by the papers that we are definitely frowning." Then she said to the Judge, "But if Mitch is going to take the knife to the heir to the throne and the idol of the people of Alalaf, and Maggie takes his mama in, here, as I suppose she will—"

"Of course," said Maggie. "Of course, for pity's sake! Alice Foster's daughter!"

"But won't that seem pro-Alalaf, at a bad time?"

"No, no," said the Judge. "I can blame my wife's compassionate heart and transcend politics, can't I?"

"Pretty All-American, that," said Duncan. "And All-American Mitch had better be right, I suppose."

Tamsen, who was following all this, knew that not everyone here could follow and it made her uneasy.

"If Mitch says that the poor little fellow will benefit from the operation, then, of course, he will," proclaimed Maggie.

"I say he *may*," Mitch corrected. "I'll need him here a while before I add up the chances."

"Say . . . uh . . . whose little fellow is this?" said Lurlene. "Excuse me, but you all go so fast." Her eyes thanked Tamsen for the phrase and Tamsen smiled at her.

17 *

"The King's grandson," said Duncan kindly. "The heir to the throne. Eleven years old. Saiph, they call him. Al Saiph, I guess it should be."

"For heaven's sakes," said Lurlene rather skeptically.

"So you'd better be right, eh, Mitch?" Rufus repeated Duncan's phrase just as if it were new and his own. But he was catching on, now.

"You're damned right, I'd better be right," said the Doctor genially, "and, if asked, I expect to be. Cool it, everybody."

"And thanks a lot, Duncan," said Phillida merrily, "for getting Mitch into this one."

"Who, me?" drawled Duncan. "Can I help it if I'm there to look at the old King's shiny new University and Alice Foster and the Princess Jaylia happen to mention that the boy's got this trouble and I just happen to have a brother who happens to be the only wizard extant? Taken them a year to do anything about it," he grumbled. He was a man who liked things done.

"Alice Foster's grandson is not my patient yet," said Mitch.

"Wait a minute," Rufus said. "Alice Foster's grandson has got to be half American. So how can the King be anti-American?"

"The child is a quarter, Rufus," said Maggie gently. "Alice married an Australian. Not long after we were graduated, her daddy gave her a trip around the world. Do you know," Maggie squinted thoughtfully, "Alice may have gone into orbit. She seems to have been going around the world ever since."

"Great old gal, Alice," said Duncan comfortably.

"So what's-her-name, the daughter . . ." Rufus was poor at names.

"Jaylia," Maggie prompted.

"Isn't she the one who married the Playboy Prince, what's-his-name?"

"Aljedi was his nickname," the Judge prompted.

"A prince of what?" said Lurlene. Tamsen opened her mouth

to tell her but Rufus kept right on. Lurlene was just too far behind.

"Wait a minute," Rufus said, "I remember now. He was the Playboy Prince who burned himself up in a racing car crash. Right?"

"Yes, he did," said Maggie gravely.

"Kind of thoughtless, wasn't that?" said Rufus. He smacked his lips together.

"Of whom?" said the Judge politely.

"Of what's-his-name, the Playboy Prince." Rufus made a grand gesture and Tamsen had to duck it slightly. "This boy's father. I mean, here is a chap supposed to get to be the king of this piddling little country. Shouldn't he have thought of that before he goes in for one of the most dangerous sports in the world? Especially when all he's got to leave behind him is the one child, didn't you say, Maggie?"

"Just the one," said Maggie quietly.

"And *he's* not quite right, at that," said Rufus sharply.

Tamsen noticed that Lurlene was watching her own husband with a certain resentful sullenness, as if he had begun to speak in a foreign tongue, and she was not only lost but spited.

"No, no," Rufus went on, as if the silence around the table had disputed him, "there is such a thing as responsibility to the people. Why did this Playboy Prince have to see how fast he could drive a car? Pretty childish. Oil money, they've got, haven't they? But could he afford that?"

Rufus was sounding painfully righteous, but Tamsen said in her soft voice, "I certainly think you have a point, Rufus."

The Judge said, in an offhand way, "I believe the King had other sons."

"One killed in a plane," said Maggie, "and one in battle, and one who just seems to have died. But Aljedi was the favorite of the people and now they worship Saiph, so Alice says. Oh there *is* another heir, a nephew, you see."

19   *

"Ah, lots of characters in that country who wouldn't mind being King, either," said Duncan easily. "Don't worry about it, Rufus."

Maggie rang her little bell.

"Yes," said Rufus loudly, "but wouldn't you think this particular idiot prince ought to have watched himself?" He turned his gaze on Tamsen suddenly. "What do you say, Chief?"

"I don't know," she said feebly.

"There may be," cut in Maggie, "a great many things we don't know. But we do seem to know that Alice Foster's grandson (and the King's, too, of course)"—Maggie dismissed kings as mere in-laws—"cannot live very long unless an operation can help him."

"Well, that's too bad, naturally," said Rufus.

The Judge had switched Phillida to the subject of her pet projects for helping unfortunate children, when Rufus burst out again.

"But if that's so," he said, as if no one had spoken since his own last sentence, "it looks to me as if Mitch has got a little pressure. What if Mitch says to the King, what's-his-name, 'See here, I am an American and I'm not going to operate on your grandson until you let those Americans out of your jail.' How about that?" Rufus was looking crafty. He expected praise.

"How about that?" said his brother Mitch mildly.

"Well, the way their minds work . . ."

"The trouble is, Rufus, old boy," said Duncan, "I spent a whole week there, a year ago, and even I, child-prodigy that I am, haven't the slightest idea how their minds work."

"I was there a whole day, a week ago," Mitch said, "and I haven't, either."

"But you couldn't," gasped Tamsen belatedly, "use a little boy's life . . ." For pressure, her thought continued, or for blackmail!

"Kinda mess up the image of the All-American compassionate heart. Wouldn't it, just?" drawled Duncan, sending her his smile.

"Oh, say," said Lurlene, who by now had caught on to some of this, "you got to have reverence for life. I mean, don't you? Especially of a little child."

And now Rufus was staring at his wife.

"Sure you do, Lurlene." Duncan was the quickest and he broke the somewhat wincing silence. "Mitch is in that business, so don't you worry." Then he called the table's length, "Hey, Maggie, are you going to have to dedicate this dump they are naming after you?"

"Alas," said Maggie, becoming tragically weary of her worldly burdens, "since I am still alive, I suppose I must."

"Oh go on," said Phillida. "You'll love every minute—"

"Of course," said Maggie in the same tragic tones, "and so will my audience."

Her children laughed at her, as (Tamsen realized) they had been intended to do.

2

TAMSEN, savoring the evening behind them, was quiet for the first part of their long ride home. Duncan Tyler didn't mind, having other things to think about. He was startled when she said, suddenly, "What does your brother Rufus feel?"

"Feel? Oh, you mean because he didn't have his pretty wreath to lay on the family altar?" Duncan had expected this to come up, sooner or later. "Don't worry, honey. He's used to that."

"Is he? Really?"

Duncan knew the shades of her soft voice. He began to declaim, being free to do so with his bride of six months, and enjoying the exercise of the privilege. "Rufus," he said, "was born what you might call one of the untalented of this world. Nice fellow, but . . . well . . . not bright. The folks had to squeak him through the easiest college courses known to man, and it took persistence, believe me. On their part, that is. Well, of course, he couldn't qualify for medical. Dad did wangle him into law school, where he washed out almost immediately. In fact, I think it *was* immediately. As for science, since I doubt he realizes firmly that two and two will usually make four—"

"Oh, Duncan!"

"No, no," he said, wondering if she could have been hearing

meanness in what he thought of as his humorous vein. "Honey, an IQ is an IQ, rough measure though that may be. Everybody knows it's not his fault."

"But if it's not his fault . . ."

"Then nobody blames him," Duncan finished for her.

They were trundling through the western section of the city. Duncan was thinking it was hard for Tamsen to understand the family attitude. He must, he supposed, teach her.

"What *has* he done?" she asked in another moment.

"Well, Rufus thought he'd start at the bottom in industry and work up. Turned out it takes some yeasty kind of thing to rise, and he didn't have it. So he dropped that and thought he'd be a salesman and make a wad, which is respectable, you know. But there seemed to be some kind of self-starting energy involved there that he doesn't have, either. They lived with, or on, Lurlene's mother for years."

"He just keeps on failing?" Tamsen said, in mourning tones.

"Well, no. I think he's just stopped trying," said Duncan cheerfully. "After all, why should *he* pursue that will-o'-the-wisp, security, when he's got about as much of it as humans get. He's got the family. He's got some comfortable friends of his own, I presume. And of course, he's got Lurlene, and he *is* devoted to her. Well, she never has, and still doesn't, demand too much intellectual brilliance, would you say? So Rufus may be a whole lot happier than any of us miserable strivers."

"I don't think so," Tamsen said.

"My love, my little bleeding heart," said Duncan, "mind, when you empathize, that you allow for the fact that the other fellow isn't just like you."

"But he has to feel accepted," she said stubbornly.

"As what and by whom?" said Duncan, who had known that he must come bluntly to this, sooner or later. "Must he be accepted as what he isn't, by people pretending to be what they are not? Which is to say, as uninformed and unintelligent as he?"

"Oh, Duncan, that's cruel," she cried, bending forward in pain. "I think that's cruel!"

"We do, too," he said, deliberately misunderstanding her.

They went along silently for a while.

"Wait a minute. *You* didn't get fooled, did you?" Duncan asked her, suddenly.

"What?"

"You do realize, for instance, that Maggie knows she couldn't make it in the modern theatre? That the Judge is not licking his chops over this 'honor'? He gets asked to do what he still can do, but he is tired. As for Mitch, he hasn't even scratched the surface of what he intends to accomplish before he's through. And Phillida gave up her own career, years ago, to be a pretty darned good wife and mother. If she has energy left over and does these charity things, it's not *her* name she wants in bronze. And look at me, the bright young educator. Believe me, I am one who knows better than most how terrifyingly ignorant I really am. And I guess you don't consider yourself on top of the world of art, eh?"

"It bothers me to pieces," said Tamsen promptly, "that the one they chose to hang is not the one I like the best."

"All right," Duncan chuckled. "Granted, Rufus seems to have fallen into fast company. Also granted, it did seem on the sore-thumbish side tonight. But, as the Chinese used to say, 'No blame.' And we were not beating him down, for the fun of it. He's one of us."

They began the descent into the canyon, where they lived in a brown-shingled house of mad design that delighted them both for its charming unorthodoxy. Duncan parked the car where it must stand, beside Tamsen's Volkswagen, because there was no garage. He went around and took her out, into his arms.

"Do you and I," he said, into her sweet-scented hair, "make ourselves miserable because Mitch, our brother, has *his* marvelous skill to save that little foreign prince? Ah, no! Rejoice! Rejoice!"

"I do," Tamsen said into his shoulder. "I do."

Dr. Mitchel Tyler was a fast driver; he liked the freeways. Phillida said, as they sped the long way, in order to get home sooner, "Lurlene! Lurlene! How she does get herself up!" Phillida had begun life as a dress designer and now shuddered. "Has science discovered whether good taste is hereditary or environmental?"

"What Foundation has cared enough?" said her husband. "I don't know what the dickens Rufus is doing these days. Not making any money, I'd imagine."

"It doesn't take money," said Phillida, "to eschew orange roses on chiffon, *plus* rhinestones, for a Sunday night on the terrace."

The Doctor pursued his own thoughts. "I tried to find old Rufus something to do, but if he won't sink in his teeth or persevere . . ."

"No room in my business, either," she agreed. "Even a do-gooder has to be good at it." She, too, had once tried to find Rufus a job.

"Oh, he'll never be a charity case. The family sees to that."

"Maybe he's been overprivileged."

"Oh, come on." There was no such thing, in the Doctor's opinion.

"Of course, he early made his bed by marrying Lurlene when he was what . . . twenty?"

"No accounting for tastes." The Doctor grinned. "That's not been researched."

"It wasn't shotgun, either," mused Phillida, without malice. "Or where's the evidence?" (Rufus and Lurlene had no children.)

"Oh, Rufus is all right, I suppose." The Doctor turned his head. "When shall we go ahead and have our fourth, Phillida?"

"Whenever you have time, dear," said his wife cheerfully.

They swooped down into the underground garage and left

the car, and rode in a deep and comfortable silence up to their very modern and spacious apartment in one of the newest high-rise buildings in the City of Los Angeles.

"Is Rufus all right, William?" asked Maggie suddenly.

The Judge regarded her fondly, where she sat in negligee, cozily near, in the corner of his own huge bedroom where it was their habit to share a nightcap. "I should think so, Maggie darling. He didn't mention money."

"But then, I suppose in all the excitement we forgot to ask if he needed any." Maggie sighed and then said the opposite of what she was thinking. "What a perfect triumph of a Tyler evening."

He answered her thoughts. "Not everybody needs a career, Maggie darling. Nor would relish the bother of it."

"I wish he could find at least a hobby that . . . would engross him, you know?"

"Not the sort of thing that can be found *for* him."

"But oh, I wish I could have told them . . ."

The Judge, who was used to skipping along beside her, waited patiently to know where her thoughts had gone this time.

"I didn't much like hearing poor young Aljedi so unhappily misunderstood."

The Judge made the jump. "The Playboy Prince? Condemned under that cliché? It was a state secret, Maggie darling, and not ours to tell." The Judge thought that Rufus was not to blame, this time. Some secrets made for misunderstanding.

"Not even our state," Maggie agreed. "William, do you suppose he flirted, poor afflicted fellow, with that flaming death because he knew he hadn't long to live in any case?"

"I see that you suppose so," said the Judge, amused at Maggie's way of stating her answer as if it were the question. "Perhaps it was his hobby to risk a life that wasn't going anywhere."

"I would, too," she said darkly.

"Same defect the little boy has, wasn't it? Late diagnosis, and no known cure. I'd say that Mitch thinks there is a chance for the lad, in these latter days."

"It's if they can wiggle things around so that it can be 'politically wise' to send him to America and an American. Of all the idiocy!" Maggie's voice condemned politics. "Never mind," she said, as if it had been the Judge who had mentioned politics. "Alice Foster is a very strong-minded character."

"I had heard that the King of Alalaf was an Absolute Monarch," he teased her.

"Oh, there's always some woman modifying all that," said Maggie airily.

The house was one-story and, although newly painted, old-fashioned. It sat on an unhandy triangle of land, too near a commercial street. The most desirable thing about it was its postal address. It lay on the very fringe of Beverly Hills. Lurlene had been wild to have it, a year and a half ago.

Rufus let her out at the front. She used her key and put up the light in what she still thought of as the "front room." She stepped out of her shoes at once and padded through to open the back door for him. Then she took a can of beer out of the refrigerator, went back to the front room and sat down rather heavily in her upholstered rocking chair.

The front room was furnished well enough. She kept it scrupulously clean. None of the furniture was shabby. She usually felt the effect to be fine. But it's another world, she thought, remembering the terrace scene. Yah, if you have money . . .

She had her bra unhooked and was sitting there, with her stout legs apart, when Rufus came through, bearing a can of beer of his own. He sat down in his accustomed place, angled away from the cold fireplace toward the television set.

"Um, boy," said Lurlene, weary of trying to watch her speech all evening, "that Tamsen sure thinks she's pretty cute. I see she had her hair up, at least. How come a grown woman goes around most of the time with her hair hanging down her back?"

He didn't speak, but Lurlene somehow knew it was perfectly safe, tonight, to attack Tamsen. "What kind of stuff does she get 'hung'? Those fried-egg-looking messes, I suppose. I mean, who needs them? And listen," she continued, "how come Phillida has to go around getting money out of other people? Why don't she just give out some of her own? I guess your brother makes plenty, right?"

Sometimes, when she got off like this on the subject of his family, he'd start laughing and tell her to just relax. Sometimes, he'd look a little bit sad and tell her she didn't know them like he did. Tonight he didn't say anything.

"They sure are some bunch of high-flyers," she muttered. "Pretty fancy."

Rufus got up and turned on the TV. It was a talk program. The M.C. was wrangling with some inarticulate volunteer, and cruelly, for entertainment values, preventing the poor soul from making his point.

Lurlene didn't bother to try to follow the argument. She surmised, with some shrewdness, that Rufus didn't want to talk, and TV gave the sense of life and noise that relieved you of that responsibility whether you paid attention to the tube or not.

Lurlene herself couldn't help feeling low, or like gypped, or something. Every time they went to one of these family deals at Maggie's, Maggie always put on all that dog. Lurlene always went to a lot of trouble to gussy herself up, and usually left her house feeling some self-confidence. And then ended up by coming home with this lousy feeling that she had been off-base again.

What do I do? She was brooding, now. Didn't do one damn thing I shouldn't have. *I* was well-dressed. *I* was polite.

The man on TV was shouting, "And the criminal, he not only gets off, but *he's* the one who gets his name in the papers."

"What is your point, sir?" snapped the M.C. "If you've got a point, kindly come to it, unless it's on the top of your head."

"I'm only saying—"

"You're not saying anything, pardon me. Next questioner, please."

"They talk so damn fast," said Lurlene aloud. "Tamsen was right about that. You sure can't catch on to what the hell they're talking about. And *I* don't think that's very polite."

"Tamsen," said Rufus, in a funny way.

On the screen, the next questioner had begun to drone, entangling himself in so many clauses that all hope of a sentence was soon gone.

Lurlene said, gloomily, "Even *her* name's getting in the papers, I suppose. Um, boy, like I say . . . It don't mean that much," she added sourly. "So what is it, to get famous or something? So long as you lead a decent life and raise up some decent . . ." She stopped.

"Who needs fame?" Rufus rolled his eyes.

"What I mean!" Lurlene settled down to souring the grapes, pleased to think that he was with her. "You want your name in the papers, what the heck, all you got to do is go ahead, be a criminal, like the man just said."

"Steal a million dollars?" Rufus said, with a saucy quirk of his lips. "Blow off the Statue of Liberty's head?" He seemed to be pleased and relaxed by this fancy.

"Hey!" Lurlene admired his imagination. "Or you take a big gangster," she continued.

"Sell top secrets to the enemy?"

"Or even you get in death row," said Lurlene cheerily, "like who was this killer? In the headlines for twelve years, already? Some world." She sighed luxuriously over the sins of everybody else. "No place to raise a kid, I'm telling you. I'm just as glad."

Rufus got up and went into the bedroom. Lurlene pricked up her ears. In a moment, she heard the water running in the bathroom and she sagged.

29   ✱

But when he came back and threw himself down into his chair, she recognized a certain sulky sly look.

"Say, uh . . ." she began, "when you seen the doctor Friday, did *he* think it was so smart to keep on taking that stuff?"

"He doesn't think I'm smart," said Rufus. "He doesn't think I'm stupid." He spoke with a strange cheer.

Lurlene began to think it was time to butter him up a little. "Well, how can I blame you?" She sighed. "Tonight was pretty hard to take. Pretty tough."

"What was?" He was already going off into that limp state? Lurlene didn't like it too much and that was the truth.

"Oh, I mean the whole pack of them, boasting how smart *they* were. And not one of them willing to give you any 'in' on their rackets. Their own brother. They could give you a break, once in a while." She often complained for him. Sometimes, he listened.

This time he said, "No, no, I'm lucky."

"Huh?"

"Just to belong. Tamsen said so."

Lurlene snorted. "Maybe Tamsen will give you lessons, how to mess around with some gobs of paint. So you can be immortal, too."

"Get my name into the pages of history?" he said, dreamily.

Sometimes he lost her. Sometimes, he took on a voice just like the rest of them, and Lurlene got lost.

"Yah," she said. "Well," she got up, "you coming to bed?"

"No, no," said Rufus. "I'm going to sit here and contemplate immortal fame."

"Yah," she cried, suddenly furious with him. "You do that, why don't you?" Lurlene walked toward their bedroom on her aching feet. "Um, boy," she said viciously, "I thought I was smart, glomming on to a Tyler. But I sure got the lemon in the basket."

3

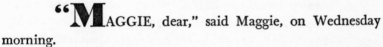

"**M**AGGIE, dear," said Maggie, on Wednesday morning.

She was reading her mail, aloud, as usual. The Judge always enjoyed hearing Maggie take on the personality of the writer. It tickled him, now, when her voice became slightly nasal and began to tumble over itself with dips and swoops of energy. He didn't have to be told that the letter was from Alice Foster.

"I'm about to tip you off to all the trouble you have let yourself in for. Our small package is being shipped, at last. Hooray!"

"Hooray!" piped Maggie on her own, for punctuation.

(The Judge put in no "hooray" but began a quiet bracing toward the immediate future.)

"It must come undercover," she continued to read. "Please ask William whether he knows ways-and-means to keep eager snoopers from noticing anything odd at your end? At this end, it is just going to be easier, all around, if nothing is known about what's going on until it *has* gone on and is successfully over."

(The Judge let notions of ways-and-means to keep the American press from noticing the arrival of a small foreign prince, and retinue, ripple across his mind.)

"It may be awkward," said Alice Foster in her letter. "We have had 'unrest' in Alalaf, you realize. These are fierce people.

31 ✳

With less luck, more blood might have been shed in the University riots recently. Just to give you some idea of the prevailing sentiments, you, my dear Maggie, by virtue of your citizenship alone, are not only an evil-minded infidel, but a fiendishly clever barbarian, with all modern improvements at your nasty fingertips. Your folks are quite capable of having used a racing course as a murder weapon. Oh, yes!"

"Oh, no!" said Maggie, as Maggie.

"Prejudice is prejudice," murmured the Judge, "whether pro or con, to or fro." (This affair was going to be awkward, all right, he thought, as had been said before.)

"So anxiety will be high, in high places," Maggie read, "without added tension of a populace in an uproar. So it may be impossible, but it is important, so please don't, if you can help it, let the newsmen in on this."

(If we can help it, thought the Judge soberly.)

"The mother has already written the Doctor and they will set the date. The plan is to get our party off so quietly that it won't be known, in the marketplace, that they have gone away at all. They will transfer to a commercial flight, traveling tourist. We hope that will make it possible for them to arrive without any bugles blowing there, either.

"I'll list for you who is coming. Six, in all. Mother and child, who will try to be inconspicuous. Inga, who looks after him, you know, is of Scandinavian descent and might as well have come from South Dakota. She's no problem and she'll be in the hospital with the patient. But there will be, alas, three of these Alalafian hawk-profiles along, as Western garb cannot disguise. At least two of them will be flashing their dark eyes suspiciously at all times. J's maid (her name is Zora) will come to you with J, and be useful, I hope. But the pair of young men, faithful watchdogs who were insisted upon by you-know-who, propose, I fear, to sleep at their master's feet, and heaven knows how they are to be coped with. The best I could do was to see that the chosen two understand and speak English.

"I beg of you, please try? If the hospital has a suite of some kind, that might be part of the answer. Perhaps William knows what else might be done, or whom to tell.

"Now, if it does get out, and I know it may, the difficulty will be . . . you know . . . difficult.

"But if the worst should happen, *difficulty* isn't the word. I think you will have to know" . . . uncannily, Maggie's voice gained speed and agitation with the handwriting . . . "that certain jailbirds, here, will find their 'trial' postponed until such time as the package comes home as good or better than new. This is in the bargain. No, I don't mean that. It is related.

"All right, I'll lay it on the line. I am afraid that, if the worst should happen . . . and oh, Maggie, pray it won't! . . . then these streets will be running with ravening wolves, and tidbits of the proper flavor may have to be thrown.

(The Judge interpreted, with a shock. She meant the twenty-eight poor-but-honest American professors!)

"I say may have to be. I say I am afraid. I may have become, unbeknownst to myself, a foolish old woman. But passions in the blood of the people, that some cool hand or other has been using for a handle, may get *out* of hand. As William, I think, would agree.

"Well, fear is fear, and no point living by that, do you think? What I believe in, of course, is the happy ending. Or I wouldn't be having anything to do with the plot, now would I?

"I am not coming. You understand. I stay where I am, in my apartment in the city, which, I daresay, has modern improvements, as for instance bugging. But I have my methods. So I'll spider it up and keep an eye on, from here. While there . . .

"Oh, Maggie, I know how much this puts on you and yours. I wish it needn't. I wish it were simpler. All devious and calculating and undercover as it has to try to be, it is still the shortest distance to our dearest hope. May he live! Toward which hope I trust your devotion, and thank God for it. As ever, your devoted, Alice."

33   ✳

Maggie read the last lines sharply and let the paper fall. She was not weeping, but the Judge patted her anyway. (It was a habit he had. He enjoyed it, and Maggie never seemed to mind.)

"Secrecy is very desirable," he said soothingly. "We can manage, or have a good try, eh? Let me see. No entertaining, or acquiring debt by being entertained, while Jaylia is with us. Humph. As soon as we know the day, I think I must come down with some ailment that keeps me close indoors, at home. You, of course, will refuse to leave my side."

"Why, I wouldn't think of it!" she said at once. "I'll cancel *everything*. People will simply have to understand."

"Meanwhile, I'll make a little list."

"Oh?"

"Alice is right about that. Sometimes the best way to keep a secret is to tell the right people, at the right time, all about it."

"You take care of that, then," said Maggie, becoming the executive. "Duncan must meet them at the plane, I think. Jaylia knows him, and he *is* so civilian."

"Yes."

"Jaylia and her maid will have the west wing. We can trust Sam and Hilde, of course."

"I think so," said the Judge, with his mind full of forebodings.

"If there was no such thing as trustworthy devotion in this ridiculous world," burst Maggie, speaking to his thoughts, "it couldn't operate *at all!*"

"No, of course it couldn't, Maggie darling," he agreed. "Still, since it does, in a fashion, there must be such a thing." On all sides, alas, he was thinking.

Maggie was often a mind-reader. "O.K. We'll gamble there is enough, on our side."

The Judge had seen through the ever-changing masks to the hard-core Maggie before. "Yes, sir-ma'am," he said.

So Maggie became, perversely, as totally female as could be, putting everything upside down and backwards. "It will be suit-

*   34

able," she decreed, "for you to have the gout, just like some old millionaire in a comic strip. Nobody will dare come near us, because you shall be so mean and cross and moody, and uncooperative, *and* stupid *and* selfish . . ."

The Judge blushed under these crude compliments, but there was no denying that he did enjoy them.

When he left her, finally, counting his blessings on one hand and his worries on the other, he went into his study, ticking off on his toes a name or two that, from the top, might cut publicity close to the root if that danger arose.

He did not care for Alice Foster's notion that there were hostages. Or rather, morsels kept on hand to appease. In the event a doctor lost a patient? (As if he willingly would!) Yet sillier things than this had happened in the world.

Say the boy died in the United States of America, as had his father before him. Say the people of Alalaf went into riot, blaming the King for having put their darling secretly into the power of the dog, which is to say, the hands of the evil and untrustworthy barbarian infidels. Say the King tossed them twenty-eight American "spies."

Would Ibn-Ibrahim-Abd-er-Rahman, the Servant of the Merciful One (otherwise known as Al Asad) do such a thing?

The Judge wondered why, since the possibility of this surgery had appeared when Duncan was in Alalaf a year ago, the old King had not in the meantime influenced his people toward a softer attitude, just in case. But who could know why not? Perhaps he could not.

Al Asad, fierce in independence, played on his small scale the east against the west, and on this balance kept his tiny state aloof from the pressures toward and from the U.A.R., as well. Which wasn't easy. Nor could it possibly last forever.

The Judge realized that he did not and could not know how that mind worked. Supposing that the King did do such a thing? Say he fed the professors to the wolves. Or, supposing his people took, or were allowed to take (and who could ever say which?), those prisoners by force? As in lynch? In either case, must not this country do somewhat more than frown?

The Judge winced. He knew very well that no sequence of events was totally predictable, but he thought it not a bad idea to nip the possibility of this particular sequence as early as possible. But not, he mused sadly, quite at the root. Mitch could not possibly refuse to try to patch that poor little heart, if non-political factors gave him hope of success. No, not any more than he could possibly will to fail.

None of us will do either, he said to himself.

Meanwhile, the Judge, lest Maggie read his mind one day, kept himself from verbalizing his strong suspicion that Alice Foster herself was (or believed that she was) to be held hostage in a foreign capital.

4

ON the following Tuesday, a little after noon, Lurlene finally found the house number, parked her car, inspected her makeup in the rearview mirror, drew on her gloves virtuously, and then found herself mincing across the short dooryard on redwood rounds, inspecting everything she saw with a sharp assessing eye. For heaven's sakes! The house was just an old shack covered with rusty-looking brown shingles, and it didn't have any property, either, practically jammed in down here at the bottom of the canyon, with a steep hill behind it.

She couldn't find the button for the bell, but before she could make up her mind to knock, which might not be ladylike, Tamsen opened the door and said, "Oh, Lurlene! Hello. Come in. It's *so* hot, isn't it?"

Lurlene had to admit the dark interior seemed a little cooler than the car. Sure *was* a hot day—too hot to drive in traffic while encased in a new girdle, to have on nylons and heels, and a synthetic silk dress, when everybody knows cotton is cooler. She had sacrificed. But here stood Tamsen, in a plain white cotton shift, her bare feet in sandals, and wearing her hair hanging down her back in that childish way. Lurlene thought *she* looked as if she were just off to the beach.

Tamsen led her out of whatever room it was (Lurlene had a shocking impression that from the front door she had put her foot into the kitchen!) into the big front room, and Lurlene arched her neck and peered, in the somewhat better light, for the sight of the other guests. There seemed to be none.

"Sit down, and let me bring you something cool to drink. And take off those hot gloves, won't you?"

Lurlene began to take off her gloves, already feeling off-base. She had thought she had been invited to a luncheon. But it wasn't going to be a luncheon, obviously. The room wasn't even neat. It was big, all right, practically the whole wing, and it was shaped like an L, and it had a step up, at the L's right angle, and the walls, wherever there was no window, were completely lined with bookshelves and the books were just stuffed in, any old which way. Wait a minute—looked like a little bitty piano, up there in the top part of the L.

Lurlene drew in her neck as Tamsen came back with a tall glass. "You know," said the hostess, "if Maggie and the Judge are going away, even if only for a while, the rest of us are going to have to close ranks, aren't we?"

Lurlene said she thought so, too, with no very clear idea of what was meant. The drink had ice in it, anyhow.

"And you haven't even been here," said Tamsen. "But we only found it three months ago, and I don't know why, we just never seem to entertain much. I haven't got what it takes to put on a dinner, I'm afraid. Isn't this a crazy house?"

Lurlene thought it certainly was, but she said nothing of the kind, of course. Tamsen explained how the entrance room *was* the kitchen, and how the bath opened off the kitchen, which was pretty weird, and the bedroom may have once been a garage. "That's just about all there is," Tamsen explained, "except for my shed, out back. We just love it, though. I'll hate to leave."

Then she went on to tell all about the fancy modern house that was being built for them on the new campus. Lurlene listened to the count of bathrooms, the details of the modern kitchen which, Tamsen said with a phony shudder, was going to be like the dashboard of a jet plane.

"I like the creative part of housekeeping," Tamsen said, "but I don't always like the routine."

Lurlene, who didn't think she was making any sense, took care to be cooingly agreeable to everything.

Then Tamsen took her outside, through the large square dim kitchen, to a tiny bit of pavement behind the house, which was roofed with a skeleton of timbers over which vines were tumbling. Lurlene sat down gingerly on the redwood-slatted chair and tried to keep her mind off the possibility of falling bugs. The backyard was no wider than the house, but it did go back a little way, until the steep hill stopped it. Lurlene thought it was crazy. Shut in, and (although they were so near the ocean), no breeze, and just no view at all.

Tamsen brought out plates of salady stuff and iced tea. They discussed food. They deplored the weather again. The conversation limped along. Inevitably, they came to Maggie.

Maggie was wonderful. Maggie had a beautiful home. It was hot over there, but Maggie had air conditioning. And servants. Perhaps that was why, Tamsen said, the younger Tylers didn't seem to get together anywhere else. "Maggie makes it so comfortable for us all."

"Well, I suppose we get together *this* Sunday?" said Lurlene. "Or is it the week after. Did you hear yet?" It was always Sunday because of Mitch, who had a better chance of getting there on Sundays.

Tamsen said, after a funny little hesitation, "I think Maggie's probably going to skip it for a while. She's having house guests, I believe."

"Is that so?" Lurlene didn't ask who. She thought, Well, *I* don't mind skipping it, believe me.

But Tamsen stood up kind of suddenly. "Would you like to see where I work, Lurlene?"

"Huh?" Lurlene was startled. It hadn't occurred to her that Tamsen *worked*.

"The shed where I do the painting?"

"Oh. Oh, I sure would." Lurlene struggled out of her chair and followed Tamsen, who seemed to gambol lightly as she led the way—like some little kid, thought Lurlene, whose heels were sinking disagreeably into moist earth.

"I'm afraid it's awfully warm in here this time of day in summer," said Tamsen apologetically, "but it's perfect in the early morning."

Lurlene thought it was perfect *shed*, all right. Just the bare boards, inside. Stuffy, too, and stinking of painty smells. Lurlene tried to manage her nostrils politely. There was an easel, and shelves full of cans and bottles and Lurlene didn't know what-all. All kinds of pictures, some hanging on the walls just on regular old nails. Others standing on the floor, and some turned so that all you saw was the back of them. Lurlene was hard-put-to-it to be admiringly impressed, but she tried.

"I think," said Tamsen in her soft voice, and now she seemed to have gone away somewhere, standing there, looking around at what she called her "work," "I want you and Rufus to have one of my things. If you would like that. I gave one to Phillida, you know. And Maggie, of course."

"That's very nice," said Lurlene, not unpleased, and her eyes began to travel rapidly, assessing what she saw with new interest. "I sure like that one," she said, pointing impulsively. The one she said she liked was hanging on the wall. In fact, it was the only one Lurlene could plainly see.

"Oh, not that one," said Tamsen quickly. "Oh, I'm sorry, but that one is going to a gallery."

"Oh?"

"Yes, you see, about six of them are going to a gallery, and they'll be for sale, you know."

Yah! thought Lurlene. *I* don't get to have one that might sell and make her a little money, eh?

"Well," she said helplessly, "I don't care. I mean, whatever you say."

* 40

"Why don't I paint one, just for you?" said Tamsen thoughtfully. "Something you would *really* like?"

"Well, say," said Lurlene, tottering on her high heels and hoping they could get out of here pretty soon, "I kinda like scenery, you know?"

"Landscapes?" Tamsen was being very attentive.

"Well, like some fields, and oh . . . like a little farmhouse, and some of those . . . you know . . . little round trees?"

"You mean a primitive," said Tamsen alertly.

"No, no," said Lurlene. "I mean like Grandma Moses. I think they're cute."

"I see," said Tamsen gravely. "Well, I can try. Shall we go back to the house? I'm afraid it's too hot and close in here."

Lurlene's mind was not quite on what she was saying as she took a good breath of the open air. "Wow, it sure smells in there." Then she spoke her real thought. "Listen, you never been to my place, either. Maybe you should know that my fr . . . my living room is done in all different pinks."

"I see," said Tamsen in a moment. "Then, would you like snow?"

"Snow!"

"I mean for your picture? And the sky a winter gray? Do you think white and gray would look well in your room?" Tamsen was speaking very politely, but Lurlene didn't like it for some reason.

"That would be just perfect," she gushed. (I can be a phony, too, she thought.) "Just wonderful of you to go to the trouble."

"I would like to please you," Tamsen said softly.

Lurlene didn't know what to make of that, so she began to talk about the long hot ride home, and how she had better get on her horse.

As they went back through the house Tamsen seemed to Lurlene to be feeling let-down, or low, or something. I guess she tries, thought Lurlene, in sudden charity. She does the best she can, I suppose.

Lurlene thought of something else. "Oh, say, I wanted to ask you, Tamsen—"

"Yes?"

"I was just wondering. I mean, it's probably a big favor. But would you mind giving Rufus some lessons?"

"Some . . . what?" Tamsen's voice was feeble.

"I mean, show him how to paint pictures," said Lurlene.

"I couldn't!" said Tamsen in a low shocked voice.

"Oh?" Lurlene couldn't help bristling.

"No, no," said Tamsen. "I can't teach. But I'll tell you what I can do. Let me give you my teacher's name. He's awfully good. Of course, he doesn't take on everybody. But Rufus could go talk to him, and I'm sure he'd get some excellent advice."

"Oh? Well, thanks." Lurlene felt stiff as a board. She had been only half-serious in her request, which Rufus had not commissioned her to make, but now all kinds of suspicions raced in her mind. Tamsen probably didn't want anybody else *in* on her racket. Or Tamsen didn't want to be alone with a man. And if so, why not?

"Is Rufus really interested?" said Tamsen, sounding warmer.

Lurlene took the slip of paper. "Well, he could be. I don't think he's feeling so hot these days."

This was true. For some reason Lurlene felt she was wise to say so.

"I'm sorry," said Tamsen. "Is he worried about anything?"

"No, no," Lurlene said quickly, assuming that money was meant. "We don't"—she had read this many times—"care so much for material things. If it was that," she went on, "I could have got a job a long time ago. I just happen to think that a woman ought to stay home and keep her house clean, you know, and things put away?" She had not meant to show a claw; she hadn't been able to resist it.

But Tamsen smiled at her. "Of course," she said.

"I guess I'm just what you'd call a homemaker," said Lurlene piously. "The thing is, if Rufus had something . . . to, you know, fool around with . . ."

"Like painting?" said Tamsen sweetly.

"You couldn't just kinda get him started?" Lurlene said, with hard eyes.

"No, I *couldn't*," said Tamsen earnestly. "Some people *can't* teach. I don't even know how *I* do it. I . . . I'm busy, trying to learn."

"Oh, well, I know you're busy," said Lurlene. "Thanks just the same and thanks for a lovely, lovely luncheon." Lurlene knew her manners.

She went back along the redwood rounds and, sure enough, the car was about 180 degrees inside. She turned down all the windows and unbuttoned the top of her dress and rolled it lower. And the hell with it, she thought sulkily. Who cares how *I* look, anyway?

When she had run the car into the garage, she came in at the back door, kicking her shoes off petulantly the moment she was under the roof.

Rufus was in the kitchen. He had a piece of waxed paper spread on the kitchen counter, and it was covered with funny-looking tan lumps.

"What in the heck are you doing?" exclaimed Lurlene. "What's that? *Fudge!* For God's sakes!" Rufus had never turned a hand in the kitchen in his life.

"It's inedible," he said gloomily.

Lurlene was interested. She came closer and reached for one of the lumps, but he actually slapped her hand away, although lightly. "It's impossible," he said, and lifted the waxed paper and dumped the whole mess into the sink.

"Hey," said Lurlene, "how much sugar you throwing away, there? Look, probably you didn't stir it enough. Let me . . ."

But Rufus was washing his product down into the garbage disposal. Lurlene licked her finger and put it on a leftover crumb, but he slapped her hand again in the same light way.

"Listen, mister," she said, sounding furious with him but feeling a pleasant release of an anger she had carried all the way home because of a lot of things, "how come you're so free with them mitts? Nobody slaps *me* around."

"You're the only one in the world who would put it in your mouth," he said in a funny way, "and you don't count."

"I certainly appreciate the compliment," said Lurlene, picking up her shoes. She gave him his compliment for the day. "Hey, Tamsen don't want any part of you. She can't be bothered to teach *you* how to paint."

"Who asked her?" he said dully.

"I asked her."

"Why?" He rolled his eyes and Lurlene began to feel uneasy.

"Oh, I just thought I'd see what she'd say. Um, boy—what a jolly time *I* had! What a phony she is!"

"Why did you go?" he asked absently.

"Say, listen, I have to be nice to her, don't I?" said Lurlene.

"That won't put your name in the history books," he said, dreamily.

Lurlene flounced into the bedroom to strip off her finery. Still on that kick, was he? Say, listen, a joke was a joke, but Lurlene was sick of it. Maybe he was looping, really looping, with those damn pills.

God knew she had tried. . . .

Lurlene powdered her hot face and began to look at it intently. She thought, I'm not old. I could easy lose five or six pounds. Even ten. She didn't quite permit herself to realize that she was contemplating widowhood.

He was in the front room when she emerged. Lurlene spotted the mess he'd made on the coffee table with a sharp housekeeping eye. "*Now* what did you think you were doing?" she demanded. "What *was* that? The alarm clock?"

"I don't understand how it works," he said in that listless way.

"You sure fixed it." She scowled at the mess of junk on the newspaper and began to fold the paper up around all those parts and pieces. She looked at him, where he was sitting dejectedly in his usual chair. "Don't tell me you were thinking about getting up and going to work, or anything *rash?*" she said nastily. She carried the mess into the kitchen to dispose of it. One thing about Lurlene, she kept house.

Something he had said was nagging at her, although she couldn't remember what it was now. She began to survey their fifteen years of married life rather gloomily.

When Lurlene told the tale of Rufus' career, it came out crystallized. How they had gone back east, ten years ago, where Rufus had had this wonderful offer. But the company had turned out to have a very poor policy. So then they had gone to Lurlene's own hometown, in Iowa, and stayed five years, comforting her mother until that lady had died. But in the end, of course, the place was just too small for a man like Rufus Tyler. No opportunities. They had tried Tucson, but Lurlene couldn't stand the summers. So, for her sake, they had come back to Los Angeles, oh—a year or more ago. Rufus was not really settled yet. But it was so nice to be near his people.

She had almost come to believe this version herself—except for that last statement. No, it was *not* nice to be near his people.

Lurlene had never been to college. She had been a waitress in a hamburger joint where the college kids used to come. She had gone after Rufus Tyler because he was clean, well-dressed, rich, and not snooty. And from a good family. Yah, yah, she thought.

Oh, he had fallen for her, all right. Moonlight and roses! But she had put up with a lot that hadn't been so darned rosy. Yes, she had. Now, if Rufus was going to start being sloppy and messy around the house, that was going to be just great, that was.

45   *

She took up the kitchen sponge and began to clean the counter righteously. He hadn't mopped up all the crumbs of his fudge. What did he want with candy? Her forefinger hesitated over one of the crumbs, but then she whisked them, every one, away into the sink and polished vigorously.

She thought, If I'm going to start dieting, I got to start. Some grim resolution was forming. It must be this. If I'd have had a kid, she thought, a precious Tyler . . . um . . . boy . . . then I'd have been somebody, I'll bet. Nobody ever wants to know how *I* feel.

For just one scary moment Lurlene realized that she didn't want to know how she felt, either. In another moment she had squeezed out a tear, and this evidence of true suffering made her feel better.

When Duncan came home, on the late side, their big room was dusky and Tamsen was curled up on the couch in a mood to match the sadness of the light.

"Fiasco?" he said alertly, forcing himself to take account of her state. He snapped on a lamp and sat down beside her. She swayed over into his arms with a sigh.

"Pure frustration. Lurlene asked me to teach Rufus to paint. I said I *couldn't*. She thinks I *won't*. But you know the difference between teaching and doing."

"Indeed. Indeed," he soothed.

"If I had talked for three solid hours I could *not* have got that into her head," said Tamsen vehemently.

"I believe you." He was comforting her with voice and caress. "The difference between can't and won't, eh? Now, a teacher looks the other way." He was lecturing to soothe her. "I should say that the greater percentage of our so-called students is made up of those who could-learn-but-won't, and those who would-learn-but-can't. So, it follows that a whopping hunk of our valuable time is spent just trying to tell the difference."

"What do you do when you find out which is which?" she murmured, soaking up comfort.

"We coax the one-who-won't to want to—which is our art. When we are sure of the ones-who-can't, we throw them out— which is our duty."

"Besides, then they're not *your* problems anymore."

"Then, they are problems-at-large," he said, "and this society has got to find out what is to be done with them some day soon." Having calmed her with abstractions he now said, "Honey, chalk up one noble effort and mark it failed."

"So I just throw her out," said Tamsen, "and that's the moral of it?"

"With," he said pompously, "the stipulation that the language is immoderate, I'd say yes, I suppose you do. That is, you put Lurlene out of the running as an intimate chum of yours."

Tamsen sighed, and then she giggled. "Or *she* throws *me* out, when she sees my Grandma-Tyler."

But her tension was gone and Duncan, feeling his task accomplished, interrupted. "They're here," he announced.

"Oh, I forgot!" she squirmed. "Did it go all right?"

"Slick as could be," he told her, letting loose his own mood, which was exultant. "I borrowed Dick Sadler's station wagon to hold the whole pack of them in one load."

"Did the foreigners look awfully exotic?"

"Well, of course—not so much in an airport. But Alice Foster was right about the dirty looks they were casting. Expecting Indians (American variety) or at the very least, Al Capone. I . . . er . . . got a little foxy. We fetched the luggage to the curb. Mounds of it, by the way. I made Jaylia and the boy and his Swedish nurse stand in one group, and the other three, the exotic ones, stand a little bit apart. When I came by and scooped them all up in one car, pretty fast, nobody seemed to notice anything odd."

Duncan thought to himself, But it *was* odd.

47 ✳

"And the little boy is in the hospital, *now?*"

"Sure is. I got to drive in to the ambulance entrance, and Mitch was there and we were all whisked up in a back elevator. They're in a suite, all right. Very private. I think the hospital uses it for movie stars who have had face lifts, or something equally top secret. Arrangements seem fine. Saiph's got one bedroom. Inga's got the other. The two characters who are supposed to be his bodyguards are going to have cots in the sitting room —that is, if they intend to sleep at all." Duncan laughed in sheer excitement.

"But his mother isn't going to stay there?" Tamsen marveled, slightly.

(No, no, thought Duncan, you don't understand. You just don't understand.)

"No, no," he said aloud. "I drove her and the maid to Maggie's. Wait till you see Zora. Chiffon bloomers."

"Oh, Duncan, no!"

"Oh, she was *wearing* a blue suit, but Zora's got the aura." He was in high spirits. He didn't know quite why.

Tamsen fell in with his mood and rejoiced. She thought it was wonderful that something was being done, and being done through the Tylers, to help the poor child.

But Duncan Tyler knew that, marvelous though this might be, and conducive to rejoicing, it wasn't the true source of his own exhilaration.

"Hey, this cloak-and-dagger stuff works up the appetite," he announced, dumping her from his lap. "What's to nibble on?"

"Steak. I'm starving, too. I served a very genteel lunch," said Tamsen, scampering before him into their crazy kitchen. "And I swear unto thee, I don't know why."

"It was your tender heart, wishing to please."

"No," said Tamsen, "or yes, maybe. Or no, I don't really think so."

"How about searching your soul after supper?" he said cheerfully. "Hey, Maggie wants to know will I bring you by, Thursday evening, to meet the Princess?"

"Oh, I'd love to!"

"Phillida's coming too. Maggie thinks she'll be a great comfort. The Doctor's wife, you see, calm as cucumbers."

"It's 'cool' as," said Tamsen, "and Phillida *is*. But what about . . . ?"

Nothing was said.

Tamsen unwrapped the steak.

"Maggie's privilege," Duncan said, "after all."

"So it is," she agreed, "but it seems too bad to leave them out, when it's not their fault."

"Whose fault is it," he said with a touch of impatience, "that they wouldn't be of the slightest interest, or use, to Jaylia? Nor she to them, for that matter."

"Why not she to them?"

"Because they would be forbidden to name-drop," he said cruelly.

"Oh, Duncan—"

"Communication would be nil," he said. "The Princess is simply another order of human animal. And that's not *her* fault, either."

Tamsen heard a note in his voice she did not understand at all, and it frightened her a little.

5

THE big house in San Marino had two wings that bent inward, on the street side. One entered at the far left of the central block, to a wide hall which continued (under the stairs) all the way to the garden side and glass doors there. To one's left, visible through two archways, lay the enormous living room, the entire ground floor of the west wing. To one's right lay the Judge's study, a long narrow room in the central block, on the street side. Behind this, toward the garden, there was a room that Maggie called the lanai. It was both an informal sitting room and the passage to the east wing, where lay the big dining room, the kitchen beyond that, and the little breakfast room that overlooked the east terrace and the swimming pool.

Upstairs, on the street side, as the house bowed in, there ran a long passage the whole way. All the bedrooms looked out on the garden side and were not subject to the intrusion of glances from passersby. Maggie's servant-couple, who inhabited an apartment over the garage, were not in the house except when serving. The whole establishment was kept to itself within boundaries of shrubbery so that, although Maggie's hospitality was famous, this place could be a quiet fortress, and very private indeed.

They were gathered in the lanai, which Maggie considered appropriate in the summertime, with its light gay furnishings and its windows standing open to the peaceful lawns.

Tamsen was quiet in her corner, a looker and a listener. Meantime, she was trying not to turn in her mind the knowledge that she had been somewhat misdirected by her husband.

She had seen Zora, a young person with, indeed, the look of her people, but Tamsen had sensed no chiffon-bloomer aura about *her*. She was obviously devoted to her mistress and, by now, also devoted to Maggie, who had probably arranged this without half trying. Zora came and went, being of service in a happy way, and then vanished, and was not missed, and that was that.

It was quite obvious to Tamsen *who* had the chiffon-bloomer aura, if that was the name for it. Jaylia Foster, or whatever she was called now, a princess who had once expected to be a queen, spoke pure American, taking after her mother, no doubt, and her speech habits further reinforced by an education in New England. She was a dark blonde, with a great hank of hair wound around a small head that tilted nicely on a mobile neck. She was not tall but, in fact, almost as short in stature as Tamsen herself. She was a lot . . . well, *fatter* wasn't the word. Rounder? She was, if not perfectly beautiful, certainly striking, thought Tamsen, who had known at once that she might paint that face and that body seven times, and never catch Jaylia's aura.

Tamsen tried to view with detachment the two kinds of magic present here. Maggie was being the protecting angel, strong and serene, indulgent of her protégée's right to hold the center of the stage, so long as Maggie chose not to have it herself. Jaylia's magic was not that kind. It was simply that here sat a woman possessed of a magnetism of the flesh (that, no doubt, thought Tamsen wryly, wasn't her *fault*) but which drew men, any and all men—including Duncan Tyler, husband to Tamsen.

It was the psychic equivalent of chiffon bloomers, the now-you-see-it-now-you-don't fascinating promise of what? Of touch, Tamsen decided. Or just plain yumminess. All right, spell it sex. It wasn't youth. Jaylia must be hovering around thirty. It wasn't provocative clothing. She wore a dress of a brownish print, conservative to the point of long sleeves in the summertime. It was just . . . what? It was there.

Jaylia, however, was talking what Tamsen supposed must fall into the category of either politics or intrigue. Duncan and the Judge (the only men present), and sometimes Phillida, were involved in this conversation. Tamsen only looked and listened, and Maggie was keeping her wings furled benignly.

Duncan was asking about the last batch of riots at the University. Were they, he wanted to know, connected with any particular issue? Or merely the result of young exuberance, and the sheeplike nay-saying of youth to the establishment, whatever it might be?

"They were confusing," Jaylia said, one shoulder (no doubt unconsciously, thought Tamsen) moving very slightly, as if to say, But wouldn't it be more fun to go to bed than to wonder about this sort of thing? "We suspect, of course, that somebody was behind them. It remains just the usual suspicion."

"The usual," the Judge said, smiling upon her.

"Infiltration? Divide and conquer?" said Duncan, rocking backward. "Or local talent? Subversion? Rise of the military?"

"Al Asad *is* the military," said Jaylia gently.

Phillida said, in her bright way, "Did—uh—anybody really believe the American professors were agents, inciting to riot?"

Jaylia said pleasantly, "Who knows what—uh—anybody really believes?"

"What do *you* think Al Asad thought?" said the Judge, coming in bluntly. "You are among friends, my dear."

"I know," she said with a fluttery little gasp. "But it is foolish to try too hard to guess, I think, when it is only imagining. My mother, I see, has been writing letters. Of course, she is a born intriguer."

"So are you, dear," said Maggie calmly. Jaylia cast her a startled glance. "So am I," said Maggie, wing-tips stirring.

When the ripple of amusement had subsided, Duncan, with the intention of abandoning questions that the lady didn't seem to want to answer, asked another. "What kind of chap is this Dhanab? A nephew of the King's, isn't he?"

Jaylia said, "You didn't meet him, did you, Duncan? Oh, he is in his early thirties. He sometimes seems young for that." (As you do not, said her flesh.) "He is serious-minded—I'd say."

"A born intriguer?" said Duncan, grinning. "Or just power-mad?"

(All right, thought Tamsen, *he* is attractive, too. I should know.)

"He wants to do what is good for his country," said Jaylia evasively. "About those American professors. It hasn't occurred to any of you that they might have been in danger?"

"Might have *been?*" said Duncan alertly.

"Oh, in the rioting, perhaps. If some unknown parties had wanted to make awkwardness. Or just be rid of American influence in the—uh—curriculum."

"You mean to suggest that the King put them in *protective* custody?" said Duncan.

"I mean to suggest that he may have," said Jaylia. "It's not impossible."

"But I understood your mother to be . . . imagining . . ." said Phillida, "that they might possibly be in great danger later on."

"Al Asad will not let them go until later on," said Jaylia, avoiding, as had Phillida, the definition of "later on." "But you ought not to imagine that *he* won't be in charge of things. He really is quite a marvelous old person. Although a person, with the power of life or death, is bound to be approached a bit gingerly by most."

"Indeed," said Duncan. "You say he *is* the military? Not, then, the anachronism he seems to be? Yet a hereditary monarchy . . ."

"Unless otherwise decreed," she murmured.

"It's the religious element that holds?"

"Oh, yes."

The two of them seemed to have lost the others. "Are you . . ." Duncan began. Jaylia was a convert.

But at this moment Mitch came in. Tamsen couldn't help being quite glad to see him.

The Doctor was greeted but not pressed with the question, although the question hung in the ceiling corner like smoke.

The Doctor chose to answer it almost at once. "He's a good little animal, Jaylia," said Mitch, "in every way but one. I think I can say that he looks to be a classic case."

"What does that mean?" Jaylia straightened and sat tall, looking with frightened eyes at a person with the power of life or death.

"That means I see a high probability that he can successfully be patched up," said Mitch. "Of course, there'll be many preparations. I can't and won't attempt it for several days."

"Aunt Maggie?" said Jaylia in a choking voice. Her face looked shocked, thinner, almost tragically alarmed.

So Maggie simply turned the spotlight elsewhere.

"Now, Mitch," she said plaintively, "I suppose you will poke and will pry, and the poor little boy won't have the faintest idea what you are doing. No patient ever has. Is he happy, Mitch? What in the world will he *do*, between pokings and pryings? He can't look at the wall at the age of eleven. Unless, of course, there is television. But *is* that enough?"

Maggie had put on tragic concern over what was of so little importance, compared to such great hope after long despair.

"You're right, Maggie," the Doctor said. "You are absolutely right, as usual. What he needs is a playmate. He is an awfully smart little boy. And he would sure like to see something of this foreign land. He would like, in fact, to take a jaunt to Disneyland, like everybody else. But, because he is so unfortunately unable to sight-see, I wonder . . . He could certainly use an American companion."

"Mickey?" said Phillida. All of them were turning to chat of this kind because of Jaylia's stricken face.

"Well, now, Mickey," said the Doctor, and aside, "That's our ten-year-old. Mickey is not quite . . . In the first place, he is in school."

"He could take time out," said Mickey's mother, "with no permanent damage."

"Oh, certainly," said Mickey's father, "but I don't think he has . . . well . . . the maturity. Fact is, I was thinking of Tamsen."

"Me!" Tamsen sat up, startled.

"She being about the nearest thing to a *mature* child we've got handy," the Doctor said fondly. "How would you like to drop by, in the afternoons, and play with him?"

"Why, I'd just love to!" she cried. "Could I, really?"

Jaylia looked at her and said, "You!" She began to turn her head to look at all the faces. "You . . . *all* of you?"

"Do you know," said Maggie, flowing to her feet, "I think that makes a very effective exit line, my dear. I think that you and I will go quietly upstairs now."

"Aunt Maggie?" said Jaylia again, reaching out to her.

"It is very difficult," decreed Maggie, "to bawl in public and not be mortified in the morning. Come with me."

Jaylia rose. Her hands flew out, in a begging gesture. But Maggie said severely, "Unnecessary," and silently led her away.

The people left behind sat stunned for a moment.

"How great the strain has been," said the Judge finally. "Good news can be devastating. Poor girl. It *is* good news, Mitch."

Mitch was making himself a cooling drink. He grinned. "Never any guarantee, but I don't have too many qualms. He's got a lot going for him, including his attitude."

Tamsen, who had been looking at Duncan, now rose quickly. "We don't need an exit line," she said. (Because one face, peeled naked, in this room had been enough for one evening.) "Just tell me when, Mitch, please?"

"Make it two o'clock," the Doctor said. "For an hour. Teach him to paint, eh?"

"Oh, we can mess around, gloriously," she promised.

"No, no," said the Judge.

"Religion," croaked Duncan.

"Come along, Duncan," said Tamsen. "Although a *mature* child, it is early to bed for me, these days."

"Good night, Tamsen dear," said Phillida affectionately. "Good night, Duncan."

They went out to the car. They drove through sleepy Pasadena silently. They took the Pasadena Freeway to the Harbor, to the Santa Monica, toward home.

Duncan was driving faster than usual, waiting for what he knew would come. Tamsen had not chosen, so uncharacteristically, to take the center of the stage for no reason at all.

She said, at last, "Did you fall in love with her a year ago?"

"Yes," he said.

"But you came home and married me?"

"Yes."

"Why?"

"Because I love *you*," he answered.

"*Too?*" said Tamsen keenly.

"Yes."

"All right," she said quietly, in a minute.

Duncan increased speed, cutting in and out of lanes recklessly. She said nothing. After a while he was able to subdue the car to a steadier pace.

In silence they finally descended into their own terrain, and the car came softly to rest beside their door. In silence they went into the silent house, arms around each other.

But when he would have fallen fiercely upon her in their bed Tamsen said, "Not at this time."

He drew away warily.

"Because we will have so many other times," she finished, clearly.

So Duncan left the room. He went out into the little backyard and sat there, alone, in the darkness. To be thoroughly understood and, worse, accepted, as the confused and ambiguous creature you really are . . . This was not, he found, as delightful as it was cracked up to be.

6

---◆---

AT two o'clock the following day, Tamsen Tyler fell in love.

The little boy was dark-haired, dark-eyed, and if his skin was not as dark as the skin of his bodyguards (two youngish men, who watched Tamsen like twin hawks for ten minutes, and then suddenly left off watching her) the little face was handsome in much the same way as their faces. He sat up in his high bed without really wiggling, but radiating energy just the same.

Inga Bjornsen was a big woman, forty, at a guess, whose long bony face fell into dour lines until she smiled at her charge. Then she was seen to be enslaved.

Saiph, accepting Tamsen with one quick look that melted her immediately, began to bombard her with questions. It wasn't long before she had to beg mercy and restrict him to one question at a time. His curiosity was intelligent and full of fun. He was a joyous child, who came forward to meet a stranger with an endearing trust seasoned with moments of bright suspicion that she might be inventing such outlandish answers. But, if so, he didn't really mind. He was prepared to enjoy that, too.

His father had been, Tamsen supposed, a world citizen during his short life. The little boy spoke American very fluently, with only now and then a British twist to a vowel. But he did not think of himself as even a quarter of an American. He was of the royal family of Alalaf. He didn't mind being so. The knowledge he had obviously carried for a long time, that he might die in a very few years, had not bothered him, either.

Tamsen was a goner.

When her hour was up and she dutifully rose to depart she said, "Tell you what. Why don't you write down all the questions you'll think up before tomorrow?" It was in her mind to give him occupation.

Saiph said, "I can remember them. Even a hundred."

Tamsen laughed, because he was teasing her. "I wouldn't put it past you, at that," she said. Then she must explain that old-fashioned idiom to his complete satisfaction before she could get away.

Waiting for the elevator, Tamsen blew out her breath and began to wonder what charm was. Whatever it was, that little human being had a double dose of it. No wonder his people adored him! No wonder he had become a magnet that drew to itself their natural love of country and had become, therefore, their most dearly beloved, both in fact and as symbol. Oh, how dangerous!

In the elevator she found herself to be in a state of passionate prayer. When she got off at the ground floor, Tamsen had to hide her face as best she could while she scurried out into the parking lot. She sat in the car, unable to see. Duncan is right, she thought in a while, about the heart *I've* got. It could do with a little hardening, just for practical, everyday purposes.

She remembered, then, about the night before, and was soon stiffened enough to judge that she could, now, safely drive a car.

When she came into her house the telephone was ringing.

"Are you having lunch with Lurlene tomorrow?" Phillida wanted to know.

"Yes, I am."

"It's a restaurant? At noon?" Phillida seemed to be finding this hard to believe.

"I told her I'd have to make it early."

"I see. Well," said Phillida, as if she were saying, So be it, "I'll see you there, then."

"I guess *I* started all this . . ." Tamsen began.

"Saturdays," said Phillida jauntily, "don't mean as much to me as to some. We shall gather. Did you have fun today?"

"I can't *tell* you!" burst Tamsen.

"Yes, I know," Phillida said. "A lamb. Maybe *I'll* have an engagement at two tomorrow also. That might be a good idea."

"All right," said Tamsen, and burst again, "I don't *like* . . . sneaking around."

"You mean lying?" said Phillida. "Oh, you'll get the knack of it."

Phillida hung up and called Lurlene back. "I've found my little book," she lied cheerfully, "and I see that I *can* make it. Thanks so much, Lurlene, I'll be there then."

"I'm so glad you can make it," said Lurlene, and added helplessly, "Thanks so much."

She said to Rufus, rather defensively, "But I'm not going to ask Maggie. Anyhow, she's supposed to have house guests."

"I would have asked Maggie, too," Lurlene was saying, "but I happen to know she has house guests. And I wouldn't want her to feel, you know, pressured?" She smiled archly.

Tamsen's heart had jumped, but Phillida said, "The food here is not half-bad."

Tamsen sensed the noncommunication. Phillida had meant this in praise of pleasure. The hostess was taking it for condescension.

Lurlene said, "It's nothing fancy. But I thought—just some quiet place where we could talk, you know?"

The middling-good restaurant was sparsely populated at the early hour and, so far, quiet enough. They had a table in the middle of the room. Tamsen was wearing a gray seersucker suit, and Phillida was effortlessly elegant in what seemed to be blue linen, with sleeves. Lurlene had chosen a sleeveless dress of shocking pink, and the air conditioning was putting goose pimples on her bare upper arms.

But if they were here to talk, someone must speak, and they had already discussed the fact that it was much cooler today. So Lurlene moistened her mouth and said, "Say, I was reading this article about the little Prince of Al . . . How do you pronounce that?"

"It doesn't matter," said Phillida, quickly and softly. "Don't let's pronounce it."

"It didn't say anything about his being sick," said Lurlene, rather more loudly than she had been speaking. "I certainly do hope that Mitch is going to be able to—"

"Shut up," said Phillida.

Lurlene said, in a startled way, "What's the *matter* with you?"

"Just don't shout," said Phillida, "other people's business."

"Well, I'm *sorry*," said Lurlene, in outrage.

Tamsen realized that Phillida was very angry indeed. She was struggling with the anger, but it was rendering her speechless at the moment.

So Tamsen said to Lurlene, softly, "Maggie didn't want us to talk about it, that's all."

" 'Just for the family,' eh?" Lurlene quoted the code phrase in a huffy manner. "I *know* that. Pardon *me*, if I thought this *was* just the family."

"This is a public place," snapped Phillida. "No names, if you don't mind?"

Phillida was furious. Lurlene had been deeply offended. Tamsen was frightened and miserable.

"Nobody's paying any attention to us," she said as lightly as she could. "Don't worry."

Phillida's eyes met hers with a stab of rage, but then Phillida won her battle, blinked and smiled.

"What in the world's so secret about it, when it's in the papers?" Lurlene muttered.

"What is in the papers?" said Phillida, coolly.

"Nothing," said Tamsen quickly.

"I won't mention any *names*," said Lurlene loftily, "but I can't understand a white woman getting mixed up with those people in the first place. And I don't think she's so beautiful, either." Lurlene had seen an old picture of Jaylia, in an old magazine.

"People are different," said Tamsen gently. "You *can't* understand, really. People fall in love, for instance."

Phillida had become herself again, and she said, "Oh, they do. They do. Will you forgive me, Lurlene? I shouldn't have jumped down your throat, really."

But Lurlene had no grace available for accepting apologies. "If I'm not supposed to say one word to you girls, then Maggie should've left me out of it," she said sourly. "I'm very sorry, I'm sure, Phillida."

She had no grace to make an apology, either. Phillida held herself still.

Tamsen said, "Duncan was telling me about the University." She thought the air must be cleared, and some chatter that might circle harmlessly around the subject would do it. "Do you know that the . . . uh . . . founder had a couple of years of schooling in England in his day? And the . . . uh . . . son was educated all over Europe? But it seems that this is not considered good enough, or proper, for the grandson. So, nothing loath, the grandfather up and caused there to *be* a university. I think that's touching."

"Expensive, too," said Phillida, still busy with her own temper. "Although, in my opinion, the grandson is worth it."

"Of course," said Tamsen, as her heart jumped again, "once you start educating people, anything can happen."

"I guess I wouldn't understand what it feels like—to be beautiful or educated," said Lurlene darkly.

"Oh, Lurlene," said Tamsen, searching backward to the remark that had caused this response, "I didn't mean *you* couldn't understand. I meant *one* couldn't understand."

Phillida said, "Why don't we get off the subject and stay off? The enemy has ears, as they used to say in some war or other."

"What enemy is this?" said Lurlene, and added, in what was close to being a snarl, "Me?"

She was set to quarrel; she was going to quarrel. Her party was in shreds already; she didn't care anymore.

Phillida put down her teacup and said quietly, "Lurlene, you are not to say one more word about those people, or that situation, to anyone, anywhere. And if you don't understand why not, you had better just take my word for it."

"Oh, I understand why not," said Lurlene angrily. She was going to be sarcastic. Just because you say so, eh? she meant to add. But Tamsen jumped in.

"Good," she said warmly. "I thought Maggie must have made it clear. And nobody heard, here. Everything's all right."

Tamsen simply was not sure yet how much Lurlene knew, and she was, in part, probing to find out.

But Lurlene said to Phillida, "*I* didn't know you went with Mitch."

"Went where?"

"To the place of the name I'm not supposed to say out loud," said Lurlene loudly, "and can't pronounce anyway."

"No, I didn't go," said Phillida. Her eyes sought Tamsen's. Perhaps Phillida had made a mistake or two.

"*Mitch* says the little kid is worth it, eh?" Lurlene looked shrewd.

"Yes, he does," said Phillida.

"So I suppose Mitch thinks he's going to live long enough to go to college—" Lurlene was very loud.

Phillida coldly surrendered. "Lurlene," she interrupted in a low but emphatic voice, "your ignorance is going to make trouble. So you'll have to know. The boy is here, in the hospital se-

63 　✱

cretly, and his mother is Maggie's house guest. It is a secret and very important that it stay a secret. You mustn't say one word that anyone could possibly overhear. Do you understand?"

Lurlene was staring. Color came into her face. "But *Tamsen* knew all about it, eh?"

Tamsen said, "Oh, Lurlene, it's just that Duncan knows them. And Mitch does too, of course."

"And *my* husband don't?" said Lurlene belligerently.

"But there was no need. Surely you see," Tamsen pleaded, "the fewer who know, the better."

Phillida was letting Tamsen do the pleading. Her tall body was rigid. Tamsen, however, had reason to despair of ever getting into Lurlene's head the reasons for silence. So she veered, to try another path.

"Now that you know, you couldn't possibly do anything to hurt a child. *I* know that." Tamsen was nearly whispering. "If it gets out, he'll be so pestered, Lurlene. It could keep him from getting well. Please?" Tamsen leaned back. "Oh, what am I saying? *I* know how much you love children."

Lurlene's mouth moved, whether smirk or sneer there was no telling.

"I've so often wondered," Tamsen leaned toward her again, her soft voice dripping sympathy, "if your heart wasn't just about to break sometimes." Tamsen touched the bare forearm. It winced but did not reject. Lurlene's face was losing the look of hard anger, softening with surprise. "I mean, because you haven't had one of your own. I know it isn't my business, but you *would* make the most marvelous mother."

Lurlene's eyes were filling. "Nobody ever seems to notice how *I* feel," she murmured.

"Oh, I *have* noticed," said Tamsen. "But it's not easy to say anything. I've been pretty sure it hurts you—a lot. There may be some strange women who don't love children, but that wouldn't be you."

"It isn't me," whimpered Lurlene. "I been to doctors. I

mean, I tried. I guess God just doesn't want me to have any."

"But you are young," cooed Tamsen. "I just know how you would protect a child. Any child. That's how I know you'll help us protect this little one."

Lurlene found her handkerchief. "Of course," she sniffled. "Sometimes, you know, I just don't understand . . ."

"But you are much too young to give up hoping," Tamsen cooed on.

When Lurlene left them in the parking lot and they walked in another direction Phillida said dryly, "You're getting the knack, aren't you?"

"I couldn't think of any other way to make the point," said Tamsen miserably. "It was awful. I must have sounded like daytime television."

"Never mind," said Phillida, "as long as it works. I must say *I* couldn't have done that."

They were standing, now, beside Phillida's car.

"Oh well, you don't have a heart that bleeds every hour on the hour," said Tamsen, "as Duncan says *mine* does."

Phillida said, "I won't have Mitch bothered. That's the truth of it. What a fool I was," she added ruefully. "I must practice being as angry as that."

"You're *not* used to it, are you?" said Tamsen innocently.

Phillida eyed her a moment, then smiled and went away.

Lurlene came into the house and found Rufus watching daytime television. She said nothing.

Becoming aware of this, he stirred and said, "How did it go?"

"Swell," she said bitterly. "Just swell. Guess what? That little Prince Saiph—and holy cats, what names they got, that you aren't supposed to mention! Well, they *got* him, right here in the hospital, and his mama, the big old beeyootiful princess, is staying at Maggie's, and you and me aren't supposed to know a thing about it."

"That so?" He was not perturbed or especially interested.

"Because we're ignorant!" she said furiously. "We'd tell the enemy, or something. We're *stupid!*" she screamed at him.

"I don't *know* any top secrets to tell the enemy," he said. "How about that?" She could have slapped the silly look off his face.

"Well, I'm telling you, I've *had* it," she cried. "Fifteen bucks, it cost me. For what? To get insulted."

"Who insulted you?" Rufus blinked as if, at last, he paid some real attention.

Lurlene said, with hot eyes, "Dear little Tamsen."

Because butter was butter, and on the way home Lurlene had recognized the aftertaste.

7

IN the Monday morning newspaper there was a paragraph at the bottom of page one.

BOY PRINCE IN HOSPITAL FOR SERIOUS SURGERY

It was a very short paragraph and said little more.

Jaylia saw it and moved her shoulders. "Here we go," she said. Maggie wailed dismay. The Judge went into his study and got on the phone, but the people he called had already seen the paper.

Phillida saw it, and paced her apartment.

Dr. Mitchel Tyler heard about it at the hospital, where Secret Service men had multiplied and become visible. The elevator was severely guarded now. No one, no one at all (except the Doctor), got off at the fifth floor without being first questioned about, and then escorted on, whatever legitimate visit he had to make.

Duncan saw the paragraph and exploded where he sat.

Tamsen said, "Oh, no . . . I hope . . . Oh, no, I hope . . . Oh, no . . . I hope . . ." She was a broken record, but he didn't stop her or try to comfort her. He dashed to the phone. He dashed out of the house. He was not going to the University this Monday morning.

Lurlene saw it, and was pleased to contemplate her right to

say, "Some secret! Yah! I told you so." Upon reflection, she did not mention this to Rufus.

Rufus didn't see it. He was reading the sports page. He had gone to the ball game yesterday, and he liked to be told what he had enjoyed.

When Tamsen arrived at the hospital at two o'clock that afternoon she had to prove her identity and her privilege. It took her twenty minutes to proceed from the elevator to the suite.

There was another Secret Service man outside that door and she had to prove her identity and her right to enter all over again.

When she was inside, Hayyan and Kasim fastened fierce looks upon her face, went with her into the boy's room, did not leave it, but stationed themselves to watch her every eye blink. Inga was sitting at the bedside and she did not rise. Her face was dour.

But the little boy greeted her as usual. Tamsen didn't know whether to mention all these changes in the atmosphere or ignore them. While she was still trying to decide Saiph decided.

"Tamsen." He liked to use her name and did it rather shyly, always with a sideways glance as if to say, "Do you want to take back your permission now?"

"Yes, old-timer?" This was a form of address that had made him laugh one day.

"Do the people here want to kill me?"

"Oh no, no, *no!*" Tamsen rocked with dismay. "We want you to be *well*. We want that very much." (But, of course, in view of all the fuss that was being made, this would not do.) So she said, "The trouble is, Saiph, there are always some crazy people. And it is just that we not only don't want, but we just won't *let*, anything bad happen to you. We're not taking any chances."

"I understand that, you know," he said reassuringly. "There are crazy people in Alalaf, too. Drug-eaters, for instance."

"Yes," she said miserably.

"But if you aren't taking any chances, why are you so un-happy?"

"I just wish," she said, "that it was still a secret."

"Do you *like* secrets?"

"No, I don't *like* them," she answered honestly, "but they can sometimes be a good thing."

Saiph said something to his bodyguards in their own lan-guage. They both grinned wide and murmured appreciation.

"What does your name mean?" asked the Prince in a moment.

"My *name?* Oh." Tamsen settled back in the visitor's chair. "Once upon a time there was a girl's name, Thomasina. That would be 'Little-Girl-Thomas,' do you see? But it was easier to say 'Tamsen.' And that's what people began to say. And then they began to spell it the way they said it. My mother thought it was a pretty name. So she gave it to me."

"I think it *is* a pretty name," he said politely. "Do you know what my nickname means?"

"No."

"Al Saiph. That means 'The Sword.'" There was mischief in his eye.

"Oh?" Tamsen was wondering how she could bear it if any-thing bad happened to him.

"No crazy people are going to come walking in here," said Saiph somewhat wistfully. "Or at least I don't think so. Do you?"

"They'd better not," she said.

"That's right. They'd better not. So I wish you wouldn't worry"—he hesitated—"Little-Girl-Thomas?"

"I think you're right." She braced up violently, lest she bawl. "O.K.," she snapped.

"O.K.," he said with a snap. It was a bargain.

"What shall we do today? What would you like to do?"

Saiph, politely ignoring her inner turbulence, considered her question gravely. "I will teach you a game, if you like," he

69   *

said. "It is easy to learn, but it is very hard to play." He was challenging her. Tamsen was fairly sure that he thought she ought to have her mind engaged, so that her female twitterings would be put aside.

Sure enough, she found herself being taught the rules and objectives of a game she had noticed the two guards playing mysteriously, with little heaps of pebbles. It was mathematically based and Tamsen, to whom mathematics was a dim thicket she had never really pierced, was forced to try very hard to understand. Her teacher, although he kept advising her on the best strategy, respectfully did not make mistakes himself, to let her win.

On television that evening, the boy was identified as the son of his father, of whom there were lurid remembrances. And of his mother, who had had her share of publicity in earlier times. Her presence here was not revealed, nor was the Doctor's name mentioned, nor the precise nature of the boy's problem. But the King, his grandfather, was mentioned. Then the case of the twenty-eight American professors was tacked on, although not specifically connected. The result was hint, for wonder, for gossip, for warning, of Big Story coming up!

Tamsen watched the eleventh-hour news and turned it off.

Duncan was not at home. She knew where he was, but she was feeling almost unbearably alone. She had not phoned, not spoken, to any member of the family all day. Duncan had suggested that it might not be wise. She was ready to climb the wall when he finally came in.

"How are they?" She was dancing with nervousness.

"Rolling with it," he said. "What else is there to do? The only good thing is, as Maggie says, the whole damn world looking over Mitch's shoulder isn't going to change the tiniest muscle in *that* hand, thank God." Duncan sat down, looking exhausted.

"But the world . . . The hospital hasn't given out Mitch's name."

"Aw, come on," he said wearily.

Tears began to stream down Tamsen's face. "If it was my fault . . ." she quavered.

Duncan looked at her, with neither condemnation nor comfort. "It happened. Oh, it went through Rufus, all right."

Tamsen squealed with pain.

"Oh, for God's sake," he said, "it happened the way it happened. I've been all day tracking down exactly how it happened. I've got every link in the chain, and it leads right smack dead-on to my brother Rufus."

"And so to Lurlene?" she whimpered, "And so to me?"

"All right," said Duncan, in his exhaustion. "You are a miserable sinner and ought to be drawn and quartered. Is that what you want to hear?"

Tamsen took hold of herself. "No," she said thinly, "but I'd like to be sure exactly what I *did* have to do with it. How did it happen?"

"Well." He gave her a somewhat gruesome smile as apology. "I finally found the fellow who brought in the story to the newspaper," he said drearily, "and it took some chasing around and some persuasion, but I finally got hold of his source. And when I got to the source of the source—it seems that Rufus went to the ball game Sunday with a couple of his cronies. And when the inning was getting a little dull he, evidently making small-talk," said Duncan bitterly, "or just for the hell of it—broadcast the whole business."

Tamsen had stopped crying. It had become obvious that she could not just keep on crying. "Did you talk to Rufus?"

"I did not. Wouldn't trust myself not to wring his fool neck."

"There are guards all over the hospital," she told him.

"They are more conspicuous, eh? Oh, the State Department was never about to let anything happen *here*. Don't worry about Saiph. They're not going to let a mosquito get at him. It's what might be going on in Alalaf."

"Oh, Duncan, what might?"

"Dad says to me, *privately* . . ."

"All right," said Tamsen.

"That Alice Foster isn't safe there. How's that for openers?" He got up. "Phillida says that *she* told Lurlene, and that *she* judged it to be necessary. Phillida says she laid secrecy on the line and you did your best to persuade Lurlene to keep quiet. So nobody is blaming you. Unless"—now he was sad—"you absolutely have to blame yourself?"

"Not unless I see I absolutely have to," she answered bravely.

"Good." He kissed her brow. "Honey, I'm bushed. I'm going to bed. Stewing and fretting and assigning blame isn't going to help one damn thing in the world."

But Tamsen's brain had clicked. "Then why did you spend all day tracking down the source?" she asked.

He reeled and answered. "So that it won't happen again," he said patiently. "So that we can know what we have to deal with here. So we can do better next time. Why else?"

Tamsen said, "Is she . . . terribly upset?"

"No, no," said Duncan. Then he realized that neither of them doubted that the other understood the pronoun, and he grinned at her painfully. "But *I* am," he confessed. "It makes me pretty sick to know that it got out through the family. I don't blame myself, and I don't cry easy. But *I* am a very upset fella."

"Go to bed," said Tamsen gently.

8

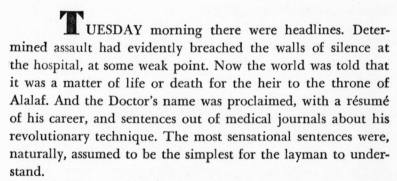

TUESDAY morning there were headlines. Determined assault had evidently breached the walls of silence at the hospital, at some weak point. Now the world was told that it was a matter of life or death for the heir to the throne of Alalaf. And the Doctor's name was proclaimed, with a résumé of his career, and sentences out of medical journals about his revolutionary technique. The most sensational sentences were, naturally, assumed to be the simplest for the layman to understand.

Two columnists analyzed the American image, as seen from Alalaf. One viewed the record with alarm and assessed a possible future improvement if American know-how saved the royal child. The other assessed the record as spotty, and viewed with alarm the possible future damages "if anything goes wrong." The one outlined Al Asad as a human grandfather, after all. The other painted him a primitive tyrant, unpredictable in his powerful ignorance.

By afternoon the news was out that severe rioting had taken place in the capital, and Al Asad, in the course of putting it down with a ruthless (or firm) use of the brutal (or loyal) military, had restored order with the loss of only three lives, although a dozen or more nameless natives had been (more or less) critically injured.

The hollow-cheeked, hollow-eyed prophets of doom on television, that evening, began to speculate openly on the consequences if the young prince did not survive the very tricky, very dubiously new, surgical procedure. "Worry, worry," they said to their viewers.

On Wednesday morning the story was rehash, but it kept the tension going. It had "heart."

On Wednesday afternoon Rufus was driving in his normal style, not very fast, and wandering rather dreamily from lane to lane, as the whim took him. But Lurlene felt so nervous she wished she had taken another tranquillizer. They had been summoned. She had dressed carefully because it could be that they had been summoned to meet this princess. But the truth was Lurlene didn't know what to make of such a summons. It had never happened before.

The Judge opened the door himself and said, "Come in," gravely. He was not smiling. The spacious house seemed very silent. You could practically hear the dust motes floating in the air. They were to go into the study. Lurlene hung back, with leaden legs, but Rufus went on into the room and she heard him say cheerfully, "Hi, Maggie."

"Go in, please," the Judge said, behind Lurlene. So she had to go in.

Maggie was sitting on the big black leather couch that was let into a niche among the bookcases. She was sitting tall; she was not smiling.

"Sit there, please," the Judge said, indicating the two leather chairs angled toward each other, across from the couch, a cozy conversational grouping of furniture that was arranged here in the center of the long narrow room. The Judge's big desk was at the far end. He did not go to his desk, but sat down beside Maggie.

"What's up?" said Rufus. "Who else is coming?"

"No one," said Maggie. Her voice was like a bell tolling.

"Well, say," said Lurlene from sheer nerves, "this is an unexpected . . ."

But Maggie's look stabbed all the way through to Lurlene's frightened core and she couldn't finish. She tried to relax, but the big chair was so tilted for lounging that when she put her back against its back, she felt like a stuffed doll, limp and helpless, her stomach humping up and her legs dangling.

The Judge said to Rufus, "Exactly when did you find out that the Prince of Alalaf was here, in the hospital?"

"Oh, that?" said Rufus. His lips were moist. He smiled his little chirrupy kind of smile.

(He don't know what it's all about, his wife thought. He never, never did. And she made, within herself, a hard resolve.)

The Judge knew that his was the role of reason and justice. Maggie was probably going to let loose later on. But she conceded him his turn, and first. So the Judge put his mind to it.

"Will you answer the question, please?" His deep voice was not impassioned.

"Well, let me see." Rufus began to slam his skull with his palm in that idiotic gesture that means "I am jolting my memory to make it work," as if a memory were a balky piece of machinery in a case. (The Judge was feeling very sad.) "Must have been the day Lurlene took the girls to lunch," said Rufus. "When was that, Lu?"

"Saturday," she said shortly.

"They told *you*, Lurlene, at lunch that day?" asked the Judge, who knew this already.

"Yes, they did," she said, as brightly as she could.

"They also told you that it must be kept a secret?"

"They sure did. I thought it *was* supposed to be a secret but, I mean, I see in the paper . . ."

The Judge lifted his hand to stop her; his eyes were sharp. "You told Rufus, that day?"

"Well, certainly," said Lurlene, bridling as best she could in her semireclining position. She began to struggle to sit up straighter. "Why shouldn't I tell my own husband?" she said, with wide eyes. "He's a Tyler, too, ain't he?"

"Yes," said the Judge, "he is. Did you tell anyone else at all?"

75   *

"Of course not," she said. "I certainly did not."

Rufus had been blinking and looking from face to face. "You know, I don't get this," he said unnecessarily.

"You went to a baseball game on Sunday afternoon?" the Judge said to him. "You told a man named Ed Duveen that the boy was here, and you told him why?"

"I did? Well, yes, I guess I did. I must say I didn't realize it was that much of a secret." Rufus was turning a bit pompous.

"You should've," murmured Lurlene, her heart pounding visibly.

"The fact is," Rufus went on, "Ed Duveen is a very close friend of mine . . ."

The Judge said, "Do you remember your mother warning us all that what she was about to say concerning Alice Foster's letter from Alalaf was 'just for the family'?"

"When was that?" said Rufus, frowning a little.

"You know what that phrase means to us?"

"Certainly I do," said Rufus promptly. "Look, I'm sorry if I spoke out of turn, but I can't see . . ."

"Because you spoke out of turn," the Judge said, "all the news media are now telling that secret to the entire world."

"Because of me?" said Rufus.

Lurlene had taken courage (because Rufus *was* stupid, and she felt protected now). "Pardon me, Judge, but how do you know it was because of him? It didn't have to be, did it?"

"I know it was," said the Judge quietly, "because Duncan spent all day Monday tracking it down. There is no doubt about it."

"What do you mean, Duncan tracking it down?" Rufus, still bewildered, now began to be resentful. "I don't get this!"

"We had to know whether it was a member of the family who betrayed this secret," said Maggie icily.

"You could have asked me, Mother," said Rufus, and his back slapped the back of his chair with a sharp sound.

"Or *you* could have told us," said Lurlene, "all about it, in the first place." (She kept thinking that she didn't have to sit here and take this, and then realizing that she *was* sitting here and taking this.) "Or else the girls should have kept still and *not* told me."

"I believe that I have heard," the Judge said patiently, "what was said at the luncheon table, and why. I am ready, of course, to listen to your version."

"I don't see any point in telling any version," Lurlene muttered. "You've got your minds made up," she added sullenly.

"I believe that you, too, Lurlene, heard Maggie's warning. And I believe that you have already told me that the girls did warn you. And very carefully."

"Yah, but *I* didn't tell," cried Lurlene. "*I* didn't go around telling. I told Rufus, that's all. I already said that, didn't I?"

Maggie said, in that voice of ice, shimmering cool and far away, "Did you, very, very carefully, explain to Rufus that it must be kept secret?"

"I *said* I did," cried Lurlene, "and if you're going to call me a liar, on top of everything . . ." Lurlene began to weep.

The Judge suspected that she was a liar, to some degree. He said to his son, sadly, "But you did not realize?"

"Maybe I wasn't paying too much attention," said Rufus. "I don't understand why it was supposed to be such a secret." He was querulous.

"You need not understand," his mother said. "When you are told a secret, and told that it is one, then you ought to keep it. Is it possible that you do not understand that?"

Rufus began to flush. "Well, I'm sorry. I know I'm stupid."

"But that is so very simple," said Maggie, and her voice mourned. "A matter of principle, very simple."

The Judge himself was wincing now. Rufus was looking blank.

Lurlene said, sniffling, "Are they pestering the poor little boy? Honest, I wouldn't have had him *pestered* . . ."

"He won't be pestered," the Judge said.

"But then," Lurlene looked up from her handkerchief, "I don't see what the fuss is all *about*, really. I mean . . ."

Maggie let loose her wrath. "I had assumed you were not malicious. But I hadn't known you were dangerous. It is our luck, and yours, too, that your brother will not be affected, that you *cannot* make Mitchel do less than his best, which is very good indeed."

Rufus said boldly, as if he had been stung at last, "Then what *is* the fuss about—if no harm's been done?"

"That's right," chimed Lurlene, in support. She thought it was a darned good point.

"Harm was done," said Maggie with a frightening drop to a sad calm. "There are three people, dead on the streets of Alalaf, who might not have died if you had held your tongue. The fact is, you ought to have held your tongue, and you did not. I can only conclude that I was quite right not to tell you 'all about it' in the first place, and wrong to have given you even the slightest hint.

"You are my children," Maggie continued with a curious grace. "You are welcome here. And always will be. But it is dangerous and unwise to tell you secrets, isn't it? For that I am sorry, but it is not I who can help it. Excuse me, now?" She rose and she left the room.

The Judge rose. "I think that is what we wanted to say." He felt helpless and sorry.

In the car Lurlene said, "Um, boy! The good old Princess, she probably bawled *Maggie* out. That's probably at the bottom of it." She glanced at his face slyly. Rufus was driving more erratically than ever, but his face was blank.

"I guess Maggie's not so crazy about being bawled out," said Lurlene. "You want to know something? Neither am I. And I don't think they were very fair to you, hon. Honest, I don't."

He didn't speak. Well, he was dumb. He *was* stupid. Lurlene could rely on that.

"Listen, sumpin's phony about the whole thing though," she

*   78

went on. "Tamsen tells me it's because the kid could get pestered. So now the Judge says that's not true. What are *we* supposed to think?"

He didn't answer. She moved closer to him. "Gee, honey," she said, "I guess you shouldn't have ever married me. Your family thinks I'm some kind of slob, all right. Well, what's that they put on ashtrays? 'I may be a slob, but I'm sincere.' " She laughed, in a tense way.

"My brother," said Rufus, talking like *them* somehow (as he sometimes did, although on the whole he had long ago fallen into Lurlene's speech habits), "my brother Duncan tracked me down."

"And didn't even have the decency to come and *ask* you," she supplied. "And Tamsen and Phillida, oh, sure . . . They go blabbing to the Judge, everything that was said at *my* party. Believe me, you don't catch me giving any more luncheons for them two. Well, I guess you and me are o-u-t out."

"Tracked me down." Rufus seemed stricken by this, in particular.

"And Duncan, he goes blabbing to the Judge and Maggie, too," Lurlene was happy to continue.

"But *Mitch* was in the paper this morning."

"Yah!" said Lurlene. "Yah, and here *you* went ahead and killed off three of them Arabs, or whatever they are, just while you're sitting at the ball game, thousands of miles away." She began to laugh a little hysterically. "I don't *believe* that. That's ridiculous, that is. I don't know what they think I am, but *that* stupid I'm not."

She glanced at his face again.

Rufus said, "She *acts*, you know."

"What? What do you mean?"

"The whole thing is phony."

He had such a funny look on his face that Lurlene didn't dare prod him to explain this. She simply agreed with him.

9

ON Thursday, Saiph's smiling face decked the covers of two news magazines. The morning paper quoted rumors of mysterious inside seethings in Alalaf. There was a rumor that American women and children were quietly being evacuated. There was a rumor of bombings. A rumor of a possible coup in progress. Rumors of rumors, flying among the people, that the Little Prince had been spirited away to the U.S.A. by his foreign mother on false pretenses, never to return. That the King, being senile, had been deceived. That the young man, nicknamed Dhanab, was preparing to seize power and act as regent for the boy, as in any case he might do when the old King died. Once in charge, Dhanab proposed to insist that the boy return at once. Dhanab was a strong man. Dhanab was weak, but a patriot, and riding the wave of the future. Dhanab was a mystery. All these rumors were unconfirmed. But there was some hard news of mobs screaming anti-American slogans.

In the privacy of the suite on the fifth floor at the hospital, that same Thursday morning, while elsewhere Dr. Mitchel Tyler applied himself to his delicate work, the women sat waiting. There was Jaylia, the patient's mother; Inga, his nurse; Tamsen, his playmate; and Maggie.

It was Maggie who kept talking, rambling in a gentle voice over many inconsequential topics. The two guards sat on the floor, their fierce eyes frustrated; yet they listened now and then. Maggie kept on talking.

At noon there was a news special on TV, a so-called roundup. Lurlene and Rufus, eating their sandwiches and drinking their glasses of beer, sat before the little window to the world.

"Before this broadcast is over, we hope to be able to bring you a bulletin from the hospital, where an American surgeon is now . . ." The situation was rehashed.

Then all the rumors were repeated, and a few added. There was a rumor that a bomb may have been thrown at an apartment house where Mrs. Alice Foster, the Little Prince's American grandmother, was alleged to be staying. The bomb had been a dud. Or, no dud, but little damage. Or, guards on the building had made the bomb ineffective. All these rumors were unconfirmed.

When the supply of rumors ran out, the commentators began on the boy's family tree. When that ran out, they began on his doctor's. And, by now, time was running out of the allotted hour.

"Dr. Mitchel Tyler is the brilliant son of Judge William Rufus Tyler, who is well-known all over this country as . . ." and so on and so on.

"Dr. Tyler's mother is the incomparable Maggie Mitchel, the famous actress, who . . ." and so on and so on.

Time was running as fast as the last grains of salt. The commentator was reaching. "Dr. Tyler is married to Phillida Tyler, prominent directress of many charitable . . ." and so on.

"Dr. Tyler's brother, Duncan, will be one of the youngest men . . ." and so on.

"Duncan Tyler's wife is Tamsen Tyler, voted by some to be the West's most promising young artist of our time . . ." and so on.

"For those who tuned in late, we are awaiting some news from St. Genevieve's Hospital, where the eleven-year-old Prince of Alalaf . . ." and so on and so on. Then staccato—"*Just a minute!*"

The commentator put a hand out of the picture and plucked a strip of paper from unseen regions.

"The operation has been performed," he announced, "and was successful! The Little Prince is in the recovery room and will be in intensive care for some time. He is doing well! Doing well! This is good news. Ladies and gentlemen, this is good news! The Little Prince is doing well!"

In the hospital, Jaylia was on the phone to the Palace in Alalaf.

In the other room, Maggie was on the phone, calling the family. The Judge at home. Phillida at her office. Duncan at the University.

Lurlene answered the telephone.

"Oh, Maggie," she said, rolling her eyes around to signal Rufus. "We just now heard it on TV. But thanks for calling. Um . . . I'm sure *glad*. We . . . we felt awful. I mean, Rufus didn't mean a thing, you know? But we both felt just awful about it."

"I thought you would be glad to hear," said Maggie. "It has been a long morning."

"Oh, it sure has! I'm real glad. I think it's just wonderful!"

"Yes. Give my love to Rufus."

"Oh, I sure will!"

But she did not. Lurlene hung up and went over to the couch and flung herself face down. The special on TV was over. She never paid much attention to commercials.

Rufus said, "Was that Maggie?"

"Calling up to tell us the good news," said Lurlene. "Nice of her, I guess. Only *I* thought they weren't going to tell us the time of day anymore."

"She was upset the other day," he said vaguely.

"Yah, sure. Me, too. But nobody wants to know how *I* feel."

"Lurlene," he said earnestly. He must have moved. He was standing over her. "You were always the girl for me. You're Mrs. Rufus Tyler, and don't you forget that."

"I'm not *going* to," she snuffled.

"And I promised you . . ."

"Don't bother. Just don't *bother*." She turned her face into the upholstery.

"Honey-Lu?"

"I notice how they said 'and the doctor's brother, Rufus Tyler.' I notice *that*, all right."

"Don't worry, hon."

"What have *I* got to worry about?" Lurlene was bawling. "Your father pays on the mortgage. That's all *I* need, in this world."

"Don't worry," he kept saying dully.

At the hospital Maggie, having announced that there were too many people here, stepped with Tamsen out of the building into a pack of newsmen. Maggie handled them with an awesome grace.

She had come with Jaylia, in a chauffeur-driven car, accompanied by a Secret Service man, so Tamsen got into it with her to be taken to where Tamsen had hidden her own Volkswagen, some blocks away.

"He isn't perfectly safe yet," said Tamsen, "is he?"

"He never will be, and who ever is?" said Maggie with an exhausted sigh. "We must give thanks and rejoice for so much, so far."

"And Mrs. Foster is all right, too. Alice Foster?"

"So far," said Maggie. "She sounded happy on the telephone."

"You were wonderful," said Tamsen. "And his mother was wonderful, I thought."

"What was so wonderful?" said Maggie musingly. "He might have died. He still may. Any of us may, at any moment."

"Though true," said Tamsen dryly, "that never did comfort *me* much."

Maggie was cheered immediately, and she laughed. "Then don't you let it," she said gaily. "Don't you let fate keep kicking you in the teeth, without making some human protest. Otherwise, what's the fun of it all?"

"Mitch protested," said Tamsen, "didn't he?"

"Yes, my dear. He did, indeed." Maggie kissed her a fond farewell and announced that she was going home to interfere with the destiny of one clump of iris. Maggie was going to thin it out, because she was alive and, for the duration, she chose to consider her garden *her* garden.

That evening Judge Tyler spoke calmly about brinkmanship in human affairs which, being the art of sensitive, quick and bold response to whatever should happen to happen next, could never be explained to the general populace because it never stood still long enough. His mellow discourse made Jaylia nod, and Maggie smile.

That evening Phillida Tyler paced her apartment and used some unladylike words. Her husband had done damn brilliantly well but, alas, the shame of publicity was upon him, and now he must live that down, damn and blast! Her explosions made the Doctor chuckle.

That evening Duncan Tyler lectured to his wife on the subject of news columnists. "You've heard that the Devil can quote Scripture to his purpose? Likewise, whatever somebody wants to 'see by the papers' that 'they say' (or, in other words, whatever he needs to reinforce his original prejudice), he can find it, in one column or another. The fact that those boys are working stiffs and must turn out the daily stint, who thinks of that?" It pleased Tamsen to hear him holding forth in his old vein.

That evening Rufus Tyler entertained Ed Duveen and his wife with boastful accounts of the prowess of the members of his remarkable family, and how their names were destined for the history books, all right. It made Lurlene nervous for some reason.

10

OVER the weekend the news broke that the coup, or whatever it had been intended to be, had failed in Alalaf. But—mild sensation—Dhanab had not been seen for forty-eight hours. He had vanished. Nobody knew whether he was dead or alive or, in either case, where. The old King rode high. But the little country was rumored to be on a brink, from which it must tilt onward or fall back. The great holes in its fabric, between jet plane and donkey, between howling wilderness and air-conditioned office building, must be filled in and smoothed over. But with whose help?

Meantime, the American professors still languished in their cells, for reasons unknown but guessed at. The guesses were then analyzed, as if they were not guesses at all. The East accused the West, and the West the East, as usual, of some dirty fingers in the small, but "significant" pie.

"Jaylia, dear," read Maggie aloud, on the following Tuesday morning. "Share this with Maggie and William, and tell them, all over again, how I am rejoicing over Saiph and how I bless them and theirs.

"I am happy to tell you that the foreign press is beginning to be believed around these parts. After all, fifty million Frenchmen, Britishers, Italians, Egyptians, Israelis, Indians, and who-have-we can't *all* be wrong. So it is getting through, in spite of a great deal of nonsense to the contrary, that Saiph is not only alive and well, but in better health than he has been.

"For the rest, don't worry too much. The Lion is the King of Beasts, as usual. However, the aforesaid nonsense was (for nonsense) too consistent and too evenly spread to have sprung up spontaneously. Somebody was trying to use your secret departure. But who, ah, who?

"The one out front may have seemed to be that which drags behind. But right from my little webby nest I could a tale unfold. Although I won't, until time untangles.

"Meanwhile, there, take care, let him heal, and when he is perfectly strong, bring him home.

"Love. And love to all Tylers. Your devoted Alice."

"Now really!" said Maggie in exasperation. "What on earth is to be made of *most* of that?"

"Oh, Mother loves to be cryptic." Jaylia was smiling. She hesitated and then added, "I suppose you may not know that Al Asad means The Lion?"

"Oh?" said Maggie. "Well, *that* was clear enough anyhow."

"Anything else, meaning what we may not know?" drawled the Judge, cheerfully suspicious.

"Oh," said Jaylia, "not much." She laughed aloud. "My mother is priceless. She is really priceless."

"So she is, but does she know what she's talking about? Or, I should say, *not* talking about, so that a lay person such as I am can figure it out?" Maggie was sputtering.

"She has her methods," said Jaylia mirthfully, "as she keeps saying."

"Spiders it up, eh?" said Maggie, beginning to smile, too.

But the Judge thought that some news had been conveyed to Jaylia in the letter that Jaylia considered none of their business. Still, whatever it was, it was making Jaylia merry, so he fell in with the mood of gaiety here at the breakfast table, intending later to do his duty and pass along, for what they were worth, what on-the-spot observations he had gleaned from Alice Foster's letter. And so he did.

But the Judge was a shrewd old party, and inclined to persist. He settled in his leather chair, with the fat unabridged dictionary before him, and through its pages he pursued this and that. When referred, he pursued the reference. At last he came to a certain definition and he, too, laughed aloud.

He didn't understand the news entirely, but the way it was put was certainly amusing.

Tamsen had not been allowed in the hospital for several days. When she appeared, on Wednesday, she found her little friend pale and obviously still weak from the ordeal, but in good spirits, accepting life as easily as death, and glad to see her. She sat beside him and, in order to ask no effort of him, told him stories. When her hour was up, Saiph promised her that he would be thinking up questions for tomorrow.

"And tomorrow and tomorrow," she said, rejoicing.

"And when I am strong, I may go and see?" he said wistfully to the window.

"I don't know, Butch. *I'll* see you tomorrow."

"O.K., old-timer," Saiph said. "It's a date."

The guard on the door to the suite said to her urgently, "Mrs. Tyler, maybe you better get on down there."

She looked toward the elevators and recognized that there was an argument of some sort going on. So she hurried.

"Mrs. Tyler," said one of the guards, "is this man a Mr. Tyler? He refuses to show identification."

"Oh, yes," she gasped. "Rufus, what are you doing here?"

"Just thought I'd come by and be neighborly," said Rufus. "I don't get all *this,* believe me." His face was red and his eyes were rolling. He seemed to have a candy box under his arm.

"This is the Doctor's brother," Tamsen said.

"We have no instructions to let him pass," the guard said, at the same time.

"Oh, Rufus, you should have phoned," she said. "You can't see Saiph today, I'm afraid. No visitors allowed."

"What are *you* doing here?" he said truculently.

"Let's go down to the coffee shop and I'll tell you."

"I brought him a little present," Rufus grumbled. "Just trying to be . . ."

"No gifts," said the guard sharply.

"That was awfully kind of you," said Tamsen, "but please . . ."

"Well, we wanted to pay a little attention—being family." Rufus looked haughtily at the guard.

"Of course you did." Tamsen was anxious to get him away. He had been in enough trouble. The guards were bristling. "Come on downstairs with me, Rufus, please?"

Rufus got into the elevator with her. "Say, who *are* these men?" he demanded.

"Oh, they are guards. Government people."

"What for?"

"Well, that's a very important little boy," she said. "They can't have people bothering him."

"No visitors?" He looked angry and suspicious. "Not a soul, eh?"

"Well, of course, when his mother comes, every morning and every evening, sometimes Maggie or the Judge comes with her. But even Phillida comes by only once in a long while, and she *never* stays."

"Duncan?"

"No, he *never* comes." (Duncan was minding his own business these days.)

"But *you* can get in, eh, Tamsen? You were in there with him?"

"Come on. Let's have a coffee break and I'll tell you. And you can tell me how you've been, too. I haven't seen you for so long."

She led him into the coffee shop, where they took a small table. "You see," she said, when the coffee cups were before them,

89   ✳

"Mitch asked me, long ago, to come by and play with the little boy for an hour every day. I've been doing that, ever since he got here. Today's the first time I've come, since surgery—but that's my job. So that's all about it. How have *you* been? But first, tell me, how is Lurlene?"

Tamsen hated coffee breaks, but she had settled herself to seem cozy, and to please and comfort him, if possible.

"She's fine." Rufus had a changed look. Perhaps he had not been feeling well. Tamsen dimly remembered Lurlene having said something to this effect. His face looked thinner. Now that the flush of anger had receded, he looked pale.

"And you've been keeping well and busy?" she said.

"Oh, yes. I've been fairly busy." He smiled, not at her, but at the table top. "Doing some homework. Research, you could say."

"That's interesting."

"Yes, it . . . uh . . . keeps me busy. So that's a very important little boy, eh?" He sucked in coffee. "I guess so."

"All little boys are very important," said Tamsen sentimentally. "This one happens to be—well, you could say—in the spotlight of history, poor child."

"We . . . uh . . . This happens to be homemade candy." Rufus smacked the pound box he had before him on the table. "All kids like candy, we thought."

"Wasn't it good of Lurlene to go to the trouble," said Tamsen in her soft voice.

Rufus was staring at her as if she had startled him.

"Oh, I'm sure you *will* meet Saiph, before he goes home again," she comforted.

"How soon will that be?" He pulled himself up.

"The Doctor hasn't told us. I suppose it depends on lots of things."

"They'd have blamed *me*, you know," said Rufus in tones curiously too flat and dull for the meaning of his words.

"Oh, I'm sure that's all been forgotten." Tamsen, who herself had forgiven and almost forgotten, was quick to cast backwards. "Don't you agree, it is obvious now that something was going to be troublesome in Alalaf, sooner or later, no matter what?"

"The old King should step down," Rufus said, eyeing her craftily.

"Do you think so?" she murmured. "I don't know very much about Al Asad."

"But a little kid can't rule the country," Rufus continued didactically. "This Dhanab might. He's got modern ideas."

"Has he?" Tamsen kept her eyes lowered, because she couldn't believe that Rufus was an authority. Yet she felt he needed her respectful attention. "You don't think he is dead, then?"

"No, no," said Rufus, expanding. "No, no, he's lying low, choosing the right time, consolidating his support."

"I see," she said softly. "I didn't know."

But when he said no more, she looked up and caught the anger on his face.

"You have made a study of it, haven't you?" she said. "More than I have, surely." She forced herself to a belief in what she was saying. It might be so.

He said, "Say, Tamsen, you go up and see this boy every day? Your job, you say? Why couldn't you take him his present?"

"Oh, I wish I could," she said, "but it wouldn't be permitted, really." Tamsen tried to soften this. "He has to keep to a very strict diet, for one thing. It would have to be doctor's orders. Why don't you talk to Mitch, and see when he thinks you could come by and meet Saiph? Next week, possibly?"

He was moving his jaw in an odd way from side to side, without opening his mouth at all.

"I might do that," he said in a moment. "Say, uh . . ." His brows rode up, his eyes popped. "Why don't you take the candy home, then, Tamsen? Somebody might as well enjoy it." Bright idea? his expression was asking.

She thought, I simply must not reject him again. He has been rejected just too many times. "Why, thank you very much, Rufus," she said, summoning enthusiasm. "That's awfully kind. May I, really?"

"Do that." He nodded and got up, bumbling and striking his thigh against the table.

"Are you all right?" she said. It occurred to her that he might be feeling dizzy.

"Fine," he said absently. "Fine." He didn't thank her for the coffee, although she had been the quicker to produce the money. Instead, he left her abruptly, went out and started down the corridor toward the street.

Tamsen followed in a moment and turned the other way, toward the parking lot, the box of candy in her hand. It seemed to her to be a pathetic object. It was also, for her, an object to which clung an aura of inexplicable loathsomeness. There was a porter in a blue coverall hauling a very large wastebasket toward the back of the building. Tamsen slipped the candy box into the trash. "A little contribution. O.K.?" she said to the man, who grinned and went on.

Tamsen herself went on, feeling relieved, yet puzzled and faintly alarmed, and trying to track down a reason for all these feelings. Then she heard him calling her name and she let the glass door settle without going through it. "Oh? Yes? Rufus?"

"I changed my mind," he said gruffly.

"What?"

"I'll just take that candy. I'm sure you don't care that much."

"Oh, but . . ." She swallowed. She was caught and no way out. Nothing she could do.

"Oh, I'm sorry," she said. "I . . . Rufus, I was very grateful for the thought, but I never do eat candy. And Duncan's off sweets."

"Where is it?" He brushed all else aside.

"Well, I . . ."

"What did you do with it? You gave it to somebody," he roared. "Some 'nothing' kind of menial, I suppose?"

"No, no," she said, feeling terrified. "I put it in the trash."

He stared at her. His full lips began to smile saucily. "Now, wasn't that," he said, "a stinking lousy thing for you to do?"

"Yes, it was," she said valiantly. "I didn't want to hurt your feelings."

"You *are* a phony, aren't you?" he said, as if this statement had been made and was now ratified. "You don't count, though," he said thickly. He looked for a second as if he were going to cry. Then he turned and walked away, staggering slightly.

Tamsen went outside, staggering a little herself. Oh, she was thinking, oh, what I just did to him! Me and my famous old tender heart! Rejected him, just like everybody else, but *I* had to go and lie about it. And make it twenty times as bad! I see. Do I? Do I begin to see what Duncan means about me?

Duncan sipped his cocktail and listened to his wife explain herself. "I begin to see," she was saying earnestly. She was pretty cute, he thought, when she curled up and turned her delicate face to him and spoke so earnestly. "I always feel that I ought to be kind. I ought *never* to hurt a human person's feelings. So, if I think the truth is going to hurt I'll soften it. So the result is, I just don't tell the truth, do I?"

"Let's not get carried away, here," he said with amusement. "I wouldn't call you a dishonest woman."

"But I am," she said, "and I've even thought I was right to be. Now I see it may be kinder to tell the truth."

"Well, it's safer," he teased her. "That way you don't get caught telling pretty lies."

"Yes, I got caught," she said soberly. "The point is, not to let it happen again. Wouldn't *you* say?"

He laughed and embraced her. He thought it was all very well for Tamsen to have had an insight into some of her ways. But it was just her combination of delicate conscience, dear gentle heart, and unexpected humor about both, that he loved,

93　✳

even when the combination sometimes led her where she didn't always see herself going.

"I guess I'd better brace myself," he announced, "to have the truth, the whole truth, and nothing but the truth, hurled into my teeth at all times. Do I deserve this?"

"Oh, well, let's not get carried away," she said, and Duncan felt content.

When, hours later, he looked up from his book to the clock and found his instinct to have been right (it was bedtime), he saw Tamsen on the couch over there, motionless, with one foot under her, evidently in a trance of thought. He had a telepathic flash.

"So *why* did you put a gift box in the trash?" he said quietly.

"Because the candy was poisoned," Tamsen said.

"Oh, honey, honey." Duncan was much alarmed. He was alarmed for her. He thought, She can't forgive herself for hurting my brother's feelings, for having been so carelessly rude, against all her principles, so she is dreaming up a better reason. And this ain't good! "Just forget it, why don't you?" he begged.

Tamsen seemed to wake and blink. "Did I *say* that?"

"I wish you hadn't."

"I suppose I'd . . . better not spare your feelings?"

"No," he said tenderly.

"All right. I think Rufus is in a bad state. I think he is mentally ill. I think he had it in mind . . ."

"Go on." Duncan wasn't being reassured.

"To poison Prince Saiph."

"Well!" said Duncan, faking objectivity. "That's a mouthful. For what on earth reason would Rufus want to poison Prince Saiph?"

"I don't know," she said.

Duncan himself could not imagine any reason. Rufus? All right, Rufus might not have the most brilliant mind in the world, and Rufus might, on occasion, feel discouraged not to have found a talent in himself that he knew how or where to employ, but Rufus was (although bumbling) an amiable soul. There was no meanness in him. Nothing vicious. Why should there be? He was beloved. He belonged.

No, no, the problem here was Tamsen.

"But he couldn't manage, eh? So he figured to assassinate you instead? Just while he was up, eh?" Duncan *might* reduce this to absurdity.

"He does hate me, in particular." She seemed serious.

"I should think," said Duncan carefully, becoming more or less serious himself, "that if *I* had given somebody a gift, and been prettily thanked, and then found out that she had quickly thrown it in the trash, *I* would be somewhat annoyed."

"No, that's backwards."

Duncan began to feel like shaking her. He said, "But he did think better of it? He did decide *not* to poison you today? How does that go, again?"

"He stopped to think, and I didn't count," said Tamsen.

"Honey, honey—" Duncan went to her and took her hands and looked into her eyes, those brilliant eyes. "I don't think it's very good for you to go there every day, with all those Secret Service monkeyshines, and all that suspicious protective stuff. You have too much imagination. You're too suggestible."

"Oh, don't," she said. "If you think I'm crazy, just say so. I'd be very glad to know it."

"Not crazy. That doesn't mean anything. See here, can you get hold of that candy? Have it analyzed? Prove something?"

"I doubt it exists. It went to be burned."

"Nobody would have retrieved it, and eaten any?"

"Nobody eats the trash, in a hospital."

"Then you can't prove it?"

"Of course not. If I could prove it, I might know what to do."

"Do you even believe it?" he asked gently.

"But it's not *like* believing. It's more like knowing."

"Honey," he said, "could you possibly try to take it, right on your little old chin? Try this on, for size?"

"All right," she said trustingly.

"*You* don't like *Rufus*. I won't say you 'hate' him. But you loathed the idea of putting his nasty old homemade candy, full of fingerprints and all, into your dainty mouth."

She was hit. She winced. He saw it.

"So you threw it where you 'felt' it belonged. But you got caught. And you don't like the looks of yourself in this matter very much. You'd rather see yourself 'forever kind.' You wouldn't mind one bit, if you had a better reason to have done what you did. Do you think this is possible?"

She took it. Her chin quivered only a little.

"I'll agree it was an irrational act. And to say such things, to think such things now, is not rational, either."

Duncan, however, got the message. "Intuitional, eh? O.K. Even if you are right, I wouldn't fret. Rufus is too . . . well, we'll have to say it . . . too dumb to pull it off. Would you know, for instance, *how* to poison a batch of candy? With what? Believe me, *I* don't know. And Saiph never would have the chance to put it in his mouth. It wouldn't have got to him. Nothing happened. Nothing will. Sweetheart, let it rest? Your intuition could be wrong."

"Oh, Lord, I can be just as wrong as anybody else," she sighed. "But I don't think Rufus is well. I really don't."

"That much," he said, "I'll take from your intuition. You may very well be right. Trouble is, I'm not the doctor."

11

"**I**'M sorry to hear that," the Doctor said. "Haven't seen Rufus myself since the big night at Maggie's. Which was a while ago."

He sat behind his desk, courteously relaxed, but Tamsen knew she had been squeezed in between appointments; she must not linger.

"I hadn't seen him again either, until yesterday," she said. "And it struck me so . . . well, so urgently . . . how he has changed. Duncan says *he's* not the doctor. Neither of us—or anyhow *I* don't—know what to do."

Mitchel Tyler smiled at her. "Neither am I the doctor, in this case. What about Lurlene. Is she concerned?"

"I don't know. She may be. I can't, you see, just go there and be direct. I'm pretty much off on the wrong foot with both of them. The trouble with me is, I busybody too much," said Tamsen miserably, "just as I'm doing right now."

"How about Maggie and the Judge? I suppose they are entitled to go and be direct." The Doctor cocked his head. "Why isn't it good of you, Tamsen, to take notice and be concerned?"

"No, that's my failing," she said. "I am, believe me, an *awful* nuisance, to myself, too."

"We're very fond of him, you know," the Doctor said, his fine hands playing with a pencil. "But it may be true that the rest

97　✳

of us become so engrossed, so meshed into our own marching affairs, that we never do find time to stop and hold his hand."

"Maybe you shouldn't hold his hand," she said promptly. "It's only that he scared me. You see . . ." She had not told Mitch about the box of candy. She was tempted to do so now. But the Doctor had made one involuntary restless motion of his hand, so she rose. "No. I certainly mustn't hang around and ask you to hold *my* hand."

"Then I'll say thanks for alerting me." He rose and was smiling.

"Thanks for letting me in."

"Aren't you on my staff?" He walked with her to the door. "How did you find Saiph today?"

"Oh, he's making leaps and bounds." It struck her as absurd that she should be telling the Doctor. "Isn't he?" she challenged.

"He should make very rapid progress from here on," Mitch said, with obvious pleasure. "No use saying 'Don't worry about Rufus.' The most ineffective advice in the world, eh? But I'll give him the hard eye, next time I see him."

And you can't ask fairer than that, thought Tamsen in her car. She felt that she had made enough of an intrusion, without burdening the busy man with her "irrational" details. Mitch is decisive, she thought with admiration. He says he will cast a hard eye, and he will.

Well, then, she had done it. Duncan had approved. He seemed to think it was not too unreasonable a thing, for her to talk to Mitch about his brother. It was supposed to be off *her* mind, now. Maybe that was what Duncan had approved.

Of course, Mitch wouldn't *hurry*.

Tamsen found her car to be turning the other way from home.

There was a guard on the entrance to the grounds in San Marino, but Tamsen was let through at once. Sam, who opened the door, told her that Mrs. Tyler was out. The Judge was out, also. But the Princess was on the pool deck, if Mrs. Duncan would like to come on through?

So Tamsen went on through the house and out at the other side, asking herself why she had been cursed by this compulsion to be so torn between duty and fear-to-offend, between heart and conscience, and always guilty, either way. Always torn, and never decisive, and unable to mind her own business. How could she, the youngest and newest Tyler wife, go to Maggie and say that Maggie's second son was, in her opinion, losing his mind? On the other hand, how could she refrain from mentioning, to another mother, that *her* son might be in danger from an unsuspected quarter? Yet how could she, a Tyler, tell an outsider that a Tyler was a potential madman? On the other hand, if she did not tell *somebody* . . .

But she had.

She drifted across the terraces and down the steps to the pool deck where Jaylia, in two scraps of white, was lying on a long white chaise, her flesh oiled to receive the sun.

"Tamsen! How nice to see you! Come and sit down. How is my child?"

Tamsen sat down on a white-webbed chair, in a spot dappled with shade. "Oh, just since yesterday," she said, "his energy has been seeping back. You can see it coming in, like the tide."

"I thought so, too, this morning," said Jaylia, yanking at the mechanism of her chaise to pull up the back and be able to sit, rather than lie. She was a pleasant color, Tamsen thought, the shade of a lightly browned biscuit. Her teeth seemed very white when she smiled.

"How am I going to thank you?" the Princess exclaimed. "It's Tamsen-this, and Tamsen-that, when I am there. He is just delighted with you."

"Likewise, I am sure," said Tamsen happily.

"But this must be taking too much time away from your work. Your poor neglected paintings."

"They'll be the better for it," said Tamsen, her heart warming wonderfully, to her surprise.

"I wish I could come and see what you are up to. But I can very well go running around." Jaylia sighed. "I'm out of the habit, you know, anyway. 1 may have forgotten *how* to drive a car." She had her chair and knees adjusted now. "Maggie's off shopping. The Judge had an appointment. But here I am."

"Tell me," said Tamsen. "Saiph wouldn't . . . He wouldn't, for instance, take candy from a stranger? Would he, Jaylia? It worries me sometimes."

"Does it?" said Jaylia. "Yes, I see it does."

"But it doesn't worry you?"

"I suppose it must. Although I'm so used to it, I forget. Oh, yes, Saiph understands that *he* must always be especially cautious. Is that what you mean?"

"He is so young."

"Ah"—Jaylia stretched and spoke softly—"but he will grow up, now."

Tamsen had been, ever since the morning in the hospital, seeing this woman in a new light. Now there was full sun. Jaylia, here (half-naked, American fashion) in Maggie's garden, seemed to have put off that allure, or whatever it was. Because there were no men around? No, thought Tamsen, maybe not. Jaylia looked, today, like a normal healthy young woman, a little too well-padded, but attractive, and friendly and easy and also (as a woman ought to be) a loving woman.

"I think," Jaylia was saying, "there must be different . . . um . . . call them life-styles?"

"Explain that some more," said Tamsen, feeling friendly and easy, and sinking back.

"I suppose *I* always did enjoy a spot of danger," Jaylia mused. "When I married, I moved into all this sort of thing. The peril, the swarms of protectors, the constant wariness, and the obligation to *take* chances, too. Saiph has never known anything else.

Of course, it is a style of living that some people could not bear."

"I certainly couldn't," Tamsen said, with conviction.

"Your husband couldn't, either," said the Princess, gazing afar.

Tamsen was brushed by the wing of a resentful suspicion. Here! Here! Was Jaylia telling Tamsen that she was welcome to her own husband? But then Jaylia laughed.

"I was thinking that, of all of you Tylers, perhaps Mitch wouldn't mind the cold-blooded risk-taking. But oh, how he would be bored by all the pussy-footing!"

So Tamsen had to smile. "You haven't met," she said in a moment, seeing her opening, "the other son, Rufus?"

"Oh, yes," said Jaylia. "He was here, day before yesterday. Maggie gave us sandwiches and salads."

"Oh," said Tamsen, enlightened. "Oh, then maybe I understand how come he was so knowledgeable about Alalaf yesterday."

"He does read the papers rather diligently," said Jaylia, very innocently. "Yesterday?"

"Rufus came to the hospital. He meant to call on Saiph. But, of course, he wasn't let."

"I see," said Jaylia. "A reciprocal gesture. Because Maggie . . . Oh now, come, come. I shouldn't be gossiping about the Tylers. God knows what I owe them."

"I suppose I shouldn't, either," Tamsen said, "having become one of them. But I'll bet you it was olive-branchy? Maggie *would* make some such gesture, bless her."

"She would, wouldn't she?" said Jaylia warmly. "Poor man, he brought down so much wrath upon his head."

"Did you . . ." But Tamsen could not say "think he seemed crazy?" . . . "meet Lurlene, too?" she substituted.

"No, she wasn't here. We discussed Alalaf." Jaylia leaned back. "Although *I* can't really do that. It is too different. It isn't anything like this. Not *anything*. Aljedi and I spent most of a

101 ✱

year in Europe, you see. I have only begun to try to understand."

"You live there now, all year?"

"My son lives there," said Jaylia. "My son is not an American little boy."

"No, but he is a darling, and I adore him," said Tamsen flatly.

"Yes," said Jaylia, "everybody does. But I don't think you, or any other American, even including me, can ever really know some very deep part of his mind, or anticipate exactly how Saiph will react."

"Is he like his father, then?"

"Somewhat. Somewhat," said Jaylia restlessly.

Tamsen said intuitively, "*I* think you're homesick for Alalaf."

"How did you know?" said Jaylia. "This is so lovely, so comfortable, so free, and so safe. And here I am, beginning to feel as restless as a—as a snake!"

Tamsen laughed. "This is all you say. It just doesn't happen to be *your* life-style."

"No." Jaylia was glowing with the pleasure of having been understood. "Saiph is restless, too. Locked up in those four walls. We are going to bring him here, very soon. That should be helpful."

"Here?" Tamsen felt alarm. "But is this safe enough?"

"Why, it should be easier. After all, this is not a public building. Besides, they can't allow him the solarium. Here, he can have the sun. Ah, but *you* must keep on coming, Tamsen, or he won't like it at all. I warn you, he is capable of assuming that you belong to him."

"He may be right," said Tamsen solemnly. "I am going to have a fit of noble proportions when he goes away home."

Jaylia moved her head slightly, in sympathy, but said nothing.

"I'd better go home, *now*." Tamsen rose, and the Princess rose, draped herself in a towel, and led her through the house, chatting all the way. Tamsen simply could not help liking this girl. The Princess, towel-clad, stood on the front portico to wave her off, as if they had been old chums.

Maggie's car was coming in. "Oh, Tamsen," said Maggie, driver-to-driver, as they paused on opposite paths, "I've been shopping all afternoon with Lurlene. You're not leaving?"

"I must feed a husband. I've had a lovely time with Jaylia."

"Oh, good, then," Maggie approved. *"Hasta la vista."*

Tamsen drove on, feeling humble and happy. Maggie was doing the healing things, of course. Tamsen really need not shoulder the whole world, at her age.

The truth was, Duncan was not for Jaylia, and Jaylia was not for Duncan, and they knew it very well. And Tamsen knew it, too.

12

THERE had been a cooling off, or at least a scarcity of news, in Alalaf. Affairs there had either stabilized or were straining in an impasse. Reports that nothing was known to have changed faded to small inside paragraphs, if any. And the Little Prince, being out of danger, was no fun anymore, either.

When they moved Saiph, on the following Thursday, quietly by ambulance and rather late at night—the two guards riding with him, as hidden as he, and no sirens wailing—there was nobody lurking about whose business it was to notice anything odd.

Saiph was delighted with his new quarters. He sat up in the four-poster in the guest room over the east wing and poured out questions about the customs of the natives, as typified in an authentic native dwelling. Jaylia and her maid continued to inhabit the west wing. Inga had a bed in the spacious dressing room, off Saiph's room, built back-to-back with the Judge's similar arrangement. Maggie solved the problem of the two guards by charming those lately much relaxed young men into agreeing with her. One of them was stationed under Saiph's window and balcony. The other was at the bottom of the back stairs. If and when they wished to sleep, there were beds for them over the garage.

After all, Secret Service men were not only on the front door, but all around the perimeter of the property.

So the establishment settled down to be a fortress in which to entertain and enjoy their convalescing guest. Only Tylers came in and out: the Doctor, often; Phillida, from time to time; Duncan, only now and then. Tamsen made the long drive every day.

She had set aside her worries about Rufus. She had no time for them, anyway. Saiph was frisky as a squirrel. Soon, soon, he would be going home. There had been no softening assurances that Tamsen must, of course, go there to visit him. No one had been cruel enough to pretend that this would ever happen.

"*I* have got to have a baby!" she concluded. "A boy. A girl. *Two* of each. *Lots* of babies!"

Duncan said he agreed, but whoa . . . one step at a time, did she mind? After all, a poor schoolteacher, he. They mustn't forget that every darned one of those babies would, one day, need a college education. They should figure for future financial breathing spaces. He was only half kidding, and she knew it. He and I, Tamsen thought, have the *same* life-style, by gosh!

When somebody made the discovery, three days later, that the boy was no longer in the hospital, there was a bit of a flurry. *Boy Prince spirited away*. The Judge shut this up firmly by stating the truth to the press at once. The house endured a brief siege, and then this flurry died away.

Lurlene saw it in the paper. "You see this, Rufus?"

Rufus had seen it.

"Yah, *we* get to read it in the paper," she grumbled. "I guess little old Tamsen gets in."

"I could get in," he muttered.

"That's right," said Lurlene bitterly. "We are her children. We're welcome, and always will be. Nyah! Nyah! Nyah!"

Shopping with Maggie the other day had practically given Lurlene the jitters. While Maggie had bought (with the back of her hand, like) three different costumes for herself, very sure of which would suit, Lurlene had finally bought one suit for fall. And when she got it home it didn't do a thing for her. Lurlene felt she had been brainwashed, or something. So O.K., it was real nice of Maggie. So O.K. So what?

She got up and went into another room. Rufus had a new toy. He didn't know she knew about it. She didn't want to know about it officially. She was thinking now—and nobody could say she didn't try to be understanding and all—that Rufus might feel like playing with it this minute.

Sometimes she didn't want to stay in the room with him, these days.

Well, she felt sorry for him. God knows, she felt sorry. You could say one thing, he wasn't any chaser. He was hers alone. But honestly, I mean, how sorry can you feel? she thought. Rufus could be damned stubborn, and that wasn't *her* fault. He didn't want to talk. He didn't want to let her baby him, or anything. Or get out of here, for instance, and go someplace else where his folks couldn't bug him, if that was what was bugging him. Well, O.K. God knows she had tried. She would have liked to be sure how much insurance he was carrying (she forgot) but she was too superstitious to ask anybody, right out. Besides, it might not look so good—some day.

She stood at her sink and she thought, Tragedy! Here we got tragedy! And his own folks paying more attention to some kid, that's nothing but a foreigner.

It didn't occur to her that she might have said something to Maggie about what strange thoughts she kept thinking these days. *They* didn't tell *her* one damn thing anymore, did they? Well, could be they'd feel sorry for that before too long.

Rufus' new toy was a gun. Lurlene didn't know exactly what he was figuring to do with it.

On Monday burst the headline. AL ASAD TO L. A.

Then followed the speculations. The King is coming! What

does this *mean?* Is he flying into voluntary exile? Is he, in effect, abdicating? Will the mysterious Dhanab appear and take over? Or has the military given notice? What, then, of the Prince?

Or, must a suspicious old ignoramus see with his own eyes the fact of his grandson's good health and kind treatment in the U. S. A.? Must he carry back his eyewitness account to stop the flow of the deep-running rumors still current underground? (The boy is dead. The boy is lost. The boy will never return.) Did the King himself half believe these legends?

The King was deep. The King was narrow. The King was driven. The King was driving. The King had a political ax to grind. The boy was an excuse. The King was coming.

The visit was a Good Thing, because Al Asad must succumb, at once, to the obvious superiority of the American way. The Russians wouldn't like it if he did. The Egyptians wouldn't like it, either. The Americans wouldn't like it, if he didn't. What were the Communists going to think?

The King was presumptuous. Twenty-eight American professors were not out of his jail yet. There would be a strain put upon those responsible for his safety. Everybody knows that L. A. is full of fanatics. The King must have a strong reason for putting his royal foot into such a city. Placards were being printed already, rumor said, for some impassioned pickets.

Could a Head-of-State be denied entrance? Protocol? Would the White House send a greeter? Courtesy? Yes. No. Maybe. Alalaf was too tiny to matter much. Alalaf was a symbol, of great importance, because it *was* so tiny.

Duncan was sputtering away one morning. "Why doesn't it occur to anybody that an old man just might feel like paying a sick-call on his only grandson? The King has got the money. He can spare the two days. The box-boy at the market can take a little trip, if he's got the money and can spare the time. Why must deep and devious motives always be suspected and analyzed, and re-analyzed? Why do we keep on trying to figure out what the Communists are going to think, if they were to think that *we* thought *they* thought. . . . This world is getting so damned foxy you can't draw a simple breath. Whew! Why don't we figure out what *we* think, period?"

Tamsen was laughing at him. "Al Asad is stuck with his own life-style," she told him. "By the way, what *do* we think?"

"Damned if I know," Duncan confessed. "But that old rascal is up to something."

Then they both laughed.

The Judge said, "Maggie, darling, do you know what I think?"

"No, dear. Not at the moment."

"Let me see. His Majesty arrives early in the morning, on Wednesday. He goes, with entourage, to the hotel, I suppose, first. Then we can expect him here to see Saiph."

"Yes," said Maggie. "I agree that this should be top priority." She was looking mischievously solemn.

"And he flies off again, or so we understand, on the following noon. Which leaves . . ."

"Yes?"

"Wednesday evening. I think that perhaps we should entertain on Wednesday evening with a small reception. Or a medium-sized reception. A very select group of people."

"Oh, do you, William?" she said with wifely respect. He wasn't fooling her, of course.

"I think," the Judge continued, "you ought to ask a dozen or more of the very strongest egos in show business."

"Oh?"

"Yes, people much too busy at projecting their own images to notice certain other quiet guests, whom I shall invite, if you don't mind, dear?"

"The peacocks?" Maggie said. "I'm sure I can produce a dozen or more from the neighboring hills. And incur the undying enmity of some others."

"In a good cause."

"I'm sure. But will the *King* like the idea?"

"We shall ask him," the Judge said, who privately expected the King to like it very much. "Now, do you suppose it is possible to invite these guests on the contingency that the King will agree? If not, no party?"

"I should certainly think that to be quite possible." She was serene. "It won't matter if there *is* no party. The *invitation* will be the prestigious thing." Multisyllabic words, with equally suitable double meanings, wouldn't melt in Maggie's mouth.

The Judge patted her. He couldn't help it. "It should be one of those very formal, strutting, all-dressed-up and showing-off parties, where nobody sits down."

"Like a pavanne," mused Maggie. "Of course, William. But the peacocks will tell the newspapers," she warned him. "It is inherent in their natures."

"Yes, I know," the Judge said. "But there is no way to prevent publicity. The King won't blink an eye without someone assessing the dire significance." The Judge chuckled. "We shall not, of course, ask for publicity. In fact, we shall mildly deplore it. From modesty."

"Of course," chimed Maggie.

"So we shall attract it."

"And we shall saw the lady in half, before their very eyes," said Maggie merrily.

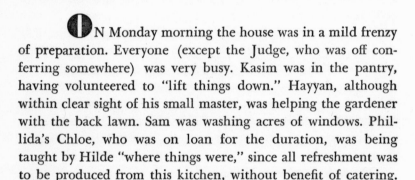

13

ON Monday morning the house was in a mild frenzy of preparation. Everyone (except the Judge, who was off conferring somewhere) was very busy. Kasim was in the pantry, having volunteered to "lift things down." Hayyan, although within clear sight of his small master, was helping the gardener with the back lawn. Sam was washing acres of windows. Phillida's Chloe, who was on loan for the duration, was being taught by Hilde "where things were," since all refreshment was to be produced from this kitchen, without benefit of catering.

Maggie and Jaylia were sitting in the lanai, discussing the King's tastes, He would drink nothing at all, Jaylia warned, and he most probably would not eat, either. But there were certain foods that might be offensive in his very nostrils. And, of course, alcohol . . .

"Oh, dear!" Maggie explained that this reception would follow the pattern of a cocktail party, simply because this was the only kind of party the natives really understood. But if it must be a cocktail party, without any alcohol, Maggie anticipated much drunkenness.

Jaylia was looking amused, but puzzled, when Sam came away from his tasks to announce that the guards had just let Mrs. Rufus Tyler through.

"Oh, have they?" Maggie went to greet Lurlene.

Lurlene said at once, apologetically, "Gee, Maggie, I guess you're awfully, awfully busy."

"We are busy," agreed Maggie, "but not 'awfully.' Come on back. I don't think you have met Jaylia, have you, dear?"

Lurlene had put on her new fall suit, the one Maggie had helped her choose. She followed Maggie into the lanai and looked around for this princess. There was a young woman sitting there whose golden legs were bare below a pair of white shorts, whose blondish hair was wound in careless profusion around her head. Lurlene found herself being presented, and was compelled to bridle and gawk. She managed to recover and produce her politeness, hold out her hand, and say, "Well, I'm certainly glad to meet you. I've heard so much about you." The hand in her own was cool, and only briefly there.

"You must excuse my costume," said Jaylia, "but Aunt Maggie is an absolute slavedriver. It's work, work, work, all the time, around here."

Lurlene, still inclined to gawk, could not find one word in her mouth to say to this. She blinked and looked away, out to the terraces. "Oh," she craned her neck. "Is that the Little Prince?"

They had set Saiph out in the sun to toast. Oiled and martyred, he was lying on his back, his eyes closed. Inga sat beside him, reading aloud.

"Would you like to come and meet my little boy?" Jaylia said. She slid the screen without waiting for an answer. Lurlene followed her.

"Saiph, here is another Mrs. Tyler."

Saiph dragged up lazy lids.

"Say, I'm certainly glad to meet you," blurted Lurlene. "I've heard so much about you."

This was a remark that suggested no reply. Saiph made none. He smiled, sleepily. Inga's voice had politely stopped. Lurlene felt lost. She felt as if she were on some kind of spot. She turned her head, and there stood this foreign-looking fellow, leaning on a bamboo rake, his brilliant eyes just practically glaring at her.

Much startled, she turned, saying, "Listen, I don't want to bother anybody, honestly. You go ahead, whatever you were doing." She went blundering back into the house.

Maggie, who was wearing a comfortable-looking pale cotton frock, sat at a card table with lists before her and a pencil touching her lips. She looked up and smiled. "Isn't he a charming little fellow?"

"He sure is," gushed Lurlene, thinking to herself, What's so charming? Just a skinny little kid who thinks he's so great he don't even have to say "hello" to common people.

Maggie said, "That does look well on you, Lurlene."

So? She had noticed what Lurlene had on. (*Finally*, thought Lurlene, soured by her own awkwardness.) "Well, that's one reason . . ." she began craftily.

"Sit down, dear."

Lurlene sat down and the dumb skirt hiked up. She tugged at it. So she had a little extra on her hips. So what? "I just happened to be coming over this way," she said nervously, "so I thought, Why don't I go and ask Maggie? I mean, what are we supposed to wear? I mean, to the reception for this king? I mean, I thought to myself, why don't I ask Maggie?"

Jaylia's lazy voice said behind her, "*Black* tie, isn't it, Maggie?"

Lurlene jumped. She didn't know whether she ought to stand up when a princess came in or not. This character didn't look anything like a princess to Lurlene. But Jaylia slid into another chair at the card table, and wound those bare legs around each other.

"Isn't it ridiculous?" sighed Maggie. "But William says some of the men will be more comfortable." (Less conspicuous on the streets, had been the Judge's thought.) "And if, as a free people, we chose to array ourselves improperly, this must be taken as symbolic of our independence. So, there being no dinner, the men will wear dinner jackets. Tell Rufus, dear." She smiled at Lurlene. "Let me see, the ladies? Hm, I should think a long dress. Not too dec . . . not too low at the top, mind. Not too

voluminous, either. Narrow, don't you think? Something . . .
oh . . . rather simple. Dark perhaps? After all, if summer
comes, can fall be far behind?"

Lurlene was swallowing hard. It was O.K. They were invited.

"*I'm* not wearing dark, Maggie," Jaylia said, looking mischievous.

"*You*," said Maggie severely, "are living out of eleven suit-
cases and will, I'm sure, be forgiven. I wonder, Lurlene . . .
Had you thought of consulting Phillida? She's good at clothes."

"Well, I . . . no . . ." (Lurlene darn well wasn't going to
consult Phillida, the big old ex-dress designer.) "I thought I'd
rather ask *you*, Maggie." Lurlene fawned. She couldn't help it.
She was nervous. "Oh, say, what time? I mean, when are we supposed to come? Wednesday night, right?"

"We are not quite sure yet," said Maggie pleasantly. "It will
depend on His Majesty's wishes. And, of course, you realize that
if he does not want a reception, there won't *be* a reception?"

"Oh, well, sure."

"Why don't you and Rufus plan to come along a bit ahead of
whatever-the-hour-turns-out-to-be?" said Maggie kindly. "Being family, you can chat with our earlier guests. By the way,
Jaylia dear, I keep forgetting to ask you. Will the King speak
English?"

"You have used the exact word," said Jaylia good-naturedly.
"He will, if he so wills. He can. But he may or he may not.
Sometimes he isn't in the mood."

"*He* won't, I suppose, wear black tie?" said Maggie, amused.

"Al Asad never wears Western dress."

Lurlene was being stricken by panic. It crossed her mind that
anybody was crazy to expect that this king might show up in
cowboy boots! What! He ought to know better than that. But
what would you *say* to a king who might speak English if he felt
like it? She said, "Oh, I wouldn't know what to say, you know.
We just . . . we just kinda want to come and sit in a corner."

"Mind your shoes," said Jaylia carelessly. "Nobody gets to sit
down."

"Oh, well, I see, I'm sure." Lurlene was scarlet. Didn't this princess figure that Lurlene knew better than to sit down, if some king should be standing up? Lurlene was feeling most uncomfortably warm. The new suit was too heavy for the temperature of the day. She didn't even feel like herself in it. *She* didn't even want to come to the dumb party. This was all for Rufus' sake, because ever since he read about it on the society page he'd been looking in the mailbox or waiting for the phone to ring. Lurlene was now giving Jaylia a black look.

Maggie said easily, "There was a friendly warning. Not that it will do a bit of good. Every woman will have on her feet some brand-new, matching shoes that will inevitably be killing her."

Yah! thought Lurlene, a flash of grim joy going through her. She got up. She had to get out of here. "Listen, I certainly don't want to bother anybody. I got to run along anyhow. Thanks a lot. And say, I was very happy to meet you . . . uh . . ." Lurlene didn't know *what* to call the woman. "Excuse me?" she finished.

Maggie got up and accompanied her to the front door, although Lurlene protested. When the door had opened Maggie said soothingly, "Don't fuss too much, Lurlene. It won't be a long gathering. It will be very quiet, just people standing around and, for the most part, saying absolutely nothing of any importance."

Yah! That's what *you* think! thought Lurlene. "It'll be a wonderful experience," she said lamely, and went away.

When Maggie came back, Jaylia said with a puzzled look, "Did I offend her?"

"No, no," said Maggie absently. Then, pencil poised, she looked far away and said, "Lurlene is no more flustered than the majority of our guests will be pretending not to be."

Jaylia leaned back and stretched her torso, catlike. She said, softly, "Have I told you lately, Maggie darling, that I think you are a bit of a darling?"

"Not since Friday, I believe it was," said Maggie severely. "Come. Come. To work."

14

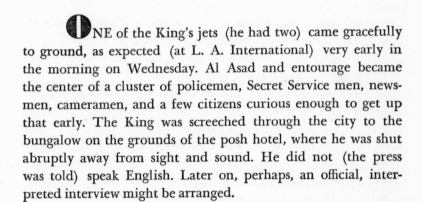

ONE of the King's jets (he had two) came gracefully to ground, as expected (at L. A. International) very early in the morning on Wednesday. Al Asad and entourage became the center of a cluster of policemen, Secret Service men, newsmen, cameramen, and a few citizens curious enough to get up that early. The King was screeched through the city to the bungalow on the grounds of the posh hotel, where he was shut abruptly away from sight and sound. He did not (the press was told) speak English. Later on, perhaps, an official, interpreted interview might be arranged.

Duncan Tyler found his mother and father watching a rerun of all this on the downstairs portable television set in the Judge's study. (Maggie and the Judge kept a portable TV on each floor of the house for use in cases of real necessity.) Duncan sensed that his parents were glad to see him this morning. After all, he *had* met the King before (as, of course, had Mitch although more briefly). Duncan had arranged to take the day off and be, as best he could, some sort of liaison.

The house was cool and in perfect order, humming along smoothly. Duncan left his parents to their viewing and ran up to look in on the boy. Jaylia was with him. They were chattering away and Duncan realized that they were both excited, and both happy to be excited. Tamsen had been right. They were homesick.

He told Saiph that Tamsen would not come to play this afternoon because of the party. (That is, if there were to be one.) He said a few words to Jaylia, who scarcely seemed to see or hear him, and went back down.

But there it was, still. The same damn thing. A man can look at a princess, he supposed, although there was nothing more that he could do. Oh, he would if he could. He didn't kid himself. But the chances that he ever could were very small. He would not be led into any further temptation. Duncan knew he had made no great and noble renunciation. The thing was and always had been . . . well, *almost* impossible. Besides, he was married now, to a beloved bride who loved and understood him. He did not and never would live on the same side of the globe of the earth as Jaylia, who . . . Well, never mind.

He went to sit with his parents, and began to watch Maggie fondly, trying to guess what role she would choose this morning. Ah, the calm chatelaine. Dainty fingertips on every pulse in the house. Would Duncan take coffee? Nothing was the slightest trouble.

When Jaylia came down to take coffee, too, Duncan was able to sip quietly, watching and listening while she tried to describe who might be coming with the King. The entourage, she explained, would consist of at least three body servants to His Majesty. They would not come here. There would also be at least three members of what might be called his inner cabinet, if Alalaf had such a thing. These would be men who were always at the King's side whenever he was visible to the people. Any people. At home, Jaylia said, there would be bodyguards with swords and daggers, or (on occasion) machine guns.

At this Maggie threw up her hands.

But Jaylia did not think the King would lead what might look like an armed invasion into this country.

The Judge wanted to know who would be minding the store,

and Jaylia made educated guesses. A very tight military watchfulness would be on in Alalaf. Everything would be kept strictly status quo; no decisions until the King came home to make them. After all, who else could?

When the sirens sounded, Maggie caused the coffee cups to disappear. Jaylia scampered up to her son, the Judge cleared his throat several times, and Duncan found himself straightening his tie.

The visitors were four. There was no doubt which of them was the King. His silken robes hung with a difference. Nothing could be seen of the body, except that it moved well for a man of seventy. The face, beaten by time, was sharp; it was stern. It had no humor. The eyes seemed cold.

But Al Asad chose to remember Duncan Tyler from a year ago. The King also chose to speak English this morning.

Now it turned out that Maggie Mitchel Tyler was a Queen this morning. Duncan was tickled to see Maggie assume a position of equality and let her crowned head be gracious to its male counterpart. He thought he saw the King's eye flicker, briefly.

Their Majesties decided to ascend the stairs almost at once. Behind them marched the one man of the four who wore trousers. He was in a khaki outfit of military aspect. He had sparse sandy-reddish hair, and a face full of freckles. The other two men, both in gowns and headcloths, remained below, and the Judge turned his hand, indicating that Duncan must go up and help Maggie do the honors while he, the Judge, attempted to entertain these two gentlemen.

So Duncan went leaping upward, in the rear of the procession.

He had missed the first encounter of the King with the Prince, not to mention with the Princess.

Saiph was sitting up in a big blue chair near the balcony doors. He was wearing white pajamas and a blue robe. Daily sunning had given his skin a glow. He looked healthy and handsome. Duncan was tickled to notice that the little face had

117   ✳

taken on an imitation of the expression on the face of the King, his grandfather. It was stern; it was keen, but the eyes seemed cold.

This east guest room was a large room; it was crowded at the moment. The King's presence was imposing. He had been persuaded to sit down in a chair facing the boy, from just within the passage door. Beside him, watchdogging the proceedings, stood this freckle-faced chap in the khaki. Inga was there, in her white uniform, drawn politely into a far corner. Hayyan was there, dutifully stiff, beside his little master. Jaylia was there, in her pleasantly designed, but long-sleeved, high-necked summer frock. Her face was proud and happy, and yet in some way humble. She had a "presenting" air. "See," she seemed to say, "may it please you!"

Maggie was there, just inside, graciously permitting everyone else to be there.

Duncan stayed just outside. He could not understand a word that was being said. The King and the little boy were not speaking English to each other. Duncan began to try to guess who could understand. Jaylia, by concentrating, was getting most of it. Inga, too. Hayyan, no doubt, understood it all. So did this King's man in khaki. But had Duncan not known that Maggie was totally ignorant of that language, he would have supposed that Maggie was understanding every syllable in an aloof and indulgent manner. He had to marvel. Maggie tickled him. She really did.

The visit was not long. It seemed formal, but satisfactory. The King rose. Duncan stood aside with an ushering gesture. The King nodded and, with a movement of his eyes, invited Duncan to come along. So the King, followed by his own man, and only then by Duncan, swept through the upper passage and down the stairs.

No, the King informed his host, the Judge, the King would not take coffee. The King would like to speak with the doctor. The Judge agreed that this meeting must take place, whenever

His Majesty wished, of course. (Omitting the news that Mitch was operating on some other child this morning.) But the Judge ventured to suggest a small reception, here, this evening. Certain people. Not many.

The King said something in his own tongue to his companions. The man in khaki said to Duncan, "May I see the house, please, on this level?"

"Why, sure," said Duncan, who kept on being irreverently tickled, for some reason.

"Colonel Heinz Gorob," the man said, with the ghost of some heel-clicking.

"Duncan Tyler," said Duncan amiably. "Come on, let me show you around."

So the Judge invited the King into his own lair. Al Asad said a word or two. The white-clad ones stood still. The King stepped cautiously, but alone, into the study. The Judge, seizing this opportunity and not much doubting it had been arranged, said quickly and privately what he had hoped to say. The King understood with an eye-beam and said that he would be quite willing to exchange a few quiet words with certain people.

Duncan, still amused but beginning to be slightly outraged, too, watched this Colonel Gorob inspect the big living room, the lanai, the dining room, even the kitchen, as if he were looking for rattlesnakes.

When they returned to the reception hall the King was waiting with indications of royal impatience. He chose to depart in a whirl of white cloth.

Duncan plunked down in one of his father's leather chairs. "Whew!"

"The party is on," the Judge said, licking imaginary cream from imaginary whiskers.

"What's up?" Duncan pounced.

"Opportunity."

"Oh?"

119   *

"Quiet words, behind the scenes."

"In the middle of a social bash!"

"Where else," his father said, "can it be done so secretly?" Duncan marveled, fondly.

Jaylia came in, body curving, face smiling.

"Did we pass?" said Duncan crossly, American to ex-half-American, and the hell with it. The trouble was that Jaylia, upstairs, had just reminded him of Jaylia in Alalaf, and the whole flavor of it had come back to him. Something so precious it must be hidden? So irresistible that it must be forbidden? Or, in itself, so unresisting that it *could* be taken? In other words, the chiffon-bloomer bit?

When she nodded now in affirmative answer to his question he shifted restlessly, not pleased that she seemed to have taken it seriously.

"Who the devil is this Colonel Gorob?"

"Oh, a German. Or he once was." Jaylia sat down. "I believe he was a displaced child at the end of the Second World War. He's been around ever since. Efficient, you know."

"No flowing robes for him, eh?"

"Unfortunately they don't suit him," said Jaylia, and her eyes added, As they would *you*, oh, handsome one. "The Colonel is not a type who wishes to look ridiculous." Now she was bubbling.

"He was looking under the rugs," said Duncan grumpily.

"Oh, he loves to do that."

"What *is* he? Al Asad's hatchet man?"

Jaylia looked puzzled. Then Maggie came in. Her erstwhile Majesty was a bit miffed; her crown had gone somewhat askew when she had been left with the women and children upstairs. "Isn't he the arrogant old b . . . bird!" she sputtered. "My word, Jaylia, does a woman have to behave like a *worm* with these creatures?"

Jaylia bent her head and looked at her own hands where they were clasped loosely. "Apparently," she murmured.

Maggie darted her a glance that answered with mischief. She then sat down and changed her face. The one she put on now was all sweet deference, but from behind the mask there steamed and there blew gusts of pure power, mockingly translated into superfeminine terms.

Duncan marveled. He felt that his mother's art had just enlightened him. But to what, he was not sure.

15

THE reception was to be at eight o'clock. Maggie, on the phone, apologized for the inconvenience of so strange an hour but, since it was His Majesty's choice, there was nothing to be done about it, was there, except to arrive promptly. The Judge, meantime, was on his own phone.

At seven-twenty Lurlene put her head out of the bedroom door and said, "Look, hon, why don't you just go on ahead? Listen, I'm having a *terrible* time with this damned hairdo. You don't want to be late."

"No, I don't want to be any later," Rufus said tensely. He had been ready for half an hour, all dressed up in his tux and walking around like an animal in the zoo.

"If you leave now you can even be early. Listen, I can take a cab. Why not? So what, if it's a little bit expensive? This damn hair . . ."

He said, "All right. All right, then."

He wasn't seeing her. He was thinking about something else. Her heart was jumping, but he didn't say anything more.

When the car had bucked backwards out of the driveway Lurlene dropped her comb on the dresser and looked at herself in the mirror, and she wasn't seeing a thing. In a moment she went tiptoeing, which was silly because she was all alone in the house, out to the tiny room off the kitchen that they called Rufus' "den." When she looked in the bottom drawer, it wasn't there.

So she went back into the bedroom and began to struggle into her new dress. It was long; it wasn't too full in the skirt or too low at the neckline. It was dark. Lurlene had thought of black, but then she had remembered something from somewhere. Somebody had once said, in her hearing, that neither black nor white was very good on television. The dress was a deep, an almost-navy, blue.

Lurlene's skin kept crawling. It kept crawling, like when you start getting the flu. She'd already had one tranquillizer. She thought another wouldn't hurt. Suddenly she was in a fever to get there, to arrive, and not miss anything. She wished she hadn't chickened out, there for a minute. She called for a cab before she swiftly did her hair.

Tamsen had chosen white, a simple dress with a high waistline. Her hair was up. She looked like a small ode-worthy Grecian, from an urn. She was in Saiph's room, and he in the blue chair. The boy had been arrayed in gown, robe and headcloth. The costume suited him marvelously well. Inga was in the dressing room, changing into a fresh uniform now that her charge was ready. To Tamsen had fallen the pleasant task of being with him. They were gay and excited.

Meantime, Jaylia was making herself glamorous (Tamsen had no doubt) in the west wing. The whole house thrummed with anticipation.

"This is going to be fun," Tamsen predicted.

Downstairs, the Judge had just answered his phone.

"William?"

"Yes. Oh, Alice! Alice Foster?"

"William, please listen carefully. Can you hear me well?"

"Yes, I can, Alice." The Judge respected urgency and cut off fripperies.

"I'm going to talk fast, because I may be monitored. Speed's the thing." Alice's words began to race. "I have with me, as you know, a certain politically important . . ."

"What drags behind?"

"Yes. Yes. I've finally got out of this poor innocent intellectual *who* must have been behind the late and latent nonsense." Alice's voice rattled and swooped. "William, it is Asiatic. You know. Those people? My young friend didn't even realize he was their cat's-paw. Idealist! Too easy to sway. Fact is, *I've* swayed him, myself."

"I'm sure," the Judge murmured.

"He's lost to them, but that may not matter. Are you getting this?"

"I'm getting it," the Judge snapped, unable to keep from responding in a comparable style.

"I've found out that somebody very close to . . . Himself?"

"Yes."

"*Somebody* has been bought out by these people. The man is there with him. The man is there, *now*."

"And who?" said the Judge.

"I can't be sure," said Alice Foster, "but for my money it's G. G.," she repeated. "G. Now, you can't announce that. You can't accuse. Not directly. I haven't the proof. But warn Himself, quietly. Can you do that, William? Warn Jaylia, too. And please watch out . . . William, can you hear all this?"

"Loud and clear. Go on, Alice. As fast as you like." The Judge's ear was sweating on the phone. He could hear her gathering force to continue this machine-gun delivery, which would, he had to admit, tend to baffle a listener whose native tongue this was not.

"It is suspected, by those people, that Himself has in mind to make some contacts. Helpful agreements?"

"That is possible." The Judge was cautious.

"He has to turn somewhere," said Alice, "but that's the last place these people want him to turn. So, now is *their* last chance.

Do you see that? Don't let anything happen there. Because here, it is absolute tinder. The whole works could go up in flame."

"In that way?" the Judge asked as she paused for breath.

"What these people will do, on the slightest excuse," she rattled ahead, "such as anything that will get into the foreign press, for instance, and hence be believable . . . then they will martyr Dhanab. Oh, *they* know where he is. And, in his name . . . which amounts to *something* . . . there will be a bloody mess. We won't have seen anything yet."

"What ought *not* to happen here?" the Judge said alertly, cutting to the point.

"Anything. Anything at all *untoward*. Either to Himself or the young one. Anything suitable for poking up the anti-sentiment that is ready to explode at any moment. Now, this hireling, you see—especially if he becomes convinced that alliances are in the wind—might even attempt to *make* trouble. Anything to break them off. How can I be clear enough or emphatic enough . . ."

"You are being emphatic enough," the Judge rattled back at her. "I'm listening. Just go on."

"*Anything* that happens in the U. S. A. that *they* can use, they *will* use."

"For what? Raids, riots or revolution?" the Judge let himself drawl, resorting to a fake humorous effect.

"A massacre," said Alice Foster. "The twenty-eight, for instance."

"And *you?*"

"Oh, they will cut *my* throat first of all," she said rat-a-tat, "if that matters."

"I will do the best I can," the Judge said without letting his voice wince. "We all will. G, you think?"

"Oh, yes, I think so. He is a mercenary, I'm betting. But now, William, let me point out what is *desirable*. Let His M. return well pleased. Let the boy return, safe and well, and his mother with him. Then the whole thing swings. One source of power, for these people, leaks *away* from them. They are set back. Don't you see?"

"It's now or never for those people, eh?" the Judge said.

"Oh, William, bless you." Her voice was running down, exhausted.

"Can you take care?" he snapped.

"I am a stranger in a strange land," said Alice Foster, "but I know what I know."

"I believe you," the Judge said.

"Have fun," she said faintly, and hung up.

Humph! This is going to be fun, all right, the Judge said to himself. Poor woman, waiting in a strange land for her death to become "desirable," if "those people" saw their chance to swing that country. . . .

When he opened the door, there was Maggie, standing at the foot of the stairs just outside, talking to Rufus. "Good of *you* to be so early, dear. Although nobody is here yet, really. Well, Tamsen is upstairs, of course. Duncan, too. He's primping in his daddy's room." Maggie smiled. "*You* look very nice. Why don't you roam around down here and see if everything is just so? Oh, William . . ."

She had already received the message from the Judge's eye: "Something urgent has come up."

"Do that for me, Rufus," said Maggie, "but don't go upstairs. Everyone up there may not be decent." She tapped his arm affectionately and said, "Oh, William, there *is* one thing . . ." By some instinct she disguised the fact that she was being summoned by seeming to summon.

Rufus grunted hail-and-farewell to his father and walked toward the garden side, skipping the stairs.

Maggie walked into the study and the Judge softly closed the door and told her.

Maggie said, "Alice has this young man, Dhanab, *with* her?"

"I don't know how or why," the Judge said, "but I had that

hunch. After her letter, I saw by the dictionary that the nick-name 'Dhanab' means 'tail.'"

"Does it? Well, we must just make sure that nothing unto-ward happens *here*," Maggie said resolutely. "What, more or less than we *are* doing, ought we to do?"

"I think," said the Judge, "that I had better warn my . . . er . . . special guests not to approach the King, at all, this eve-ning."

"Isn't that too bad, dear?"

"Yes, but it may be wiser if this treacherous fellow is not given the notion that he had better (now or never) *cause* a little trouble. We shall see, of course. That may be overcau-tious."

"I'll tell Jaylia," Maggie said, "and I think, perhaps, Duncan, too. He can speak to the King as an old acquaintance. Or, given the opportunity, I'll tell the King myself. None of *them* would suspect a woman of saying anything of importance."

Maggie was wearing a long dress of a lavender-gray, with a silvery shimmer woven into the fabric. With it she wore a Vic-torian magnificence of amethysts around her neck. She turned and took hold of her skirt, lifting it daintily in an old-fashioned gesture, and said, "There can't be any real danger, if we are just as polite as we can be—and deadly bores for about two hours."

"Do try," the Judge said, "to be dull, Maggie darling."

In the kitchen Kasim was hanging over an enormous round tray of small edibles, trying to point out to Chloe which va-rieties were, in his opinion, unsuitable. He was having difficulty. Chloe, because she was enjoying herself very much, had chosen to be obtuse.

When the tallish figure of a man in a dinner jacket went through, behind them, and whisked around the corner of the doorway to the back stair-hall, it was the stirring of the air, or perhaps his shadow only, that made Kasim look up and say sharply, "Who was that?"

Hilde said, "Who? Oh, that was only Mr. Tyler."

Kasim stared fiercely at the doorway to the spot he had been, in theory, guarding.

Chloe said, "But how can there be religious reasons? That ain't meat. And this ain't Friday." She batted her lashes.

Kasim sighed. It was his duty to enlighten this young and pretty infidel. And *Tylers* were safe; he knew that, by this time.

Maggie went up the front stairs and tapped on the door of the Judge's bedroom. She opened it. Duncan said, grinning widely, "Hi, Maggie. Am I sufficiently adorable to cope with the fairest flower . . ."

But as she slipped inside and shut the door, he sobered at the sight of her face. She told him quickly about Alice Foster's phone call. She didn't put on any acts.

Duncan whistled softly. "Gorob, eh? What could he do, I wonder, to *make* trouble?"

"He can grab at anything to upset the King," said Maggie, "who doesn't seem to be exactly in love with us adorable Americans."

"Well, we'll just have to be as adorable as *hell*," promised Duncan.

"And, also, dull, don't forget," she warned him.

Duncan realized that he "adored" his mother when she put on acts, but he loved her most when she flattered him and didn't.

Tamsen was saying, "Well, so long, old-timer. I guess it's battle stations." When she had explained this phrase to his satisfaction she slipped out of his room. All was ready there. Inga was spotless and correct. The outer little boy was beautifully arrayed. Yet perhaps he needed some quiet moments to prepare, inside. Tamsen had a suspicion that Saiph had become somewhat more Americanized than was politic, for this evening. And much of this must have been her own doing. The truth was, he did not belong to her. He belonged to other people.

When she was standing in the upper passage she was struck by the silence. Downstairs she knew the servants were buzzing softly. On the terrace she knew the musicians were arranging their chairs and music stands. All around out of doors, the fortress was ringed by defenders who were keeping a noise of newsmen at bay.

But here, in the core—here, just outside the precious boy's room—this silence was of a peculiarly thick texture. Well, of course, everyone was busy somewhere else.

Tamsen shrugged and went skipping along toward the main staircase, passing the door to the Judge's room with no notion that anyone was within, then passing Maggie's door, and so around the corner, and down.

16

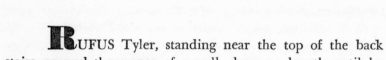

RUFUS Tyler, standing near the top of the back stairs, around the corner of a wall, drew no breath until he sensed that Tamsen had gone.

When he slid along the empty passage, rubbing a shoulder on the inside wall, he found the door to Saiph's room standing about a quarter of the way open. All that could be seen, through the gap, was a door to the dressing room and bath, there in the side wall, toward the Judge's bedroom.

But now the door of the Judge's bedroom itself began to swing inward, causing a faint shifting of air currents and a change of light in the curtained corridor. There was just room in the narrow triangle for Rufus to place his feet and draw his body out of the passage, to be hidden from any glance cast casually along it. Yet he was not visible to very much of the room behind him.

Inga was saying, placidly, "There will be ceremonies."

"I know," said Saiph, "I must wait here. But I am very thirsty." His voice was lazy, but commanding.

Tamsen, where the stairs curved and bridged the hall below, crossed over and came down sedately to the last step, where she hesitated, with the door to the Judge's study at her left, one of the arches to the living room at her right, and the front door before her. Sam, in his stiff white coat, was stationed there to bow in the guests, some of whom must have already arrived. From here, she could see a few people in the big room, and among them Phillida, wearing a satin gown of dullish green, so understated that the first impression was the elegance of the woman. Tamsen was relieved to see her. Phillida would have everything in hand. Tamsen herself was feeling very young and shy.

Then Sam said, "Mrs. Rufus Tyler. Good evening, ma'am."

There was Lurlene, and Sam taking her somewhat battered "mink" stole. Lurlene, looking quite nice in dark blue, but not at all nice in the face.

Tamsen drew in a sharp breath. She took a quick step down and she came to Lurlene. She didn't say "Good evening" or even "Hello." She didn't ask where Rufus was. She sensed there wasn't time. Lurlene's terrified eyes met hers at once. Lurlene sent a nervous tongue over her upper lip and burst, *"What's wrong?"*

Tamsen said nothing. She tilted her head. She watched. She listened. She ached to read through the skin. Sam had carried the wrap away. There was no one else near enough to watch and listen and somehow know.

"I'm sorry," whined Lurlene, "I said he should go on ahead because I didn't want to hold him up. *I* just got here in a cab myself, I mean . . ." All this was excuse, apology, alibi. *For what?*

Tamsen simply turned and flew up the stairs, as light-footed as a child.

Lurlene put her hand to her throat, blinked, and started toward the stairs. But Phillida came swinging out of the living room. "Hi, Lurlene," she said. "Come and meet some people. The King isn't here yet, but he soon will be."

"I'm . . . I'm . . . I'm . . ." Lurlene's eyes rolled. "I'm scared!"

"You looked it," said Phillida, in a kindly way. "I fly to the rescue. Come on. I know somebody who is probably just as scared. You can help."

"What . . ." whispered Lurlene, "what's *happening?*"

"Oh, we are having a gay time," said Phillida blithely. "Three movie stars so far, and all absolutely furious because they got here first. You're looking very smart and proper."

Lurlene swallowed. She felt her blood begin to flow differently. I guess he goofed, she thought, and that figures. He would. Listen, she told herself, it wasn't that I *wanted* anybody to get hurt, or anything.

She said to Phillida, "Well, I thought . . . something simple, you know?"

"Very wise," Phillida approved. "Oh, Mrs. Hardy, may I present my sister-in-law, another Mrs. Tyler?"

The Judge, who was standing, for strategic purposes of his own, near the garden doors, noticed the movements of his daughters-in-law, caught the sense of momentary panic, then of Phillida's cool hand on things.

Upstairs, the Princess wore a crown of her own hair. She was clad in gold. Her gown was long of skirt and sleeve, and high to her throat. The fabric was stiff and under the shape of the dress, the body curved invisibly. But the body was potently there, as Duncan noted with one uncontrollable part of his senses. Otherwise, he was intelligently concerned with what Maggie was telling this young woman. The young woman, he observed, was receiving the news that many people, including her own mother, were in danger, without making any girlish outcries. The three of them were clustered in the upper passage, just outside Maggie's door.

As Inga went into the boy's bathroom to fetch him a glass of water . . .

As the door to that east guest room, that had been standing on a slant, began to swing inward, opening . . .

As the boy sat absolutely still, staring into the eyes of the sudden man . . .

As Tamsen came from the stairwell, flitting in a curious way, like a blown brittle leaf, her arms working, from the elbows, angularly. Her face was white. Her lips set. Her eyes blazed. They, and the motion of her arms, canceled all thought of any of the three becoming an impediment to her purpose. She was not to be stopped! She passed them by.

Duncan growled astonishment and took strides after her.

The door to Saiph's room stood wide. A few feet inside, stood Rufus Tyler with a gun in his hand. The boy sat in the blue chair and his eyes were not swerving from the man's face, as if the man were a snake and the boy an accomplished charmer of reptiles. Someone was running water in the bathroom. A faucet thumped closed.

The man, startled, jerked up the gun. The boy raised his right arm; his robes made an angel wing. Tamsen blew in like a leaf. There was a flash, a glitter of light. She fell against the man's right forearm as the gun made a sharp little bark, and the knife sliced along Tamsen's flesh. She staggered and fell hard against the man's body. He pawed with frantic feet on the round white rug that lay on the polished floor. The rug skidded. They both fell. On the way down, the man's head hit the edge of a wooden chair. When he was down, he murmured softly and his head rolled and he was still. The white of Tamsen's gown began to soak up redness. The white of the boy's sleeve was reddening.

The only sounds had been the bark of the gun, the crack of the man's head, and a series of soft thumpings and subsidings.

Duncan went, in an apelike crouch, to where his wife had fallen on her face. The blood was welling from her upper back along her left shoulder blade, seeping into the white of her bodice, slipping down along the bare flesh and under her left arm into the thickness of the rug.

Tamsen said in a tone that was hushed, "He didn't hurt Saiph? He *didn't?*"

Duncan looked up; although he was feeling almost blind, he could see that Inga was already there, bunching the white fabric under the boy's right upper arm. The boy had not made

133   ✳

a sound. Duncan looked at his brother Rufus, who seemed to be napping peacefully. His breathing was gentle. Duncan thought that he himself must be going mad. He twisted his neck to look behind, and saw his mother in her lavender silver, and the Princess in the gold, standing together silently in the open door.

And he thought, in fierce rebellion, that wanted *noise,* If Tamsen's badly hurt, the hell with the rest of the whole damned world! But from long habit, he looked first to see what the truth was. He didn't dare touch, but the wound was more broad than deep. Tamsen's profile was smashed against the white rug. Her eye was wincing and blinking. But she was not going to cry. He seemed to know that Tamsen was not, for instance, dying.

Then Maggie Mitchel Tyler, a small and rather elderly person in silvery lavender, put out her hand and closed that bedroom door, gently, but very firmly.

Duncan recognized the instinct to conceal, to wait, to catch at one's breath and one's wits.

He caught at his own. Now the press? Headlines? American Guns Prince. . . . Prince Knifes American Girl.

Maggie had come to speak to Inga. "Is it bad? No, I see. Will it bleed?"

"It is not bad. I can stop the bleeding." Inga was blunt and factual.

Maggie looked down. "Tamsen?"

"All right," said Tamsen.

"This did not happen, you know," said Maggie, as if she were reasoning with a director at rehearsal. "Nothing, at all, has happened in this room."

Jaylia then said some quick foreign words and the boy answered with one.

And Maggie went swiftly to the doors to the balcony, opened them in a quick double swing, stepped outside, leaned slightly and called below. "Did you gentlemen hear anything strange, just now?" she inquired, with more curiosity than alarm.

"Ah no, Maggie, you can't," groaned Duncan.

He heard Jaylia speak low. "Turn up the air conditioning. Is there a spray to get the smell out?"

But Inga had towels, now, and was working with the boy.

Duncan crouched where he was, over the fallen people, the bloodied rug, the disaster.

A man's voice, American, called up from outside. "There was something, Mrs. Tyler. In the house, was it?"

"*I* thought it was outside," said Maggie. "You don't know? Oh, I hear that the musicians have come. Why *must* they scrape so! Hayyan? And the other gentlemen? Has anyone give you coffee?"

"It could have come from the kitchen," the American voice said.

"Saiph, my dear," Maggie's voice changed. "I believe I see how to prove to you what I was saying. If you could come out?"

Jaylia pounced upon her son. A wad of toweling was under his arm. His mother snatched another large clean towel and threw it over his right shoulder. The boy got to his feet. His mother was whispering in his ear.

"Mrs. Tyler," the voice said, below. "I don't know as he ought to come outside until we check . . ."

"Oh mercy! Then, *I'll* stand in front of him, myself," Maggie promised, gaily. "Now, then, my dear . . ."

The boy was on the balcony, Maggie in advance of him on the railing side. "Do you see the sky?" Maggie's voice charmed and teased. "Is that not the east? Now, do you not see the pink and the purple? So does not the sun set in the east, sometimes?"

Saiph laughed.

Duncan could almost feel the whole world relax.

"No, no, Aunt Maggie. That's only the reflection," the boy said.

"It is?" said Maggie, mock-dubious. "Well, it may *be,* I suppose."

"You were pulling my leg," said Saiph. "Do I say that correctly?"

Maggie was laughing now, in lavender silver, on a set to represent a summer evening, in a sentimental musical. Duncan, paralyzed where he was, thought, But she can't do this!

"Oh, please," called Maggie to those below. "Would you mind asking the musicians to hurry over that dreadful tuning-up? We can't have it going on when the King comes, can we?"

Duncan could almost see someone below melting, all his purposes dissolving in a wish to please her.

Then Saiph called down something merry in his own language and somebody laughed (as it were) in that foreign tongue.

Duncan marveled.

"Come in. Come in, dear," said Maggie. "Your royal grandfather should be along any minute. You do look handsome. Your mother looks most beautiful, don't you agree?"

(How could anything have happened here, where everyone was handsome or beautiful, and filled with summery laughter?)

With perfect timing, on the tail of her sentence, Maggie closed (and then she nervously locked) the balcony doors.

Jaylia was laying out another set of clothing for Saiph. Inga had her first aid kit now, bandages ready. The boy walked toward his nurse carefully. There was no sign of pain on his small face.

Maggie looked down at her son Rufus, and one flash of pain crossed her eyes. But she said, "He seems quiet. Take Tamsen into Dad's room, Duncan. Take the rug and all. There is another, exactly like it, on my bedroom floor. Fetch that here, will you?"

"Maggie, we can't—" he began.

But Jaylia turned on him. "Do as you're told." He looked up into her eyes. "How many people do you insist shall die?" she hissed. "We can't *have* this. You should realize . . ."

Oh yes, he thought, that's right. Now, I remember. Something about a massacre?

Tamsen said, "Don't let . . . the family . . . down the drain. Duncan, don't *do* that."

"We won't do that," said Maggie. "Nothing has happened, here."

"Downstairs—there's Lurlene." Tamsen was gasping.

"Does she know?" Maggie pounced, and Duncan groaned.

"She *expected*. That's how I . . ."

Jaylia said, "I'll go and see that she is seen to. I'll also send the Doctor."

"Yes, go. Do that, Jaylia," said Maggie. "And mind—you take their attention."

Duncan got to his feet, feeling furious. The boy, under Inga's ministrations, was looking keen and cold. Jaylia was pulling herself together to resume . . . what? Power?

"Damn white of you, to think of the Doctor," snarled Duncan, releasing some of his feelings. He bent and scooped up his wife, rug and all. The limp body of his brother was tumbled in the process. Duncan didn't care.

When he stepped into the passage the Princess was walking ahead of him, encased in her stiff gold, yet with a womanly swaying. He didn't know why, but as a person and in the flesh, she meant nothing to him anymore. Nothing at all.

It was Maggie who nipped just ahead to open the door to the Judge's bedroom. Duncan carried his wife, his darling burden, to the big bed and put her gently down on her face, the rug still under her.

"Mind, no blood on you," said Maggie quietly. She closed the door and put up a soft light. "Fetch the other rug, now. And something must be done with Rufus."

Duncan let his fury out on his mother. "Lug the guts into the neighbor room, eh?"

"Do not waste our time," said his mother, gently.

137   *

"She is my—"

"We cannot argue, nor can we discuss, not even plan," said Maggie. "We must simpy *do* this. Hurry, please, dear?"

Duncan went into his mother's dim and scented room and snatched the round white rug from the floor. He went into the boy's room to lay it down, spotless and innocent, where its counterpart had been.

Inga was working expertly to bandage the gouge in the flesh under the boy's right arm, where the bullet had ripped at it as the arm had been raised to throw. The wound might not be serious; it must be painful. The boy's face was stern and cold. His eyes turned. They had no guilty anguish; they did not plead to be forgiven. His voice did not apologize. It explained. "Tamsen meant to save me. I meant to save myself."

"Yes, I saw what happened," said Duncan, with control. "Now, it's save the surface and save all, eh? That's a slogan."

He bent, escaping the boy's steady eyes, and hit his brother rather sharply on a certain spot of the neck with the edge of his hand. (And why, he did not know.) Then he picked Rufus up, like a sack of beans, and carted him through the silence, the uncanny silence, of the upper passage, into the Judge's room and dumped him on the carpet.

Then looking gloomily down, Duncan felt himself flowing into a state of thaw. Now he remembered another boy. A bumbling cheerful little boy—the one whom Duncan had beaten at every game as soon as Duncan had grown old enough to play it. But the brother he had loved, just the same. Inept, and yet— no matter—one of them. One of the Tyler sons.

How had Rufus come to this? Why haven't we taken notice? Duncan thought. What has been happening, while we've paid it no attention? How could he have come to the point of doing so mad, so wicked a deed, and his own people not know how it was with him?

Maggie said, reading his mind, "Poor Rufus. What will you

do with him, Duncan? I must go down. And so must you. The time is very short."

"Telling Dad?" Duncan accepted the effort, now.

"I think not," Maggie said. "Not yet." She seemed to be brooding somberly. Having said the time was short, she was not hurrying. "Improvisation on a theme," she pronounced. "Nothing has happened."

"Nothing will, either," Duncan promised her, with sudden spirit.

His wits and energies began to operate, unimpeded by rage. He dragged his brother into the Judge's complex of bath-shower-cupboards and all the rest.

When he came back into the bedroom, Maggie had gone. Tamsen was lying there, her fingers tight on the edge of the pillow—in pain, but making not a whimper. He bloodied his shirt after all.

17

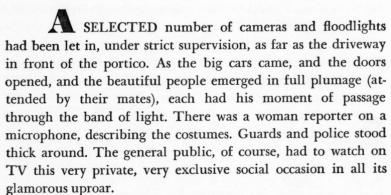

A SELECTED number of cameras and floodlights had been let in, under strict supervision, as far as the driveway in front of the portico. As the big cars came, and the doors opened, and the beautiful people emerged in full plumage (attended by their mates), each had his moment of passage through the band of light. There was a woman reporter on a microphone, describing the costumes. Guards and police stood thick around. The general public, of course, had to watch on TV this very private, very exclusive social occasion in all its glamorous uproar.

Behind the garage, there was a path and a gate. Here guards stood, thick, in the growing dusk, to let in certain other guests, who came this way, quietly, on foot, from cars they had left at a little distance. They were escorted through the silent gardens and taken up the terraces and let in by the garden doors.

These few were welcomed by the Judge, where he stood placed to intercept them, and to the male of each pair he spoke quietly, saying in effect, "Not yet. Perhaps not at all. We shall see." Then these people, all well-dressed but none startling to the eye, blended inconspicuously with the gathering crowd.

Mrs. Hardy said to Lurlene, "So that's the Princess, eh? I suppose, when the King shows up, everybody gets to stand in line and meet him, too."

"I suppose." Lurlene licked her lips nervously.

"Not me," said her companion, a thin woman who carried an aura of bitter anger. She was watching her husband, a peacock, who even now was spreading his tail-feathers (the old fool!) — waiting for the Princess to notice *him*. "What's she like, anyhow?"

"Oh, sa-ay," Lurlene began, with hint of much lore. Then she changed her mind and said, "You really mean you're not going to get in line, to meet this king?"

"Not me," said Mrs. Hardy.

This struck Lurlene as the height of something or other, to have the chance of meeting this king, and just not bothering. "Listen, *I* don't really want to, either," she confided.

"So let the rest of them line up, like a herd of sheep," said Mrs. Hardy, who may have braced herself with alcohol before she came to this arid place. "Not me, honey. Not *this* chicken!"

Lurlene had to giggle. "Well," she said, "I can tell you, *she* didn't look like so much, the other morning."

"Oh-ho! Say, why couldn't we go out there and sit down? I'd like to get the real skinny." Mrs. Hardy was contemplating the terrace. It made her sick to contemplate her husband.

"The only thing is," said Lurlene, not quite sure whether she ought to agree, "my husband is probably looking all over the place for me."

"Let him," said Mrs. Hardy viciously. "Do him a world of good."

"Well, O.K.," said Lurlene, "why not?" She giggled and slid the screen, and they slipped out to the west terrace, where "live" musicians were now softly playing "background music." The two women found a shadowy spot where there were two chairs.

"Well, I must say, this is a heck of a lot better," said Mrs. Hardy, who had no notion of the ring of eyes that watched them from stations all around the grounds. She lit a cigarette. "Now, what about this buxom lass, the Princess? And, by the way, can we get ourselves some punch, or whatever is going?" Mrs. Hardy had brought her own vodka and intended to have a do-it-her-self cocktail party.

Lurlene sighed with pleasure. "We sure can," she promised. "I know this house. Just as soon as Maggie gives the word, Sam will be going around. I'll get hold of him. You know, this princess was running around in a pair of shorts up to *here*." Lurlene was, to her surprise, having quite a good time at the party. (Well, Rufus had goofed, as usual. So why not?)

Jaylia, within doors, continued to greet the guests that Phillida continued to present. But the Princess contrived to drift her whole group close to Mitch.

"Oh, do please excuse me?" she said to the latest candidates for her acquaintance. "Doctor Tyler?"

"Yes, ma'am."

"I am to tell you that your patient would like to ask a question of monumental importance that only you can answer."

"Now, if that's so," said Mitch, smiling, "I had better go up and see what I can do."

Phillida, because Jaylia was laughing and looking amused, said encouragingly, "But what can the question be?"

"My little boy," the Princess said, charmingly, to those who stood around her, "would like to know whether he may go off his diet, for the occasion of this party, and have American ice cream."

"How cute!" "Isn't that adorable!"

Mitch smiled, with the rest. He did not hurry, but he went.

"Have you seen Lurlene?" said Jaylia, under cover of all the cooing.

"I know where she is," said Phillida carelessly.

"I hope she is . . . having a quiet time?"

Phillida's brows curled and then smoothed out. "Shall I . . . er . . . ?"

"Make sure," said Jaylia. "Oh, yes, he is quite delighted with *many* American foods."

"I cleaned the knife," said Duncan dourly, "by the way."

"Good thinking," his brother Mitchel said.

"Where's the gun?"

"Inga's got it. Bullet's in the wall. That's O.K. She moved the bureau. I'll take the knife back, then. Expect he feels naked, without it." The Doctor was leaning over Tamsen, with a lamp turned to shine directly on her wound. "Isn't much more than a slice off the white meat, Tamsen. You got skun, as in 'I skun my knee.' Bet it hurts like the devil."

"It does. It does," she gasped. "Saiph is really O.K?"

"Not bad, either. He's tough, that one. Still, I've got to get the two of you out of here somehow."

"Why?" Duncan was touchy to alarm.

The Doctor's hands were busy. He had his emergency bag of tools, always left here in his father's room. "I'll do what I can to dull this down, Tamsen. But not to knock your wits out. You may need them."

"Why can't she just lie low until the party's over?" Duncan bristled.

"When is it going to be over?" Mitch said. "And what makes you think all the newsmen will leave, at any given moment? At the least, she'll have to walk out, even if she just goes home. I'd a heck of a lot rather have her in the hospital."

"Why?"

"Oh, come on," the Doctor said. "You think yon knife was sterilized?"

"She's not going to . . ."

"No, she is not," said the Doctor sternly. "Take a look at yourself, why don't you? Get into one of Dad's shirts, and quick. The old boy must be on his way by now."

"I don't want to leave Tam."

"Yes, you do," said Tamsen.

"You know, I think I'll send Phillida up," the Doctor said, looking thoughtfully down at her. "When you do walk out of here, sweetie, you'd better look somewhat less bedraggled and torn. Bloodstains aren't being worn this season, either. Phillida will know how to fix you up."

"My hair must be a perfect *mess*," said Tamsen, with silly courage.

"Are we going to get away with this?" Duncan was out of his own shirt and getting one of his father's ready. His fingers felt thick on the studs.

"Of course we are," said Tamsen. "I feel better already."

"Trust *her*," said the Doctor, and then grimly, "Where is Rufus? Him, we *can't* trust."

Duncan said, "I've got him secured. I'll show you."

They went into the Judge's dressing room and Mitch crouched and said, "Oh for God's sakes! Listen, there is no such thing as a gag that works worth a damn." He was taking the stuffing out of Rufus' mouth. "I'll say you've got him secured," Mitch muttered.

Duncan had tied Rufus, hand and foot, and by the neck as well. Mitch was taking the Judge's white silk scarf from around that limp neck. "No need to strangle him, you idiot. Bring my bag."

Duncan did so, and stood there, putting on the clean shirt while he watched the Doctor's lean hands swiftly examine the physical thing there on the floor. "I hit him, you know," said Duncan lamely.

"You did, eh? Not too hard? Right?"

Then Mitch sank back on his heels, where, in motionless silence, he conducted a further examination within his assessing mind. "Well, we can't trust it," he decreed. So Duncan watched, while the Doctor pulled back Rufus's jacket and made an injection.

"Should hold him till the party's over," Mitch said, "Poor devil." He gave Duncan a hard look. "Come on. Time's wasting. Give me that knife."

When Mitch had slipped away to take the wickedly curving,

and now shining, knife back to its owner, Duncan bent over his wife. "How in hell can I leave you?"

"Because you have to," she said. "I can stay here . . ." She groped for words to brace him. "I should think you would have *noticed. I* do not *want* people to get killed."

"I guess I more or less begin to get the pitch," said Duncan, wanly.

In the boy's room, Mitch handed over the knife silently. The boy, using his good arm, sheathed it mysteriously within his clean garments. Mitch's trained eye checked for signs of shock. It saw none. So he smiled, in his Mephistophelian way, glanced around the room (in which nothing seemed to have happened), nodded to Inga, signifying faith, and went to meet Duncan in the passage.

Duncan was wiping his brow.

"Pull up your socks," Mitch said. "If *I'm* breaking the rules I live by, *you* can damn well be a carefree playboy."

"Right." Duncan settled his shoulder muscles. "The show must go on, eh? Our mother's sons, eh?"

"What else?" snapped Mitch. "Raised in the magic of make-believe." But his eyes were softer than his words, and he grinned, before he turned to lead the way.

They could hear the sirens.

18

DOWNSTAIRS, the guests could hear them, too.

Maggie, who had been suggesting by the power of make-believe that she had been among her guests all along, now went to the arch nearest the entrance door. The company was drawn into a pattern, facing this archway as if it were the stage, and the volume of sound in the room fell to a few murmurings.

The Judge, with Jaylia on his arm, came to join Maggie. The sirens, outside, choked off. Two of those good-looking young Tyler sons came quietly down the stairs to station themselves with the others in this semblance of a receiving line.

The Judge wondered, for a moment, where the girls were. Then he saw Phillida in the audience, and presumed that Maggie wished this kept simple. The Judge had problems of his own on his mind.

When Al Asad came into the spotlight of attention he was no disappointment. The people swayed like grass at the impact of his royal presence and watched the ceremonious greetings with fascinated eyes.

Then, as was understandable, the King and the Doctor drew aside, while the Judge brought Jaylia, and Maggie brought two of these long-gowned foreigners, into the big room to be engulfed.

So it was Duncan who edged around to be near Phillida.

Colonel Gorob did not leave the King's side until he per-
ceived the technical nature of the Doctor's discourse. His uniform, his undistinguished stature, and his freckled face did not
receive as many curious glances as did his more exotic companions. He was able to slip away from formalities and begin to
move among the standing people quietly, his freckled ears on
the alert.

Heinz Gorob had seen the handwriting on the wall, long ago,
when he had first found out that Al Saiph was not going to live
to be very old. The old King was a good master, but he was not
going to outlast the Colonel, and the Colonel had begun to
think about his own future.

He had considered Dhanab.

Gorob was a natural second-in-command. He functioned most
comfortably under a powerful master whose power was given
to Gorob to exert. But Dhanab was not a born master. He was
too hesitant and too muddled. He might do for a puppet. But
Gorob, who could pull the strings below him, needed a master
above. He had quite recently found some new masters. Or they
had found him.

The handwriting was on the wall for Alalaf. No such tiny
state could exist much longer, independent of the great modern
realities. It must be absorbed into one sphere of influence or another. Gorob envisioned himself as second-in-command to the
real masters of Alalaf, wielding (behind some front, of course)
the kind of power he enjoyed.

He felt himself to be absolutely trustworthy. The King, for
instance, had trusted him for years. But times change. His new
masters would find him trustworthy, now. Gorob himself, however, trusted almost nobody. Particularly Americans.

When he had warned his contacts, here in Los Angeles, that
the foolish old king might go so far as to believe the promises of
these imperialist-hypocrites, the representatives of his new
masters had advised him to note anything . . . anything at all
. . . about these deceitful people that might be usefully ex-

posed. So Gorob (who was a linguist) began to drift and eavesdrop.

"Wouldn't want to meet one of those fellows on a dark night. *Brrrr.*"

"They're theoretically civilized. You old enough to remember Valentino?"

"Isn't it the women who wear the trousers?"
"Yes, but not the pants, ha ha."

"Say, why don't you make a play for the Princess, Rory?"
"You think that's punishment?"

Frivolous, frivolous, thought Gorob disapprovingly.

Sam was going by with a tray. Duncan said to Phillida, "Will you?" He lifted a glass for each of them.

"If Maggie thinks it's time, it must be time," she said.

"Where's Lurlene? Hang on to your face!"

"Out on the terrace, having a gossip. I just checked. Don't know *why,* of course." Phillida was curious, but cool.

Duncan said, "If you're ready?"

"I'm fine."

"You're needed upstairs."

"Really?" Her eyebrows went up smoothly. Her smile stayed on.

So, while his eyes roved as if he were merely chattering nothings as he surveyed the scene, Duncan told her.

"Nothing has happened," he began. "Hang on to that. Rufus went off his rocker, actually shot the boy. Not serious. Tamsen deflected his aim. Boy threw a knife and got Tamsen in the upper back. Not serious. Mitch says you've got to fix her up, clothing-wise. Dad's room. *Maggie says nothing has happened.*"

"I should think not," said Phillida, who had turned only a little pale. She drank thirstily. "What did you do with—"

Colonel Gorob had just come, like a shadow, into the fringe of a group just behind them. But Duncan had moved his feet and had glanced full circle.

Duncan said, "You remember . . . which was it, now? *Through the Looking Glass?*"

"Alice?" said Phillida, brightly.

The sound of this name caused Gorob to prick up his ears and begin to listen with interest.

"Well, it's like in guinea pigs," drawled Duncan. "Don't worry about it."

"Who knows?" said Phillida, with a shrug and the wrong inflections, disguising her literal question.

"A domestic affair, eh?" Duncan smiled at her but sent his pupils sideways in warning. "Go," they said.

Phillida gave him her empty glass. "Please? And excuse me, Duncan? I ought to circulate."

"Of course. *I* should . . ." Duncan turned around. "Ah, good evening, Colonel," he said cordially. "Have you had refreshment, sir?"

The King was now across the room, standing beside Maggie. Maggie, who knew exactly where Colonel Gorob was at the moment, and also that the other two strangers were well surrounded, said to Al Asad, in the full hearing of six people, in what seemed to be purely conversational tones, very chitchatty, "I understand that there is a traitor and a spy in your entourage, Your Majesty. I think that's fascinating! Don't you?"

None of the six guests was quite sure what she had said. Maggie could, if she so willed, beam her voice into one ear only. The fact was, none of the six really cared what *she* way saying, each being occupied in trying to think of something to say for himself. Furthermore, her cadences had been the heavily accented beats that go with trivia. (What an *absolutely dar*ling bracelet!) Whereas tragedy comes in monotones. (Look, I'm sorry, lady, but your husband had a little accident, and as a matter of fact, he . . .)

The King, who had heard her plainly, said nothing.

"That's what Alice Foster says," gushed Maggie, all deference and flutter. "Dear Alice! We went to school together, ages and ages ago."

"So I have been told," the King said gravely. His eyes were fixed on her face.

"We are still in constant touch! Isn't that remarkable! He begins with the letter G," said Maggie. "So Alice surmises. She can be so amusing."

"Yes, indeed," the King murmured politely. But his glance had gone over her head, in the desired direction.

"Oh, Monica," cried Maggie. "Your Majesty, may I present a very dear . . ."

Elsewhere in the room, Mitch, hero-surgeon, was bearing up under more gushing praise than he cared for, when his wife came slipping to his side. "Are you allowing Saiph to come down, dear? So many people want to know."

"Oh, now, about that . . . Excuse us?" Mitch drew his wife away. This was understandable. Everyone hoped to see the Little Prince.

Phillida said, "Spot on your left cuff. I'm clued."

Mitch looked at his watch, and in the process rearranged his jacket sleeve. "I've had a thought," he began.

"Level, first," said Phillida, in an undertone. "Will she be all right?"

"If the knife was clean," said her husband grimly. Then louder, "I'd like to persuade His Majesty and the Princess to come up with me. I want to suggest something."

"Both of them? Away from the party?" Phillida said. "Oooh, the hostess won't like that! I had better check for neglected souls."

She moved in the direction of the hall. Mitch moved in the direction of his mother.

Colonel Gorob moved in the direction of the King. His ears were pink with delight.

That had been *blood* on the Doctor's cuff. Recent? Of course, since he must have dressed himself afresh for this occasion. So? A knife had wounded someone in this house. "Someone" was a woman. It was a domestic affair. Ah, these clever Americans! The woman's name might be "Alice." Yet, perhaps not. The Colonel was easily persuading himself that he had, all along, been sensing undercurrents here. So, blood and a knife and a woman? And all in secret. Very clever, these Americans. But not, of course, as clever as he.

Lurlene saw Phillida ghosting by again, between her and the musicians. "Hey, Phillida! Excuse me."

"Who is it? Oh, Lurlene. Yes? Mrs. Hardy, are you comfortable?"

Mrs. Hardy was very comfortable indeed.

Lurlene, having accepted the comfort of a drop of vodka, here and there, was also getting tipsy.

"Listen," she said anxiously, "I haven't seen one single sign of Rufus and I'm getting worried."

"Of course you are." Phillida bent closer. "I'm afraid he may have fortified himself a little too much. Best not to disturb, don't you think?"

"Oh, I see," said Lurlene. "Well, thanks. Gee, I'm sorry. Is Maggie awful upset?"

"She hasn't the time," Phillida smiled and glided away.

To Mrs. Hardy, Lurlene said, "You know, my husband has been drinking pretty heavy, lately." This wasn't the truth, but near enough.

"Me, too," said Mrs. Hardy, cheerfully. "The on—ly way to fly."

Lurlene, however, was not amused. She was beginning to

wonder if she was so smart to be hiding out here with this stupid dame and missing everything. *She* didn't think Rufus was
drunk. Probably those dumb pills. Because a drink or two
couldn't hurt, could it? Especially when you felt—well—let
down or something. But you were *supposed* to be having a good
time, at a party.

19

THE guest bedroom in the east wing was a large one, but it was crowded. The King was there, seated where he had sat this morning. Colonel Gorob stood stiffly beside Al Asad's chair, keeping his ears and his eyes open, even while his wits were racing. One part of his mind considered the boy, who was a factor, now, and a powerful one.

Why this was clearer to him than it had been this morning, Gorob did not know, but Al Saiph, dressed as he was now dressed, looking as he now looked—somehow older, new planes on his cheeks, somehow emerging from childhood, becoming under one's eyes a young male of the royal line, and not sickly, either—he was a factor impossible to dismiss. Nor could his mother, the Princess, standing there in her gold, be dismissed too lightly. She was a widow. Half-formed schemes tumbled in the Colonel's deep-dreaming mind.

Meantime, his eyes inspected Inga Bjornsen, who was there, drawn respectfully into the corner, spotless in her uniform, as silent and dour as ever. Gorob discarded any suspicion that it could have been she whose blood had stained the Doctor's cuff. Nor could it have been the Princess. No, not that golden glow. And not, he concluded, their hostess, who was standing there in her silvery gown, beaming in her silly fashion, a pampered so-called "society" woman in a decadent society, who would have no tolerance for pain.

All the while, the Colonel's ears were listening to the Doctor, who was saying that he realized there might be some considerations to do with this particular patient that, providing his well-being was not jeopardized, the Doctor was proposing to take into account. It had occurred to him that it might seem desirable to His Majesty, and perhaps, also, to the Princess, if Prince Saiph were to be permitted to fly home to his own country tomorrow, on the King's own plane. "Unless," the Doctor continued, "Your Majesty would prefer not to risk both of your persons in the one plane. In which case," the Doctor smiled, "we will be very glad to keep him with us."

Colonel Gorob was finding himself startled.

Jaylia did not speak or even gasp. Into the boy's face an eagerness leaped, but he said nothing.

Al Asad, with his palm over his chin, said, "If he can safely travel with me, tomorrow, that would be desirable."

Now Jaylia did gasp and clasp her hands. Across Maggie's face ran a parade of emotions—surprise, dismay, resignation, sadness, and on into unselfish-rejoicing.

Gorob, however, was viewing the prospect with some alarm. What! The royal family returning all together, with the boy looking as he now looked—landing in a blaze of glamorous excitement with joyous tidings from America, with the inevitable gratitude and a softening . . .

The Doctor was now saying that the boy's health was, of course, his primary consideration and responsibility. And to that end, he would very much like—in fact, must insist—that the boy be transferred to the hospital for the balance of this night. This to enable some tests, some final checkings, to provide all possible assurance that the Doctor, in his experienced and yet intuitive judgment, was correct. If everything was found to be healing as well as the Doctor felt sure was true in this case, then the Doctor could trust Miss Bjornsen, who was (in his opinion) an excellent nurse, to continue a regime which she well understood. Yes, after such testing—a cautious step the King must understand and approve—if all went well, the boy might go.

The Doctor turned and said to Saiph easily, "We'll just put you back in your old nest for a few hours."

"Very good," the boy said. "Then I can say good-bye to many kind people."

"Ah," said the Colonel.

But the King stopped him with a raised hand. "You will arrange this, Doctor? How soon?"

"I will telephone for an ambulance. I will alert the escorts. It won't take, I should say, more than twenty minutes or half an hour for them to come. That is, if this is your pleasure, Your Majesty."

The King's head bent, indicating that this was his pleasure and also his express command.

Mitch bowed, in his own somewhat saturnine manner, and went away.

"Oh, but my *party!*" cried Maggie softly. "My poor, poor party! Oh, I *beg* your pardon."

Jaylia said, "If I may be excused, Your Majesty? I must tell my maid to pack quickly. Perhaps I could, then, help with the party?"

"My dear, you *could*, indeed," said Maggie, as if the world had just been saved.

"Wait," said Gorob rapidly in the King's own tongue. "Your Majesty, I must give warning. A woman has been knifed in this house. The Doctor has blood on his linen. They are all concealing this fact. It is a woman of the household. Would it not be desirable to let the Prince require the women to come here, that he may thank them?"

The King rose. His eyes were cold. "What has this to do with us?" he said sharply, in the other tongue. Then he said to Jaylia, in English, "Indeed, you must be ready." This dismissed her. Jaylia left, invisibly curving under her stiff golden gown.

"But the maid . . ." Gorob began to plead. He was thinking, Suppose it is the maid, one of ours, who has been injured? They would not wish this known. "If I may ask that the maid come here . . ."

The King said, in English, "You are rude." He said to Maggie, "I am sorry for this embarrassment to your party, madame. I shall go down. During this time of waiting, perhaps Al Saiph may also greet your guests."

"Oh, that *is* kind," glowed Maggie, "so kind of you, Your Majesty, to understand what this means to me." (As silly a society hostess as had ever walked a stage, was she.) "Saiph, my dear, you must know how much everyone wants to see you, if only for a little, little minute. Oh, I *am* sorry that you will miss most of the party. Could we not send—something with you?" Maggie's lashes seemed to be batting at thoughts of ice cream.

Saiph leaned forward, his face alight. He said, "May I have Tamsen?" He was not making a request. He was giving forth, from a position of privilege, and with some boyish glee besides, a royal command.

"I will inquire, Your Highness," said Maggie gently.

"Who is this?" asked Gorob. Maggie's mask had slipped only a little, but he sensed something.

"A friend to me," said Saiph, arrogantly. "Don't be rude."

The King sat down again. So Duncan Tyler left his listening-post in the passage and walked into the vacuum Maggie had left behind her. "So you're going to leave us?" he said to the boy, after his nod had done honor to the King.

"I hope I shall be going home," said Saiph. "Not that I have been unhappy here. Will Tamsen mind coming with me to the hospital and missing the party?"

"I'm sure she would much rather celebrate with you," said

Duncan. Then to Al Asad, who seemed to be sitting very still, "My wife is putty in his hands, Your Majesty."

"Explain," said Saiph. "This is an idiom?" Then to his grandfather, he added, "I have been studying the idioms, you see, sir."

Colonel Gorob was looking stiff and sour. Trivialities, he thought. When we should be searching for the woman. . . .

In the Judge's room, Tamsen was on her feet, in a white dress that belonged to Maggie. Phillida had been circling her with a mouthful of pins, tucking and fitting and creating. Now she was hooking the bracelet on Tamsen's left wrist to a brooch that was fastened at her waist.

"Makes a bit of a sling, anyhow." Phillida put a small white satin evening purse into Tamsen's left hand. "Can you hold on to this?"

"Yes, but I can't do my hair," said Tamsen matter-of-factly.

"I'll fix." Phillida began to take down the dark disarrayed tumbling tresses. "Now, if you must move suddenly, and that dressing begins to feel icky, keep your back to some wall. Hah, brilliant thought! Let's have your hair down." Phillida turned gentle. "Honey, can you do this?"

"Of course I can," said Tamsen. "I can do anything."

Maggie opened the door softly. "Can you come now, Tamsen?"

"Yes, all but my hair."

"Then will you come? That Colonel is on to something. Saiph is helping us, God bless him. You'll see. We must simply exhibit you boldly and get that over."

"Yes," said Tamsen, "let's get that over."

So, after Phillida had whacked a brush swiftly down her hair, Tamsen went walking beside Maggie into the passage, and along it to the boy's room, which looked as if nothing had happened there. She gave Duncan one quick look and saw his face

157 ✳

go fond and proud. She was lifted into perfect confidence. Nothing *has* happened, she said to herself.

The white dress came high to the base of her neck. Her own fall of dark hair was another cover for the wad of surgical dressing over the raw place where the knife had scraped her skin away. Forget it.

Maggie was cooing respectfully, "Your Majesty, may I present my little daughter-in-law, Tamsen Tyler, who has been your grandson's loving playmate all this while." (A sentimental old fool, she was.)

"Your Majesty," said Tamsen, bending only slightly from her waist. The effect was gravely ceremonious. She gave the old King, those piercing eyes, one shy glance of her own. Then she turned toward the boy. Her back must now turn part way toward the King and the other man. She had not even glanced at the other man. She said to Saiph in her soft manner, but somehow jauntily, "I'm glad the Doctor thinks you are well. But I don't *like* saying good-bye and spoiling the whole party."

Saiph laughed. "Oh, you look very pretty, Little-Girl-Thomas," he said teasingly, "all dressed up in a party dress. But *you* can't stay at the party, either. You must come with me to the hospital."

"Oh, must I?" Tamsen was gay. "Phooey—that same old hospital?"

Inga rose and spoke from her corner. "May I say—please? Mrs. Tamsen cannot go in such a party dress. May I, perhaps, lend her a uniform?"

"Very good, Inga," said Saiph at once. "Yes, she shall wear a uniform. And she must be ready *quickly*." This was an order. "Because I must go downstairs, now. Let Kasim and Hayyan come," he said with his chin up.

"Yes, indeed, Your Highness," said Maggie, as she curtsied.

Al Asad seemed to be hiding his mouth under his palm. With a rustling of robes, he rose. Tamsen was already vanishing with Inga into the dressing room, as unmannerly as an excited child who was "going somewhere." The Colonel, who had dismissed her almost at once as more child than woman, said to his old master, "Should we not discover what woman . . ."

The King's hand moved half an inch and the Colonel shut his mouth. There was, then, one moment when the King and the hostess stood side by side, both intending to go through that open door. It was the King who bowed. So Maggie, crowned again, went gracefully before him. Their Majesties walked sedately together toward the stairs. Colonel Gorob, red in the face, stalked behind.

Al Asad did not seem to be trusting him as he should, and Gorob was no longer trusting Maggie Tyler. She was not what she seemed, he had concluded crossly, whatever she was.

Duncan Tyler, yearning toward that dressing room, said to the boy, "What's eating on the Colonel?"

"He says that there has been a woman wounded with a knife." Saiph's voice was calm and his face composed. But his left hand was holding his right elbow, now.

"Nothing of the sort has happened here," said Duncan.

"Of course not," said Saiph, without even a hint of mischief. " 'Eating on him?' That is an idiom? Or is it slang?"

Duncan silently studied him. A boy of eleven, who wore a knife at all times.

"I shall ask Tamsen," Saiph said, suddenly sunny. "Ah, Tamsen, she is very foolish." The boy was giving Duncan what might be a man's look. Foolish heart-driven women. As if a man is not prepared, and would not prefer, to protect himself. Yet, in this foolishness, we must sometimes indulge them. "I will take care of her," said the Prince of Alalaf.

Duncan bowed and went (dismissed) away. He took no offense against the boy for his attitude. He couldn't kid himself that he understood this boy. When Duncan could not even speak the language, how could he read the idioms? Behind the words would be centuries of thoughts—as strange or stranger.

159   *

If Duncan thought that Saiph "ought" to have expressed gratitude, and then regret, it was only that Duncan himself "ought," in the same circumstances.

Duncan simply felt that it was time Saiph went home.

Tamsen, standing in the dressing room, with shafts of pain running down her left arm while Inga pinned up the extra length of the uniform together with the extra length of the party dress, worn underneath, thought that she was looking very well in that mirror.

"Can you braid my hair and pin it up?" she asked.

"Yes, madame."

"Yes, of course you can," said Tamsen dreamily, considering the kind of ballet that was going on in this house, a swift cue-snatching improvisation among many people. Improvisation on a theme, and each member of the corps entrusted to come in smoothly, wherever needed, in a pattern that had never been designed, but simply grew. How lovely! she thought.

Something had happened to Tamsen, with the pain and the bloodletting. She had in some way, now (at last), been punished. So she was not guilty anymore. She felt free and not afraid.

Lurlene stood at the bottom of the stairs. She didn't know where they had put Rufus, to sleep it off or whatever, but she herself was beginning to feel miserably out-of-place. She had better locate him. After all, he was her husband. This was the fact that made Lurlene a Tyler. Maybe he was O.K. by now. Maybe he would go with her, to meet this king.

Then the sight of such descending splendor—a King *and* a Queen—sent Lurlene turning away and scurrying back towards the garden side.

Phillida was just gliding through the lanai. "Oh, Lurlene," she said, "I've been hunting for you. I believe you are wanted."

"It's about time," said Lurlene thickly.

Phillida took her arm, quite firmly, and they went through the lanai and all the way to the kitchen.

"Back stairs, eh?" Lurlene muttered, resisting that hand.

Phillida said lightly, "Why not? They're for the family."

So Lurlene went along.

20

INSIDE the big room, Jaylia had been attracting all eyes, until Al Asad reappeared with Maggie. Then all eyes were busier than ever. The party, which had bogged down for a while, seemed to revive.

In some mysterious way, everybody suddenly knew that there was now going to be a little pageant. Into the frame of the archway came two young men, in Western clothing, with Eastern faces, very stiff to their duty. They opened the curtains, as it were, and then, walking slowly, but with ease, there came the white-clad, stunning little figure of the Prince of Alalaf. Almost no eyes looked anywhere else.

The Judge, who had instinctively put out his hand in greeting, made nothing of the boy's evasion of a handshake. Customs differ. Besides, Mitch was authoritatively, and even fussily, guiding the boy to a big chair in the large room. Saiph's young voice, in its American-flavored English, began to chat gravely and charmingly with what privileged persons could wiggle themselves near enough to see and to hear.

Both choosing to be ignored, Maggie, and the old man who was a king, stood apart. "May he live forever," she said, softly.

Al Asad said coolly, "My aide, Colonel Gorob, insists that a woman has been wounded by a knife, in this house."

"Whatever can he mean?" said Maggie, seeming almost absentminded. "Nothing untoward has happened here."

Elsewhere in the room, the Colonel, although he was fuming, continued to notice everything. Al Asad really ought to trust the Colonel, who was convinced that *something* was being concealed. He was bound he would discover what it was. This was his duty, toward at least one of his masters.

He noticed when an ambulance had drawn up quietly outside, as Sam came to inform the Doctor of its arrival. He noticed the figures of two women come quietly down the stairs and stand to wait, beside the study door. They both wore white uniforms and fingertip-length blue capes over the white. Gorob knew all about *them*. The taller one was the boy's nurse; the shorter one was that little Tyler girl. Whatever woman had been hurt in this house, she was well-hidden, somewhere else. Upstairs, he judged. It must be so. Al Asad should have believed him. Gorob was becoming a little confused, between two masters.

Tamsen could feel her back on fire, but it was well-hidden, now. The Doctor was allotting only a very few minutes for this ceremony. Already he was beside Saiph. The way was being opened. Saiph, whose arm must be on fire, was walking toward the hall. He did not smile at Tamsen nor she at him. It didn't seem necessary.

The Doctor had scurried to the front door and now was letting in (of all things and in what cold blood!) a pair of news photographers.

Saiph eyed them aloofly. He turned back to face the people, who were all watching, with Al Asad front row center.

Prince Saiph made a graceful farewell speech, regretting his departure from the party, thanking his doctor, and every member of the Tyler family, who had been so very kind to him. Still, he wanted to go home. His smile illuminated his small face and all his charm went radiantly forth. His audience was almost moaning with delight. The cameras flashed, again and again; the men, crouched low to the floor almost under the King's feet, were gleeful because they knew "heart" when they saw it. Happy emotion was running high. Even Maggie Mitchel Tyler (Look! Look!) had her handkerchief to her eyes.

The Prince spoke, in a foreign language, one sentence directly to his grandfather. He made a slight bend of his head, very like the old man's own mannerism. Then, walking steadily with great poise and dignity, and followed by his entourage, the Prince departed.

Duncan Tyler, who had twitched aside one window hanging, was watching the driveway from the passage above. He saw, in the lightning of flash bulbs, how the Prince refused to be lifted. (And no wonder.) Saiph entered the ambulance. Inga climbed in, close behind him. Kasim and Hayyan spryly followed her. In a moment, the driver made the vehicle begin to creep softly, as motorcycles began to roar and the police escort took position.

Next, behind the ambulance, was Mitch's car and Duncan saw his brother help Tamsen (knowledgeably) into the front seat, as a gentleman should. Then Mitch went around and got in to drive. His car, too, was encompassed within the escorting noise.

Cameras tried for some last interesting shots as the procession moved. Then it was gone.

Duncan blew out his breath in one long sigh and went back into his father's room.

"Say, you better tell me pretty soon, what's the big idea," said Lurlene, lifting her head from his father's pillow as if her head might weight a ton. "How come Phillida dumps me down? Listen, I . . ."

"You've had too much to drink," said Duncan calmly. "So the party's over."

"What do you mean, the party's over?"

"For you, I mean. The King of Alalaf doesn't care for drunken women."

"You . . . you . . . you . . . got some crust, you Tylers." Her head fell back and it began to roll. "You don't care *what* you do, do you?" she muttered.

Duncan, who cared what he did, hated to do what he now must. "Things being as they are, may as well have a little nightcap," he said to this woman, as agreeably as he could. "Care to join me, Lurlene?"

"Drink, yah! Might as well be drunk as the way I am," she mumbled. "Oh, *I* never was going to get to meet this King. Oh, I see that now. Phillida, first, she puts me with that stupid whoever-she-was. Oh, I *get* it! I'm the . . . I'm the"—triumphantly Lurlene found the words—"I'm the skeleton in the woodshed."

Well, thought Duncan, no, not quite. That cupboard is occupied. He put the pills that had come from Mitch, through Phillida, into a glass. Could not have Lurlene blundering about. Could not afford the risk. Whatever she knew, she could not know enough. Yet, what she did not know made her dangerous.

Oh Lord, what shall we do with the incompetents of this world, in this one of Your years? With the unteachables—the ones who can't, and the ones who could-but-won't, the ones who do not mesh into the whirls of the wheels as they turn, nowadays? What shall we do when they knot up, in personal grievances, unaware of much too much, yet aware of enough to make them both miserable and dangerous? Make mobs of them? Exploit? Manipulate? No, no. We have said that they must each be understood and each valued for what he is. That is our civilized position.

And so we thought we had done, with Rufus. *We* believed it. But did he? Oh, he used to. Surely, he used to. But somewhere along the line . . .

Meantime, what am *I*, in my well-educated, intelligent and civilized wisdom, doing right now? Duncan's mouth was wry as he held the glass to Lurlene's lips.

So much for love and understanding. There had come a time when it was either too late or too soon. Too risky, at the moment, to try it on. And no faith to ask for it.

Lurlene bridled and slobbered, but she took a little.

"What's so great about this prince?" she mumbled.

"Don't worry about him. He's back in the hospital. Just a checkup before he goes home tomorrow. Relax, why don't you?"

Her head rolled.

Tamsen was leaning forward to spare her back the back of the seat.

"O.K.?" Mitch was speeding them along, inside the armor of the noise.

"Something's wearing off, I guess," gasped Tamsen. "But I'll make it."

"Howl. You're entitled, and it's safe for ten minutes, at least."

"No, no, better not." She *could* have howled, all right, but once begun, could she stop?

"I hope the King gets out of there, right fast," Mitch growled.

"Why?" Tamsen tried to switch her attention.

"Because I'll be going back to see after Rufus."

"He *was* knocked out. Do you think his head . . ."

"Knocked out, momentarily," Mitch said, "and perhaps."

"*Perhaps?*" Tamsen felt astonished.

"I'm inclined to think he wasn't much hurt. I ought to examine him more thoroughly, of course."

"But . . ."

"Duncan hit him, too. Even so, he wasn't unconscious (in the usual sense, that is) when I first saw him. I'm fairly sure he was possuming. Oh, I put him in a state to snooze a while. Couldn't trust it. But I can believe that when he fell, he possumed out on the whole business, then and there."

"Because he had failed again?" she gasped.

"Because he couldn't think what else to do, in the fiasco," said Mitch grimly. "God knows what the inside of his head is like. He had bumped the outside. That would have been a suggestion."

"That's—awfully sad," she said in a moment.

"You bet. It's sad I didn't listen to *you* harder. Sweetie, you busybodied considerable tonight. Do you realize you might have got that knife in the eye? In the throat?"

"So might Rufus," Tamsen said, wonderingly.

"So might Saiph have got a bullet in his vitals. I guess we better get profound," drawled Mitch, "and say to ourselves, 'It might have been worse.' Can you walk briskly, on your own two feet, all alone, as far as the elevator?"

"Of course," she said, absentmindedly.

21

U PSTAIRS, Duncan remained on guard. This was his function. There was no one else to do it. Mitch had gone, having functions of his own. And the Judge was both unaware and unavailable.

Downstairs, as the party continued, the Judge was absorbed in his own problem. Al Asad did not wish to leave without the few words promised him. Yet the Judge was not sure he ought to risk this conference. The most secluded gathering must arouse the curiosity of this spy, however it was managed. The Judge felt that he could fool the guests, but not the enemy. Meanwhile, the party was lasting too long.

Then the Judge observed a most fortunate happening and he began to sift through the throng, dropping a word here and there.

Upstairs, as the party continued too long, too long, Duncan found himself on edge with nerves. He had checked on Rufus, who seemed still dreaming whatever dreams might be in that sorry head. Lurlene was now snoring. Duncan covered her. At last, he was able to convince himself that the King surely would leave soon, at which moment he, Duncan, ought for his manners to show up and say a brief but courteous farewell. He could lock the door to his father's room.

So he did that, from inside, and slipped out through the small door that led into his mother's room, where he neatened himself, and then came out into the passage and the upper stair-hall. And went discreetly down.

The party, still a stand-up party, was milling gently. Al Asad was still there, seeming rooted, not contemplating departure. Duncan was trying to figure out how he could say a graceful good-bye to a guest who wasn't going yet, when Jaylia in her own way summoned him to her side.

She said, "I am sure we shall be leaving tomorrow. If I don't see Tamsen, will you tell her how grateful I am? For this, tonight, too. It was darling of her to go." Her eyes were asking if all was well.

"I'll be glad to tell her," he said, smiling to answer that all was well enough, so far.

Sam appeared with a tray and Duncan took refreshment. He then became aware of a presence at his back. Al Asad, with entourage (not Gorob, however), had made his way to them.

"I have been told that the young lady, your wife, has been most kind to Al Saiph." The King was gracious.

"She has enjoyed it, every minute, Your Majesty. She is devoted to him."

"She seems very young," the King said. But lights went out in that face. Duncan had not answered some other question.

What was going on in that mind, behind those eyes? Duncan didn't know. He felt as if he were pinned here. He knew that he ought to get away and go back to his post, yet how could he get away? People had shifted, drawing to stand politely a few feet apart, yet constituting an audience. "She is not as young, perhaps, as she is able to look," Duncan said. He started to ask if the King knew that Tamsen was a painter. But he remembered, in time, not to do so, there being a religious prejudice. He didn't know what remark he could throw into the silence to alleviate the King's faint whiff of ennui. Those eyes were scanning the room now. "Ah," the King said, very low.

Duncan saw that the Judge was making his way toward them, rather purposefully. "May I interrupt, Your Majesty?" said he. "There is a phone call for you, personally. Will you take it in my study, sir?"

Al Asad's head bowed assent. The Judge led. The King followed. The King's men followed him. The people shifted to let them pass.

"From home, perhaps?" said Jaylia. Her eyes met Duncan's with momentary uneasiness. Then she moved only slightly, but somehow invited the people, indicated that she was available. The women might chit-chat. The men might gather around, but mustn't touch. . . .

So Duncan slid easily away from this new grouping. He was thinking, Well, she does things *her* way, but not to *me*.

The Judge paused, with his hand on the knob of his study door. "This may be private, Your Majesty."

Al Asad spoke to his followers. One man turned his back to the door as if to station himself on guard. But the other one followed Al Asad as the Judge bowed them through. The Judge must put up with this. (He didn't mind. He had spotted Colonel Gorob, ten minutes ago, as that man had been walking softly up the stairs. That was when the Judge had gotten busy.)

The four quiet Americans seated inside his lair all rose, ready for serious business. "Ah," said the King.

Zora was half in tears. "But I do not know," she wailed. "I do *not* know."

The Colonel had pounced upon her in the midst of all the packing. Many pieces of luggage were scattered about and heaps of feminine apparel were there to be sorted. Zora did not seem to understand what he wanted of her. He had her by the wrist and she was twisting and writhing (as he shrewdly observed) as if she knew no pain would result from this frenzy.

"No blood? No knife? No woman hurt?"

"No, sir. No, I have not heard of this."

"Tell me," he said. "Who are the women of this household?"

"There is Mrs. Tyler, the elder—"

"The hostess. Yes. Yes."

"And there is Hilde—"

"Who is she?"

"Oh, she is the cook and—"

"*Where* is she?"

"She is below," Zora whimpered. "She has much to do. Chloe is helping her."

"Who is Chloe?"

"Also a servant—of the younger Mrs. Tyler."

"What Mrs. Tyler is this?"

"Mrs. Doctor."

"Describe her."

"She is very tall and wears the beautiful green." Zora used her free hand to indicate a slimness at the hips.

"Hah," said Gorob. He knew it could not be *that* woman. *Her* question had enlightened him in the first place.

"Now who else? Come. There is a little one, with the long hair."

"Mrs. Tamsen, yes, sir."

"Who is she?"

"She is the wife of the young son. She comes every day. She comes to play games with Al Saiph. They are children together."

"So I gathered," said Gorob, sourly. "Who else?"

"There is a Mrs. Tyler I do not know."

"Who is *she?*"

"The wife of the other son."

"A third son?"

"Yes, he came to this house one day only. I do not—"

"Where is he now? Is he here?" Gorob was not really concerned about a male.

"I have not seen him. I think he does not come here often."

"Where is this third—fourth Mrs. Tyler?"

"I cannot know whether she is here," Zora said, "I do not know how she looks."

"What other women, then?"

"No others, sir."

"That cannot be."

"Please, I have so much to do."

"Who is in the other rooms, up here?"

"No one. I think no one. I do not know."

"Get on with it," he said abruptly and let her go.

Zora was obviously perfectly whole. Not she, then.

Gorob went on to the end of the west wing, looked into the smaller room, where Zora slept, and into a storage place. No one there. But he felt sure that he was right and he meant to vindicate his intelligence, prove his zeal, and maintain his trustworthiness. He began to open doors along this passage. Mere cupboards. Finally he came back into the stair-hall and stood there a moment, listening to the party sounds wafting upward. He glanced along the center block. Everything was silent. Two doors, both closed. The Colonel began to walk that way. He had always been inclined to be thorough.

Duncan was already edging toward the hall when Maggie caught him. "Oh, there you are, dear," she said. "Have you seen Colonel (what's-his-name?) Gorob?"

"No, I haven't, Maggie." Duncan was able to sound casual. "He is not with the King, is he?"

"No, he is not," Maggie joined him in anxiety, without sounding anxious. "Sam, please?"

"Yes, ma'am, Mrs. Tyler?"

"Have *you* seen the colonel with the uniform?"

"Yes, ma'am. I think he went upstairs a while ago, Mrs. Tyler. Five or ten minutes ago."

People were hovering to pounce on Maggie. Duncan said, "Hoo, I bet he's got himself lost, looking for the conveniences."

He patted his mother's arm, as the Judge so often did. Then he went upstairs, faster than he seemed to be going.

"Oh, Maggie," he heard someone say, "I haven't had a chance to tell you what a lovely party—"

"My dear, you are an ornament to it."

"The King's had a phone call? From Alalaf?" The guest sought exciting inside dope.

"Ah, well," said Maggie, "there is a time difference. Perhaps it is office hours there. Come, have you met . . ."

Duncan huffed and stopped himself at the top of the stairs to listen to the air up here. He heard nothing. He went quickly to his mother's door and inside. The small door to his father's room was open and shedding more light than he had left in there. His toes curled within his shoes as he went softly across to look in.

Colonel Gorob was bending over a sodden-looking Lurlene on the bed. He had stripped her dress lower, to expose both plump shoulders.

Duncan roared and jumped in.

The Colonel straightened and gave him an icy glare.

Duncan said, "Please leave this room and this floor of this house. You have no business here."

Gorob smiled nastily. "You don't understand," he said in condescending tones.

"I'm afraid I do. I find you in a bedroom, undressing a sleeping woman—"

"Oh, come," said Gorob. (This was, he remembered, an adolescent nation—still as fearful and worshipful of sex as a thirteen-year-old who has just heard of it—but it did seem ridiculous, in the moment.) "I am responsible," Gorob began, "for the safety of the King. I have reason to believe that something very strange has happened in this house. It is necessary for me to know what has happened. If you will simply enlighten me, then."

"I can enlighten you as to what is *going* to happen if you do not get out of here, right now."

"Mr . . . Tyler, isn't it?" The Colonel was patient. "I have realized, for some time past, that you are all concealing an incident of some kind. What is wrong with this woman?"

Lurlene's eyes had popped open. They were frightened and puzzled, but in a minute her mouth would open. Duncan might have to wrestle this man out of here, by force. But that would tear it, as quickly as anything. The house was surrounded by police. There must not be a row.

His mother spoke, behind him. "Will you please," said Maggie's coolest voice, "explain this to me? Both of you?"

"It has become my duty," said the Colonel stiffly, "to search this house."

"My house? Without my permission?"

"Where the King is," said Gorob, with pomp and pity, "can no longer be a private dwelling."

"Let me deal with him," Duncan said. "Let me just throw him down the stairs on his—"

"I must then see that His Majesty is informed—"

"Out of the house, entirely," roared Duncan, "and if His Majesty doesn't like it, let him go back where he came from, too."

"Then," said Gorob, unimpressed by roaring, "I must ask the American—police, are they not?—to inquire what woman has been knifed in this house."

Duncan felt as if he were strangling.

But Lurlene sat up, clutching to her breast the coverlet that Duncan had thrown over her. "*What* woman!" she said thickly. "What does he mean? *Knifed!* Who is this man? What's the big—"

"Hush," said Maggie. She went to Lurlene and touched her hair, caressingly. Lurlene's eyes immediately filled with tears. "Oh, listen, Maggie . . ."

"Hush." Maggie was using magic. Lurlene hushed.

"Colonel Gorob," said Maggie cuttingly, "do what you like,

anywhere else. But you will not, in my house, disturb a woman who is ill and unhappy."

"What," said the Colonel, "is her illness?" He could not believe that *this* woman had been knifed. But he was ever thorough.

Duncan had reached the lamp and turned it low again. "Go on. Get out."

"I realize," the Colonel said, "that you do not recognize my authority. I quite understand. I may seem to have exceeded what is proper for a guest. But my concern must be His Majesty's security. I believe that this is also the concern of the guards who surround this house? Perhaps they have the authority to conduct the necessary search. I shall speak to them. I shall suggest that they look for bloodstains. I have already seen a trace of blood on Doctor Tyler's cuff. There must be others."

He was backing away. If he told the guards, it would be disaster. But he was not going the right way. He was backing toward the door to the Judge's dressing room. Where bloody towels were in the hamper, and a bloody rug in a heap with Tamsen's bloodied dress. But worse than that, where Rufus Tyler lay bound and drugged in an unconscious knot on the floor. If he looked in—disaster.

Well, Duncan was going to have to hit the man. He must calculate the quickest way to be sure of knocking him silent, because a noisy row would also be disaster.

Maggie's voice struck across the room like a lance of silver. "Nonsense. I don't believe you. You must be looking for the traitor."

The Colonel's hand did not turn the doorknob. He turned his head.

"How silly of you," said Maggie. "*He* came with the King. We all know he is in the house. He is one of you."

"Traitor?" said Gorob, with interest. (For a moment, he did not apply the word to himself.)

"Of course." Maggie taught an ignoramus. "Alice Foster telephoned. In fact, she is on the phone with Al Asad himself at this very moment. By this time, she must be sure which one of you this traitor is."

"I know nothing of this," said Gorob stiffly. He began to walk toward Duncan.

Duncan said, "I believe I have realized for some time past— er— Let me show you down. And *out?*"

"I can find my way," Gorob clicked his heels. "I beg your pardon, madame."

"I do not grant it," said Maggie regally.

"Thank you," said Gorob, not having heard her at all. He had other things to think about.

When he had gone, the room was very quiet. Lurlene was silent from sheer incomprehension. Duncan gripped Maggie's shoulder. "Wow!"

"I don't know," said Maggie, with anxiety. "I don't know. Your father is in the midst of the conference. But I *had* to . . ."

"Sure, you did." Duncan went to open the door that had not been opened by the colonel. He said over his shoulder, "Gorob will be getting out, without any fussing with guards. He knows what's good for him. That's O.K. I'll stay with this pair, Maggie. You go on down. Hold the fort. It must be almost over."

Lurlene said, with belated indignation, "Say, who *was* that guy? What was he trying to do to me? I'm not sick. Why did you tell him I was sick? What's the . . ."

"There isn't time," said Maggie wearily.

"Time for what? Time to tell *me* anything? Yah, you never tell me one damn thing. How come you didn't bother to tell me about my own husband? How come you tied him up and you don't even— What am *I* supposed to do?"

Duncan stared at her. Slowly, he turned his head and looked within the dressing room. The light was sufficient. There were only some cut pieces of the Judge's neckties, scattered on the floor where Rufus had been lying.

22

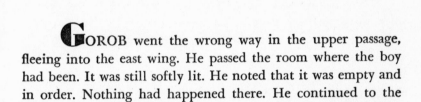

GOROB went the wrong way in the upper passage, fleeing into the east wing. He passed the room where the boy had been. It was still softly lit. He noted that it was empty and in order. Nothing had happened there. He continued to the back stairway. He came down into the space just off the kitchen. He could hear the servants' voices, cheerful and busy.

He listened only a moment. Then he slipped out of the house by its back door. A guard came out of the shadows instantly. "Yes, sir?"

Gorob said curtly, "I must leave."

"Better be checked out, sir. Around front."

"Of course." Gorob turned to go around the sprawling house to the front of it. There the police waited for His Majesty's departing parade. The TV people had gone, but there were some cameramen still, and there was light. Gorob stood quietly in a shaft of shadow. A bit of commotion, at the moment, made him wonder whether he could possibly slip past it. They seemed to be swarming around a man in a dinner jacket. The Colonel had never seen him before, and could not see him very well, at the moment, either.

Rufus was blinking in the strong light.

"No, no," he was saying. "Not yet. Not now. It isn't finished."

"Party still going on, right?"

"What about the King?"

"No, no," Rufus was mumbling, "not the King. I've got to get on down to the hospital. *I* can get in. My brother . . . Doctor . . ."

"You're not feeling so good, Mr.—uh?"

"I've got this headache," Rufus said in a drone. "I took some pills. They haven't started to work yet." He wasn't being fascinating.

Somebody shouted. Gorob had been spotted.

"Well, listen, good luck, Mr.—uh," said one of the inquisitors in a spirit of general goodwill. (Yet who needed symptoms?) He scooted, with the rest, into the new swarming gathering, now, around the Colonel.

"Is the King coming out now, sir?"

"How's the party going?"

"How is the King feeling about the kid, I mean, the Prince?"

"Is it true, sir, that the Prince gets to go home tomorrow?"

"Or is there something wrong? Why did the Doctor . . . ?"

"What is this last-minute checkup?"

The Colonel raised his hand and said primly, "It is a checkup. We are confident that Al Saiph will be able to fly home tomorrow. His Majesty is pleased. The party continues. Would you excuse me? I am sent on a small errand."

"When is the King coming out?"

"I believe, soon," said Gorob.

A policeman was now solicitous at his elbow.

"No, no," said Gorob. "No escort is necessary. I am not royalty," he added with a thin smile. "But I wonder . . . A taxicab?"

"Come with me, sir," said the cop. "I'll get you a cab."

"You are very kind."

"Turn this way, sir?" yelled a cameraman.

"Don't waste it," said another. The Colonel wasn't being fascinating, either. He didn't even *look* like one of them.

The cop set off at a fast walk down the driveway toward the street and Gorob followed.

(Someone had made a mistake. Perhaps it was he?)

Fifty yards away, down under a pepper tree, Rufus Tyler was climbing, unobserved and unpursued, into his own car.

"You're hurting me," Lurlene was whining. "You let go. You quit that. You're hurting me."

Duncan only tightened his hands on her wrists. "All right, never mind your reasons for cutting him loose. Where did he go?"

Lurlene felt herself to be in the worst mess she'd ever been in, in her life. She hated Duncan. She hated Maggie. She hated all the Tylers, and the whole damn world. "Yah, but you tied him up," she wept. "You tied up your own brother. What was the big idea? That's what I . . ."

Maggie said, sadly, "She is hopeless."

"You don't *know* why?" Duncan barked. "You don't know what Rufus did?"

"No," she said, lying defiantly. "What did he do?"

"What does he intend to do now?"

"I don't get the big—"

"You never will," said Duncan furiously. "Lots of ideas are too big for you. What is Rufus going to do? Where did he go? Stop squirming and evading."

Lurlene began to look sly. Thought he was so smart, Duncan Tyler. They all thought they were so damned smart. But they were liars! Maggie was a liar! She had just told that Colonel-Somebody one big fat lie, and Lurlene had heard her do it. "You're a bunch of damn liars," she shouted, furious in confusion. "That's what you are. And I'm *not* sick. Or drunk, either."

179   ✳

Duncan slapped her, hard.

"Don't you . . ."

Duncan said, "I need you to talk. I'd a good deal rather strangle you, and be done with it."

Maggie said calmly, "He has more sense than to strangle you, Lurlene. Did you let Rufus go and ask him *no* questions?"

Lurlene was scared, real scared.

"*I* didn't know," she whined. "I didn't know he'd done anything. Only there he was, moaning and all. And tied up. And that's not *right*." She had found one moral position and she was going to hang on to it.

When she had awakened and found herself all alone in the Judge's room, and hearing some moaning going on, she'd been about scared to death. (But what did *they* care for that?) She had dared, finally, to sneak on her stockinged feet and crack that door.

Rufus had said, "Cheap. Cheap. Cheap. Lousy bargain."

"What, honey? What? What?" (Lurlene could remember now that she had really felt concern.)

"Or else I put it together wrong. I don't know too much about guns. It looked all right."

"Where is the gun?"

"I don't know."

"Listen, who did this to you?"

"They did. Where is my gun? Where is the boy?"

"Who? Who? The Prince?" Lurlene had known who. "I don't know. Yes, I do. They took him to the hospital."

"Then when I shot, I hit him!" Rufus roused. "Is he dead?"

Lurlene had sat back on her heels and let her rage fly. "Oh, you dope! You stupid idiot!" she had raged. "So you goofed. You couldn't hit a barn. You missed, as usual. He's not dead. He's going home, tomorrow. You can't do one thing . . . not one thing. . . ." She had sobbed. "O.K. We're getting out of here." She had turned and hunted and found the Judge's scissors. "Or else, for once in your stupid life," she had raged, "you could go and finish what you started."

She had cut him loose with much sawing. She had helped him to unsteady feet. She had brushed him down with a rough hand. "The party's still on," she had said, "and the King's down there. So why don't you go shoot the King? Hah, no gun! You mislaid it. Yah!"

"I'm going to the hospital?" Rufus had said, weakly questioning.

"Augh, knock it off," she had said. "You're not going anywhere. Not anywhere, in *this* life. Not you."

She had turned her back and walked out into the bedroom, but turning her head, she had seen him fumbling around for his pillbox. And the hell with it, she had thought. Born a dope!

Then he had come, shambling. "Don't worry," he had said. "I told you. *You* mustn't worry. I promised."

He had stood looking at her and Lurlene had been ready to scream—ready to scream the roof down. Oh, *damn!* No matter what she said to him, or what she did, this dope, this stupid idiot, this lemon in the basket, he kept right on thinking he had to be in love with her. Didn't he *know?* Didn't he *realize?* Times change.

"Yah, *I'm* not going to worry, believe me." She had been sullen. "Sure, now your fancy family is going to come and get you into some jail."

"No, no. Not yet." Rufus had been, by then, at the door to the passage. "How does this open?"

"My God, you can't even work a door lock!" She had turned the little latch on the inside of the bedroom door and opened the door for him. "*I'm* not . . ." She had stood there, on her stockinged feet. "Where do *you* think you're going?"

He had looked at her and his mouth had turned into that little chirruping silly smile. "In the pages of history," he had mumbled.

Then what he'd done, she didn't want to think about. He

hadn't tried to kiss her, but he had touched her cheek and even as she recoiled, Rufus had said, "I don't matter. But you mustn't worry, Lurlene. Honey-Lu? Just remember. You were always the girl for me."

Lurlene had shut the door, swiftly. She had listened and thought she heard his steps going toward the back way down. She had remembered to lock the door again, and scrambled back to the bed and felt so sick she'd thought she was going to die.

Her heart was banging away at the moment. "So go ahead, strangle me," she whined up at Duncan. "Just because I couldn't stand to see my own husband . . . and *he* cares about me. I mean, maybe nobody else does, but *he* does!"

Maggie said, in her cool voice that cut into Lurlene's rising hysteria and seemed to cut it down, "If Rufus had walked into the guards or the police or the newspapermen, outside, wouldn't we know it by now?"

Duncan let Lurlene go then. "It would seem so," he murmured.

Lurlene couldn't stand the look on his face. She said, "Oh, *you'll* hear!"

"What?" Duncan demanded.

But Lurlene had to remember *herself*. Wait. Wait. Wait. "I don't know," she whimpered. "Nothing. Nothing. What's the *matter* with you people? I didn't do one bad thing. Nothing. Nothing. So torture me. Just go ahead. Torture me."

Maggie said, as if Lurlene did not exist, "I must go down, Duncan."

"Sure enough," he said. "Violence is stupid. That's the civilized premise." His voice was back to normal. "I won't strangle her."

Downstairs, it became apparent that the King was preparing to leave the party. He had returned to the big room, flanked by his two cohorts, and was speaking to the Princess. His phone call could not have been upsetting. They did not seem excited. They seemed to be saying a pleasant good evening to each other. They took all eyes.

The four men, who had conferred so briefly and quietly in the Judge's study, were now distributed among the guests. Only they knew that there had been no phone call.

It was the Judge who noticed that the King's third man had not yet reappeared.

Maggie came floating down the stairs, all smiles, just as the Judge started up. "What is it, William?" She put her hand on his arm, turning him to walk down beside her. The Judge could feel a certain vibration in her.

"Oh, it's that colonel, Maggie darling. I saw him go up, a while ago. The King seems to be thinking about leaving."

"Oh?" said Maggie. Al Asad had seen her and was even now moving toward her under full sail. So Maggie spoke to the Judge, but pitched her voice to the King. "But Colonel Gorob just excused himself, dear. When I happened to mention that His Majesty was on the telephone to Alalaf. I'm quite sure he came down. I have the impression that he left the house. You could ask."

The King snapped some words to one of his men who immediately slipped away through the front door into the clamor out there.

"I didn't notice," the Judge said, feeling lost.

The King came to his hostess and his host, to make his formal farewells. His eye was frosty. He was very stiffly correct.

When his man slipped in again, with a word or two for the King's ear, Al Asad smiled with thin lips. He turned toward the big room to incline his head very slightly to the entire assemblage there, dismissing *them*.

The Judge murmured to the other man, "I'm sorry that your Colonel Gorob seems to have drifted off."

"His Majesty has sent him on an errand," the man said coldly.

"Oh, I see."

The King, then, with entourage, departed. Outside, it was discovered that His Majesty (who spoke no English) was too fatigued for a cumbersome interpreted interview at this time. Al Asad wished to return to his hotel at once. Motors began to stutter. The Judge and Maggie and the Princess stood in the open door to wish their royal visitor Godspeed. The royal visitor entered his limousine without a backward glance at them.

The procession moved. Bulbs flashed. Motors snarled. Sirens wound up for screaming.

When all of it had died away, the Judge closed the door of his house against the suddenly silenced night. He saw the weariness that crossed Maggie's face and he patted her. "It went well," he said comfortingly.

"I am glad, William." She gave him a wan smile. Then she turned on her hostess-ness and began to move among her guests, urging them please to stay and, at the same time, clearly stating that the party was really all over, now, and they might as well go home. The Princess, for her part, had subdued her golden glow and seemed tired.

The Judge, saying farewell to what guests had been peculiarly his own, had for some time felt his mild elation ebbing away. It wasn't like Maggie to have said what she seemed to have said that she had said. She seemed to have warned off this suspected spy, and the King had not liked that. Besides, *when* could the King have sent Gorob on an errand? And for whom, or what, had Maggie's eyes been searching the very shrubbery outside, and why had he continued to feel that vibration in her? Humph!

At last, at last the house was left to itself.

23

DOWNSTAIRS, the servants still chattered softly as they continued to clear away the debris. Upstairs, in the west wing, Zora was still frantically packing. Upstairs, in the Judge's bedroom, the family was still gathered, together with the Princess.

Since the party's demise, several things had already happened.

Duncan had found out, by a few cautious questions to the guards, that Rufus had left the grounds and so had Colonel Gorob. But in sequence, and not together.

Dr. Mitchel Tyler had already come back to this room and gone away again. Whatever dismay he had felt, to find Rufus missing, he had not complained aloud, but in a series of sharp questions he had extracted from Lurlene the information that Rufus *had* been taking a drug, over and above any doctor's advice. Mitch had pried out of her a description of the pills and what she remembered, or had ever known, of their composition.

He had then given his opinion that Rufus, in all probability, was not going to drop dead in the street, but he must be much addled in his mind, his thought processes would be fuzzier even than normal, and his actions therefore absolutely unpredictable. Rufus might, Mitch said, simply fall apart, lose energy, and do nothing. "Except talk," he had added bleakly.

(Talk is all we need, Duncan had thought. "The civilized professor hit me and tied me, hand and foot. The Doctor left me injured. In the Judge's house, a crime was hushed over. My mother, the actress, put on an act and my talented and respectable sisters-in-law lied and lied, under her direction. They drugged my wife.")

None of this was said, at the time. Mitch had whisked off again, back to the hospital where he would set up a kind of early defense line against the chance that Rufus would come there.

Duncan had already telephoned to Ed Duveen, and certain other known cronies, and with deep caution had asked in a vein of humorous wrath that if his brother was there, would Rufus kindly come to the phone and tell Duncan Tyler whether he had gone off with Duncan's car keys. Because if he had, he was darn tootin' going to bring them back. Rufus was not, and had not been, near any of those telephones.

Jaylia had already been called to the Judge's phone to listen to Al Asad's decree. The royal plane was leaving somewhat earlier on the next day than had been previously planned. His Majesty intended to be on board at nine A.M. If the boy and his mother were there and ready, well and good. But if, for some reason, they could not be, then they must follow later.

No reason was given. Uncomfortable possibilities existed. Something they knew nothing about was happening in Alalaf? The old King was scudding before a storm that only he knew was breaking? Or something had already happened here? If so, they knew not what or where. They were waiting for a blow that may have already fallen.

Phillida was sitting with her hands clenched, and from time to time she pounded her own thigh. Maggie was lying back in the Judge's other bedroom easy chair, looking fragile and exhausted. Jaylia had refused a seat; she was too restless. At the moment, she was leaning against the wall. Duncan was standing. He watched his father. The Judge was standing. His long face was grave as he looked down at Lurlene, who, disheveled, frightened, and on the defensive, was still half-lying on his bed.

"This is very serious, Lurlene," he was telling her, in his deep and quietening voice. "You must try to understand, now. If it becomes known, if the news is broadcast to the world, that Rufus," the Judge kept his voice from wincing, "attempted to assassinate Prince Saiph this evening, there go any American hopes in Alalaf. But much more important, there go some lives there. American lives, as well as others. Don't you realize that?"

"Well, but I mean, he *didn't*. The kid's O.K., isn't he? I mean, *I* didn't even know a thing about it, so what did *I* do wrong?"

The Judge was wondering whether Lurlene, in her state, even believed that there was such a place as Alalaf, with living people in it.

"There was Tamsen, you see," he went on, since he was not speaking exclusively to Lurlene. It was useful to list things for the purpose of arranging them in order, for the purpose of reasoning about them. "The boy was wearing a knife. He threw it and hurt Tamsen. How do you suppose *that* could be explained, without saying that he threw it to protect himself? And against what?"

"Honest, *I* never . . . Listen, *I* didn't know Tamsen got hurt. I'm sor-ry." Lurlene's "sorry" was a hostile whine. Why are you blaming me? it said. Not *my* fault.

The Judge, however, suspected that it was, in some degree, her fault. "You didn't guess what Rufus intended to do here this evening?" The Judge sounded unimpassioned, still—but he would have liked the true answer to this question. He felt that Maggie would, too. Only he could know how Maggie felt. Only he knew how much this hurt.

"No," Lurlene screamed the lie. "No. How could *I* know?"

"These things were done—have been done," said Jaylia restlessly.

"Yes." The Judge sighed. But he went on. "Now that Lurlene has let Rufus go, since we were not able to keep him here until we could in some way find out how to help him—"

Yah. Yah, thought Lurlene. Tie him up! Sure. That's a big help. Her face turned sullen.

"Now that Rufus has gone off alone," the Judge went plodding on, "he will, most probably, either in the act of trying another assault of some kind, or in collapse somewhere, tell the world all about what has been done here. And when this happens, the consequences I mention may all follow."

(Worse than before, the Judge thought. Worse than before.)

"But he's crazy," burst Lurlene. "Didn't Mitch say he's practically nuts? So O.K. So how come all this stuff has got to follow?" She used the Judge's word, one not natural to her.

Phillida said, "Damn! Mitch does such wonders! Oh, damn, damn and *damn!*" Nobody hushed her. She hushed herself.

"There'll be local consequences," said Duncan, speaking as his father had spoken, gravely, filling out the list so that reason could consider the total situation, "for me, as well as for Mitch. I will almost certainly be removed from my nomination, gently or otherwise. You may not be on any more committees, Phillida. They may think better of naming the theatre, Maggie, as you realize. The Judge won't get his appointment, of course. Rufus is a gone goose, one way or another. If it gets really bad . . . I suppose Lurlene will be one of the most infamous women." He could no longer keep all anger out of his voice.

Maggie said wearily, "Oh, hush, dear. We know."

But Lurlene was falling deeper into the mattress and a small alteration was taking place on her mouth. Yah! she was thinking, that's right. Hey, *I* get it! I see what Rufus was getting at. *I'm* going to be the famous one! Now she let herself know what she had known, already.

"Where did Rufus go?" asked Duncan for the nineteenth time.

Lurlene had told them, eighteen times, that she didn't know. This time, she didn't even answer. Love takes strange forms, she vaguely mused. But you had to admit, it kind of built you up. Oh, that poor *slob!* Still, say Rufus was nuts. Lurlene wasn't. And you might as well figure what's probably going to happen to you. *She* could tell about his . . . uh . . . career, and how his folks always . . . Well, no, now . . . Wait. Everybody was going to see *that,* good and plain. Yah, the wonderful, wonderful Tylers!

"We are bound to find out where he has gone, sooner or later," the Judge said with a certain dryness. He was glancing at his watch. "By the way," he added with a somewhat miraculous resumption of a twinkle, "I'm glad you chose not to tell *me* what aiding and abetting was going on over my head."

"There wasn't time for pros and cons, William," said Maggie. "Besides, you had your part to play."

Then she lifted her chin and her face announced, by a very suspicious look at the Judge, a certain lifting of her spirits. "I'm sure you were very good at it," she said.

"Oh, I'm all right in a character bit," the Judge said, chuckling. Jaylia was turned toward him now, alertly. Phillida had lifted her head and her hands were opening. Duncan himself suddenly ceased to despair.

"There is luck, you know," the Judge said, because he was very old, he had lived a long time. "Don't forget that there are often surprises. Good ones, as well as bad ones."

"And time's going by," cried Duncan. "If they can just get away, *before* it blows!" He had forgotten Jaylia's presence. He was including her in the pronoun "they." (They, the foreigners.) "*We* could then clobber Rufus, as insane. Which he is. Does Mitch know they've got to make this plane early? I want to call the hospital. Who is going to watch Lurlene?"

"I," said Phillida promptly. "I'll watch her, never fear."

Duncan actually laughed. "OK., Tiger," he said and left the room. The Princess watched him go.

Lurlene lay very low. "And like—he *was* one of the Tylers, but he married just a poor girl—and it was a real love story and always faithful. . . ." Tears were in her eyes.

24

COLONEL Gorob, riding in the third taxicab he had taken since he had left the Tyler house, judged that he must have obscured his tracks sufficiently. He was now proceeding to a spot within walking distance of his real destination.

He was going to his new masters, or their local representatives. He had not hesitated to run out on the old. That woman had obviously been very sure of her information (which was correct, of course), and so had her son been, and the Colonel putting this together with his earlier suspicions that Al Asad had mysteriously ceased to trust him, was able to decide, at once, not to risk staying around to be exposed, or worse. In the first place, discovered and uncovered, he immediately ceased to be of any use, there, to his new masters. In the second place, imprisoned or dead, he would be of no use to anyone at all, including himself. So he was going to his new masters, and he would lay the situation before them and soften their sense of loss by presenting an idea that might still enable him to save the day.

Meantime, Gorob pondered his mistake. He realized that it had not been an error in reasoning, because he had not, strictly speaking, been reasoning. He had made a bad guess. He had chosen, from four or perhaps five remarks that one Tyler or another had made in his hearing, the wrong three to put together.

"Guinea-pigs," Duncan Tyler had said, "as in Guinea pigs." Gorob was still baffled by this. Guinea pig, in the American patois, meant something to do with science, did it not? But science, as far as he could see, was perfectly irrelevant. (Very annoying. But the Colonel dismissed it.)

Now, he *had* guessed (and not unintelligently, really) that some woman connected with the household had been in that house this evening wounded by a knife. But he had been wrong. He ought not to have eliminated the *name*.

Gorob was now coming up with a revised guess that Alice Foster was, of course, the "Alice" and that someone in Alalaf had finally got close enough to that annoying and interfering old woman to sink a knife into her. He was afraid, however, that she was not dead. He was inclined to believe that she *had* been on the telephone. That would be like her. It was possible that her would-be assassin had been captured and induced to tell too much. It was possible that he had been a fellow employee of the Colonel's and had *known* too much. The Colonel felt disgusted. Still, *he* had not been captured. Hah, that woman, Maggie Tyler, had been indiscreet, in the end.

But he must turn his mind to the future. His new masters must be served; he must, in some way, substitute for his lost usefulness. But surely the idea that had come to him was an effective service, even more valuable than his original assignment.

They would be interested to hear—as the Colonel had been interested—that, on the morrow, the old King and the young Prince would both be traveling on one aircraft. If such an aircraft were to vanish into the ocean—a fine place for vanishing, incidentally—affairs would most certainly come to a sharp crisis in Alalaf, immediately. Not only would his new masters find the ensuing confusion most helpful and no doubt an opening, into which they could leap, but the Colonel himself might retrieve his own hopes of power. For who else, as trustworthy as he, had been trusted for so long in that country?

How could this be arranged? Gorob had no doubt that his masters could provide the necessary device—within an hour or two, certainly—and he had his unique usefulness to offer them. He, and only he, might be able to enter, unchallenged, the King's plane. Supposing that Gorob went at dawn? He would appear to be inspecting, which would have been the natural thing for him to do.

Of course, now that Al Asad would *certainly* not be trusting him, there was a good chance that airport authorities and the crew of the plane would have been, by dawn, warned against him. In which case, the Colonel not only could not plant an explosive, but he would be risking capture. He knew very well that Al Asad would not trouble his royal head about any American laws against violence or, for instance, kidnapping.

But there was also quite a good chance that no one would remember to alert the crew of the plane. Gorob was the one who would have taken care of that detail, and every other. Oh, the King was going to miss the Colonel. The old man would not soon find anyone as conscientious and as trustworthy as he had always been.

The old man would not have the time, for one thing, if all went in the early morning as the Colonel now hoped it would. The Princess must, of course, be included in the "accident." Still, on the whole, it was as well to be rid of a possible nuisance. Women! *American* women! And if Alice Foster isn't dead, he thought, she ought to be.

He left the cab; he walked around a corner and down the block. The street, in an old part of town, was residential, tree-shadowed. It was difficult to find the numbers on the house. But the one he sought was directly under a streetlamp, painted on a stone. The path grew darker as he went, and he stumbled up the three steps to the door. He found the bell and rang it.

After some exchanges, they let him in.

Duncan Tyler finally had his groggy little wife on the other end of the phone. "Hey, Mitch says *you* think you're going to the airport at eight in the morning. Now, honey, you better not get too flossy."

"Did Mitch give you the list?" she said, sounding a bit drunk, "My gray seersucker suit and my old white coat. Makes me look like a hunchback, anyhow. And shoes? Did I say shoes?"

"I'm not going to have you running around . . ."

"Well, who are you?" Tamsen was complacent. "When my doctor says . . ."

"*Not* funny," Duncan began severely.

"Pretty funny if I wasn't there to see him off, after all the fuss. *He'd* understand but would *he?*"

Before Duncan could unscramble this, she said, "You don't get the plot. You'll be there, won't you? Hah, so then I get to go home with you. Please bring the clothes," she wailed, "or I'll never get home again."

"All right," he said helplessly. "I'll bring the clothes."

"We have decided that I burned myself, you know, on a . . . Well, we don't know *what*, yet. What's interesting? I mean, for the neighbors?" She seemed to be rambling. Then she said sharply, "How is everybody? How are *you?*"

"Fine. Fine." He wasn't going to tell her that Rufus was lost, that Rufus seemed, or Mitch thought so, to have got as far as the hospital and been turned away, long ago, and then had vanished again. This was an anxiety he wouldn't put on Tamsen for the night.

"Oh, Duncan, do you know what Saiph said to the King?"

Duncan could hardly force his mind to take this in. "What?"

"Ever since Inga told me, I've been laughing to myself." She sounded sleepily merry or merrily sleepy. She sounded on the yummy side to him. He stifled his groan. "O.K. What did Saiph say to the King?"

"*See you later, old-timer.*"

"What?"

"That's the English. I can't *imagine* how it turned out, in another language." Tamsen was laughing. "I have struck a blow against an ancient culture."

Duncan emitted one hollow bark that must pass for mirth. "Go to sleep," he said.

"And hairpins," said his wife.

"What? Oh, sure. Good night, honey."

Tamsen got the phone back on its cradle by dangling it and fishing for its resting place. Inga had put the phone on the floor. Tamsen had been speaking upside down, of course, in the suite's second bedroom. She dared not roll over to lie on her back. But so long as she did not do that or move her shoulder blade too much, she felt quite comfortable. The hospital had drugged most of the pain away for the night. Everybody was fine and it had been quite proper for Duncan to worry. She smiled and slept again.

Out in the sitting room of the suite, the two young bodyguards, who had started up when the phone rang, lay back as her murmuring ceased. Hayyan and Kasim knew, now, what had happened at the Tyler house. It had not been feasible to keep it from them any longer. Inga had told them in such a way as to make them not very anxious for any more people to find out about it. Had they not been appointed bodyguards to the Prince? But Inga said that the wound to his body was slight. It was nothing much. Wiser to keep quiet. Otherwise none of them, Inga said, could go home tomorrow. The two young men found themselves very eager to get along home.

So in the hush of the suite, Inga, alone, was not lying down and not intending to lie down. She had been quick to answer the phone in the first place, that had rung so late by special dispensation. Saiph had not been awakened. Inga had crept to waken Tamsen. Had crept back. Her charge was sound asleep, and safe, for now. His wound (so trifling, thanks to God) would heal. Inga would watch it. She would watch. She had the gun that had been fired at him in her own pocket. She would probably kill the next even slightly suspicious person who approached him. Now, in the sleepy silence, Inga went into the bathroom and began to scrub again. She scrubbed and she scrubbed, with patient care, to get the stains out of the fabric of his gown. It was better that few knew. But *she* knew.

As the night wore on, the big house in San Marino was quiet, although the guards (still there because of the Princess) could see some lights still burning.

The apartment over the garage was dark. Hilde and Sam, having kindly taken the trouble to pack up the belongings of the two bodyguards for their departure tomorrow, were now abed. Chloe was long gone.

The light was up in the west guest room, behind drawn draperies. Jaylia was checking over the packing, what was in, and what was left out, for the morning. She was being rather picky and peculant with her maid, Zora, who was dying for sleep. The Princess did not seem sleepy. She seemed impatient to be on her way home.

The light was very dim in the east guest room, where Lurlene was asleep in the bed that Saiph had occupied. Phillida Tyler, wearing a bathrobe that belonged to the Judge (and very smart it was on her), sat in the King's chair in that room. She had not closed her eyes.

Maggie's room was dark. Maggie was lying down, not sleeping but restoring her energies in a way known to her of old, a system of relaxing inch by inch, useful in conditions of stress.

Downstairs, the hall was lit and so was the Judge's study, where William Rufus Tyler sat, sipping now and again at a tall glass. He did not dream of sleeping. He would wait up for whatever happened.

Duncan Tyler was there with him, simply because he had not been able to leave his father, nor yet the place where news would surely come, when there was any. He must go soon, to fetch Tamsen her clothes, if for no other reason. There *was* no other reason. Duncan would have felt better in the body roaming the night, hunting and peering, expending energy, but the brain decreed that this was no good, at all.

They had the TV set with them and had watched the eleven-o'clock news. The big story at that hour had been that the Little Prince of Alalaf was going home tomorrow. The hour of his departure had not been broadcast. There had been a repeat of a tape showing the King arriving, with entourage, at the airport, then a new tape of his arrival at the party. There had been no mention, whatsoever, of Rufus Tyler.

Now Duncan told himself that it was wise to wait for the twelve-o'clock news on radio, after which he must go. He clung to the hope that every hour that passed without any news of Rufus was so much the better.

The Judge was brooding, in silence.

What have we done to our son and brother? We loved him. (He was thinking in the past tense and this seemed appropriate). Although Maggie had been hurt and I, too, and often, Rufus never did set out to hurt anyone before this. Or we never thought so. It hurt us that we had to help him so much. It hurt us that we couldn't help him more. *It* hurt us, not he, as the books say. Possibly the books are nonsense? But as far as we knew, we loved him. He could have been sure of us all. Of his brothers, too. Mitch was very fond. It is hard for Mitch to be patient, but he shows devotion in other ways. Duncan was blunt with him, but free and easy, and very fond. None of this seems to have been enough. What have we . . .

The Judge caught himself going around again and wrenched out of the groove. This was the sort of "thinking" one inevitably falls into. He mused on another track. Supposing that one's childhood home, and one's first family, can never be enough? A man, or a woman, may need another home, and another family. And a grown-up place in the world.

Rufus had had Lurlene, only.

197   *

What if Rufus had married a different kind of woman?

What kind?

Such-as-Phillida could never have felt anything but live-and-let-live for such-as-Rufus. Although, in charity, such-as-Phillida would have seen to it that he was kept alive. And such-as-Tamsen basically despised him. Had Rufus sensed as much? Poor little Tamsen. She tried so hard, she gave herself away.

Then some very meek, truly meek woman? No. There tended to be an ego in a marriage. At least one ego. Some strength.

Lurlene may have been the girl for him. . . .

The Judge now remembered the relief it had been, on past occasions, to weep wet tears. But weeping? This he had outlived, and the relief of it, as well.

What have we done, or not done. . . .

25

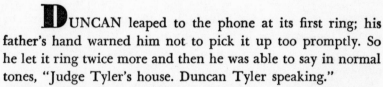

DUNCAN leaped to the phone at its first ring; his father's hand warned him not to pick it up too promptly. So he let it ring twice more and then he was able to say in normal tones, "Judge Tyler's house. Duncan Tyler speaking."

The caller announced himself as being a member of the police department. He gave name, rank, and location. Lieutenant Dennison was calling from a police station in the northeast section of the city.

"We have a Rufus Tyler here. His home number doesn't answer. He's acting a little bit peculiar. Would some member of his family care to come down?"

"Peculiar, how?" snapped Duncan. "Yes, of course, I'll be down. But what's wrong with my brother?"

"Well, sir, at first we thought he was under the influence of alcohol. But he became rambling and incoherent. It could be he is suffering from some . . . uh . . . illness. So you had better . . . It would be a good idea to come down."

"How did he get there? Are you holding him? Was he in an accident?"

"No, no. He just walked in. We . . . uh . . . don't know. I think you had better come down."

"Right." The Judge, who had been listening too, shook his

head when Duncan mutely offered him the phone. So Duncan snapped, "I'll be right there." And hung up.

His father was looking old and tired. "Save the big guns until we need them, eh?" said Duncan. "I'll go. If he is incoherent *enough,* we may be all right. Let me grab your raincoat."

Duncan turned away from the look on his father's face and went leaping up the stairs. He looked in and told Maggie, knowing that she would go down to be with the Judge. Then he covered his party clothing with the Judge's black raincoat and tore out to his car.

Duncan's spirits had risen, somewhat, because at least they knew where Rufus was. Yet the policeman had spoken with an ominous hesitation. Or rather, he had ominously refused to speak. Duncan knew he was going to have to ad lib, and fast, when he got there. But action was such relief that he felt in a swinging mood that could conquer anything, tell any number of lies, act any part, and if Rufus had spilled the beans, *un*spill them, for at least the rest of this night. And with what relief he would take Rufus where he could spill no more!

Duncan found a place for the car. It wasn't an elegant part of town. The night was cool, as nights will be in an essential desert. Duncan went in with the raincoat buttoned around him.

"Mr. Tyler?" A man got up. To Duncan's surprise, he was in plain clothes.

"I am Duncan Tyler. I spoke to *you,* did I?" Duncan looked around.

"I'm sorry, Mr. Tyler. Your brother has gone."

"Where?" Duncan felt stunned. This cop's eyes were not missing a thing. Duncan stayed stunned.

"If we knew, we'd like to pick him up and bring him back. He must have had a car. He's not safe to drive, in my opinion."

"Wait a minute. You had him here. You said he was ill. Now, you say he's not safe. I don't understand how you happened to let him go."

"We didn't intend him to go. But we had no reason to lock him up, Mr. Tyler. We knew you were on the way, and so did he. It looked as if he was willing to wait for you. He was quiet. So when he asked for the men's room, it took a while for anybody to notice that he never came back. Can you describe his car, sir?" the cop added smoothly.

"I'll do my best, in a minute," Duncan said, rubbing his head. "First, I'd like to know what happened. Take it from the top."

"Well, sir, he just came in, like a citizen with a complaint. Or a report to make."

Duncan rolled with the word "report." "Go on," he said.

"Gave his name to the desk man. Gave his father's name, his mother's name. Made a point of who his family was." The cop was watching Duncan carefully.

"Yes, yes," Duncan said impatiently.

"But then he started talking pretty crazy. I was called in on it. It wasn't a case of being drunk. He looked . . . well . . . worse than that. At one point I thought he was going to pass out. I'll have to ask you if you ever suspected that your brother took . . . well . . . say . . . goof balls?"

"I suppose anything is possible," said Duncan gravely, gazing over the man's head. "But why did he come *here?* That's what I can't . . ."

"He said there had been a crime."

Duncan said nothing. He simply stared. A thought of his mother crossed his mind, unexpectedly.

"I . . . uh . . . took a few rough notes, anyhow at first. Let's see." The cop had a piece of paper and he looked at it. "Said there had been a crime. A 'big important crime.' Something about 'kill.' Something about 'boy.' 'Kill.' 'Boy.' And then 'shot.' Or 'shots.' 'Wouldn't let me go.'" The cop looked up. "Then he started to . . . well . . . cry. But he kept saying 'don't matter.' That I remember."

" 'Don't *matter*'!" Duncan let himself be sharp.

"Well, I got the idea he meant that *he* didn't matter. Like—frustrated?"

Duncan said, after a moment of blankness, "Well, it beats me. What do you make of it?"

"He could have had a bad trip," the cop said. "LSD?"

"I don't want to believe that," Duncan said restlessly. "How long since he left? How far could he get?"

"Long ago and far enough," the cop said ruefully, "that he's not in the neighborhood. About his car, sir?"

"Oh, yes, that's right." Duncan rummaged in his mind for the make, model, and color of Rufus' car. He announced that he did not know his brother's license number. The cop said that most people didn't know their own.

"Maybe he went home," said Duncan suddenly. "I'll run down there. Perhaps find some record of that license for you."

"Oh, we can get that in a very short time. Now . . . uh . . . your brother is not, as far as we know, a suspect, Mr. Tyler. But he may be dangerous to himself, and to innocent people. Would you . . . or your father, say . . . advise us to pick him up?"

"Do that," said Duncan decisively, with an air of relief. "And when you do, call my father, please? I'll be in touch with him, too." Duncan turned to go.

"What do you make of it, Mr. Tyler?" the cop said, rather stubbornly.

"I don't make too much," said Duncan heavily. "I can tell you this. His wife took sick this evening. At least she . . . well . . . retired from the party. Now, I don't know what may have happened between them. You see, the family was entertaining at somewhat of an occasion."

"I heard about it," the cop said. "Say, how is the Little Prince?" (The Little Prince was this man's darling too?)

"The boy?" said Duncan, deliberately using this word. "Oh,

he is fine. He has been OK'ed to fly home in the morning. Had you heard?"

"I heard it on the air ten minutes ago. So they took the tests already, did they?" This cop was genial, but he had not stopped watching.

"They must have," said Duncan cheerfully. "Anyhow, the Doctor has said that he may go, and everybody's happy." He then caused his grin to be wiped away. "My point was . . ." He frowned. "It's possible that my brother was more upset than any of us had time to notice, with the house so full of guests. My sister-in-law is still there, you see. She's been put to bed. Whether her trouble is emotional . . . At any rate, my brother was certainly out of the party mood for some reason, because he left the house in the midst of things, without saying a word. I wonder . . . It's hard to believe that he could have been feeling depressed or desperate enough to have taken something."

"A serious quarrel, was it?" the cop asked, not believing in this very much.

"I don't know," said Duncan. "But there was something. Must have been."

"You don't know about any crime, then?" The cop was obviously suggesting that this could be the "something."

"I don't know what he would have meant by 'a crime,'" mused Duncan. "A lay person uses that word loosely."

"Yes," said Lieutenant Dennison, "but he said 'important.'"

"It's too bad," said Duncan, careful to speak without suggesting reproach, "that you couldn't have got a clearer statement out of him. I'm sure you tried," he added with a quick smile that didn't last. "But the point now is—if poor old Rufus is in *that* bad a way, I had damned well better find him."

"We'll try to pick him up," the cop promised. "If you and Judge Tyler say so, I'll get right on that." But Duncan noticed that he was putting his piece of paper, with the notes on it, very carefully away.

203 ✳

Duncan, however, thanked him crisply and went out. The night air made him shiver. He did not know how well he had done in there, with his hints of some marital crisis. He knew that he must hunt the streets, he must race about the city after all. Call the Judge, first. Then try to find Rufus before the police picked him up again. Because Rufus was trying to talk, trying to tell, trying to confess. And he might not seem so "rambling and incoherent" another time. Didn't drugs wear off as time went on?

Duncan had not gone three blocks before he gave up watching curbs and parked cars and what few pedestrians had dared the darkness. It was absurd to imagine that he could find his brother that way. This city was the city-that-sprawled. Duncan had no idea of what route Rufus had taken, to what destination. Both were multitudinous. So Duncan settled to going along, as swiftly as was not conspicuous, toward the house where Rufus lived, and perhaps now was.

The house was dark. Duncan parked at the curb and walked down the drive toward the garage, his flashlight in hand. The garage doors were open; there was no car inside. Duncan went up to the back entrance; the door to the service porch was not locked. So he was able to stand within the shelter of some walls and go to work on the back-door lock. He got in by using one of his credit cards, in a hoary method well taught in fiction. He was a little surprised that it worked.

Once inside, he boldly turned on the lights. He was Rufus' brother, after all. The small house depressed him. It was very neat and clean. The only disorder was some trace, in the bedroom, of Lurlene's having dressed for the party in a hurry. But there seemed so very little trace of Rufus here. No collection of pet objects, no pet books, no accumulation of papers. No life?

How did he live? thought Duncan. What did he keep on his mind? Why don't I know? Was it my ever-loving duty to have snooped into his habits, to have taken it upon myself to judge him for the way he used his twenty-four hours a day? Then to have advised him? Or led him to something more productive, more satisfying—satisfying to whom? His tastes, and his needs, aren't the same as mine. How shall I be wise for him, and teach him his *life?*

The place depressed him, just the same.

Also, damn it, he thought rebelliously, some of us are busy. I want to teach the front-runners, and learn with them. How much energy can the race spare, to turn around and understand and straighten out and patch, just to bring some people up to what? To average? Yes, Mitch does it, brilliantly—but even to do that, some of us must go groping ahead into the dark that's in front of us. And in fear and trembling, too. So-called successful people *can* be the most harassed and miserable of creatures. Why isn't that known? Well, it compounds, I suppose. The very ones who cannot are the ones who can't imagine how it's done. And there we are.

(But this was my brother.)

He stopped his sorry thoughts and used the phone to call the Judge, who had heard nothing. Duncan had given his father the news flatly, almost an hour ago, and his father had taken it calmly. The Judge was still calm. Maggie was fine, he said.

Duncan said he must now fetch Tamsen's clothes, against the morning, and change his own. He would call back soon again.

There was no point in staying here. If Rufus finally came here, he would most probably simply collapse. Duncan had no idea where else to search for him. How had he lived?

He tried cruising the neighborhood, slowly, but the hour was late, the streets were very quiet. There was no sign of Rufus, or his car. No likely neighborhood hangouts that Duncan could spot. So he drove to his own house.

He put up the lights and felt the difference hit him in the face. All over this place lay the evidences of the living inhabitants and what interested them. Or did Duncan just imagine so because he knew, so well, what interested these people?

Does Rufus know how *I* live? Or care? What lets *him* off caring, or trying to understand?

Duncan dismissed any more angry and unprofitable brooding, sat down and called the Judge, who had heard nothing yet. It was nearly two o'clock in the morning. Duncan said he would go to the hospital. Rufus might have returned there.

He went into the bedroom and found the things for Tamsen; he put them into a suitcase. He changed into slacks and sport coat. He picked up the case and put his father's raincoat over his arm. He went into the kitchen and drank a glass of water from the tap.

He was a mile away before he remembered the hairpins. He did not go back.

The hospital, at 2:45 in the morning, was hushed. No Rufus had come there a second time. Duncan gave the suitcase to an orderly and reminded him that the guards must inspect it before it went to Mrs. Tyler. After asking here and there, he finally found his brother Mitchel, sound asleep on a couch in the Doctors' Lounge.

Mitch woke to full intelligence with the ease of much practice. He listened and pursed his lips to whistle but did not. He told Duncan that tests had, indeed, been made, because the exertion of that knife-throw was not exactly what he would have ordered, for this patient. Although lucky for Tamsen that it had not had the force it might have had. But no harm had been done. The boy was all right. Tamsen was all right. If her scar was too bad, there was always skin-grafting. Everything was all right, if only . . .

"As a matter of fact," the Doctor said in hard appraisal, "if Rufus hasn't spilled the beans by this time, where it counts, our chances are getting better that he won't." Mitch advised Duncan to sleep for a few hours instead of running futilely around town. He offered him a couch.

So Duncan called his father once again. The Judge had heard nothing yet. He sounded tired but hopeful.

Then Duncan called that cop.

Lieutenant Dennison was grateful for the call. He had no news. He said that there had been no accident report. That, in all probability, Rufus had not crashed anywhere, and was not lying, injured and undiscovered, beside the wreck.

Duncan said, "Well, all I can figure is, he must have realized he wasn't too steady and gone to some friend. He's probably sleeping it off in a borrowed bed. Where, I don't know. That's all I can *think* of."

"You may be right, Mr. Tyler," the cop said smoothly. "But we'll keep checking."

Duncan reminded him to call the Judge if anything turned up. He then put himself down on the scratchy couch. He thought he could not possibly sleep. He considered the advantages of being here in the hospital. In the morning he could, for one thing, borrow a razor. For another, he and Tamsen could go together to the airport. This would be in many ways an excellent thing. It would "look good." It would also *be* good. So Duncan slept.

To the many parking lots at the airport, there was not much difference between day and night. The many cars stood in their ranks. Nobody bothered them. Sometimes one left. Sometimes one came.

26

WHEN light was just evident over the mountains, a gray sedan slid to the entrance of the building and a man got out of the back. Colonel Gorob had come to the moment of truth. He was wearing his usual uniform to assume his authority. It made him somewhat conspicuous, but that could not be helped. The gray car slid away. It would hesitate somewhere, ready to pounce back for him. But it would not hesitate forever. He knew that.

The Colonel was carrying a fat briefcase. He stepped briskly into the building and went to inquire about the procedure. How was he to go, in order to approach the royal plane belonging to the King of Alalaf, the Colonel being who he was?

The young man who told him how and where to proceed did so without any visible qualms. So the Colonel approached the door to the outside spaces of the field itself and addressed the man stationed there with some confidence.

Then he was through and walking rapidly in the chill of the dawn toward the familiar plane, which had already been wheeled into position. The crew knew him, of course. They were full of good cheer, doing their duty, delighted to know that the Prince was flying with them. Nobody had warned them.

So the Colonel went up the portable flight of steps and entered the plane. The steward knew him, of course. He had been cleaning and polishing, as was his duty. He was now cheerfully obsequious. The Colonel began to make suggestions for the comfort of Al Saiph. He took care to make a great many. He then swung the length of the huge bird, through all its various compartments.

When he returned, the steward awaited judgment. Gorob said that everything seemed in excellent order but the man must be sure of so and so. And so.

Gorob swung down and away. He had left the object in a good place. And left the steward busy. He walked briskly back, in the growing light, toward that door where the guard let him through with another "Good morning, sir."

The Colonel walked through the building and out at the street side. He stood at the curb no more than a minute before the gray car came sliding toward him. Gorob got in, pulled a topcoat over his shoulders to hide the uniform. The car went saucily around the designated ways for getting out of the airport complex. Inside the car, no word was spoken. Gorob felt that he had been worthy of their trust. This was gratifying.

The thing was set to go off in two hours.

In a little while, television men with cameras, and one remote-truck, came to the automobile gate to demand entrance to the field itself and a spot from which they could photograph the departure of the Little Prince, which the whole country would want to see.

Up in the coffee shop, a man seemed to be watching the time, in a stupid sort of way. He was clad in a mussy dinner jacket, and he had not shaved this morning. The waitress raised her brows to her fellow workers. This guy was either hung over, now, or heading for a beauty. He looked pretty owly and kept rubbing his nose and snuffling. But he was no trouble, just some harmless slob. At the airport, they had already "seen everything."

By a quarter after eight, the TV cameras were ready; a crowd of still photographers had gathered with an equal number of reporters. The broadcaster from the local channel, which alone was going to do this "live," was there, with a scarf wrapped around his precious throat. The field swarmed with guards and policemen who kept all others some distance away from the royal plane.

The first private car to come through the gate was driven by Duncan Tyler. With him was his wife, Tamsen, looking like a little pink-nosed rabbit, huddled in her white coat. Once past the guarded gate, the car was first impeded, and then actually stopped, by the swarming newsmen, who were glad to see things looking up. The local TV camera even turned its hungry eye in their direction.

The young Tylers chose, they said, to wait in their car. So the guards brushed everybody aside and directed Duncan to where the car might safely stand.

"So far, so good," breathed Duncan, "O.K., honey?"

"I'm fine," said Tamsen, trying to make herself believe this. She knew about Rufus now, and she was doing a night's worth of worrying, all at once.

"*They'll* be O.K. No matter what he does, they'll make it now. Watch it! Fix your face," said Duncan. "Here comes the interview."

But before the newsmen could pounce on them again, the second car came through. It was chauffeur-driven; a Secret Service man sat with the driver. In the back, sat the Princess, her maid, and Mrs. Mitchel Tyler. This car was permitted to draw closer to the plane and the swarm was drawn to it. The three women got out; the car turned and, in a stately manner, departed.

In a moment Zora, carrying last-minute small bags, went meekly toward the steps and up into the plane itself, and vanished. The newsmen were after the Princess, who was beautifully enveloped in a traveling costume of soft beige. The Doctor's wife was smilingly there, but only (as was Phillida's way) decoratively standing by.

"No," she said to the only newsman who addressed her directly, "Judge Tyler and Mrs. Tyler are not coming. They think the family is well enough represented."

"Say, what's it like to be married to a Tyler?" he said inanely (being very young and unable to get anywhere near the Princess because everyone else had seniority).

Phillida just kept smiling faintly until he flushed and turned away.

Jaylia was already on camera when the Doctor's car came through. Mitch was alone in it. He drew it over to where Duncan and Tamsen were waiting. He got out, but could do no more than salute them with his hand before he was engulfed by eager stragglers.

Duncan said, "I guess it's time. Now, I'm going to be right behind you."

"All right," said Tamsen gratefully. She was feeling very nervous. As they got out of the car and walked toward the Princess, she eyed the big insect, so lumpish on the ground, that would so gracefully use the sky. The crowd opened to let them in. They greeted the Princess and she greeted them. Duncan stood at Tamsen's back, guarding it from any touch whatsoever.

The "live" broadcaster was happily identifying everyone for his viewers. By this time, a crowd of ordinary people had gathered just outside the automobile gate. They were not let in. They would, of course, have seen more at home, and *would* see more, when the millions watched the news tapes run this evening. But to be, for instance, a couple of yards from the Little Prince when he came by— Well, that was distinction.

Maggie and the Judge and Lurlene were in the Judge's study with the TV set tuned to the local station, getting this "live."

The Judge was holding his thumbs. Not much more time to be endured in this much tension. Once the royal party took off from American soil, the situation would improve a good deal.

Maggie was watching intently and analyzing everyone's performance. "Tamsen is too timid to take her own stature," she declared. "Phillida doesn't want to be there. That *is*, sometimes, effective. Mitch looks dour, doesn't he? Duncan comes off best, don't you think? Jaylia is the most professional, of course, but she certainly overdoes *some* things." Maggie clicked her tongue.

Lurlene sat there, in the couch corner, keeping quiet and looking sullen. *She* was a prisoner. Phillida had watched her practically all night, for heaven's sakes! Then, before first light, when Phillida had taken off home (to change her precious clothes, and what a clothes-horse *she* was!) then Maggie had taken up the vigil. Maggie might be a little less nasty about it, but she watched, just the same, and don't try to fool Lurlene. What am *I* supposed to do? she was thinking.

What she had done this morning, under Maggie's bright suggestion that amounted to an order, was to cut off her new long dress and hem it to be a short dress. So now, here she was, wearing it, and watching TV. And look who was *on* TV, this morning.

Yah, look! "Dr. Mitchel Tyler who . . ." and so on.

"Duncan Tyler, the Doctor's brother, who . . ." and so on.

Not one word about any other brother. *They* wouldn't say there even *was* a Rufus. No, they wouldn't do *that*, in this world!

"The Doctor's wife, Phillida Tyler, who . . ." Blah-blah-blah—

"Tamsen Tyler, who is becoming one of our . . ." Blah and blah.

And was there any Lurlene Tyler mentioned? Naw, *she* wasn't there. She had to sit home with the old folks and watch the whole thing on TV. And the whole thing was phony, if you asked *her!*

The picture jumped to a long shot. Almost together, there were now arriving the King's car and the ambulance in which the Little Prince was riding. Motorcycles could be heard, roaring distantly, but that noise stopped short of the gate, where the King's car deferred to the ambulance. But when both vehicles had entered, the car came to a stop first. Three men got out of the King's car, walked to the plane, and boarded. They were only servants. The King, and two cohorts, waited in the vehicle, deferring to the Little Prince. The camera soon understood this and looked to where the swarm was buzzing around the back of the ambulance.

Duncan said quietly to the Princess, "While we have the chance, good-bye, Jaylia. And happy landing. You'll make it."

Jaylia said, with no coquetry at all, "Thank you all, for everything. Good luck."

Tamsen said, "Good-bye. Good luck." It was Tamsen who kissed the Princess. Duncan was already intent upon what was happening over there.

Hayyan and Kasim climbed out of the ambulance and turned to help Inga down. Inga turned, at once, to help the boy.

Saiph appeared on his feet and in full regalia. He looked lively and well. At some screaming suggestions, he remained poised, his hands clasped together in a very appealing way, standing higher than the crowd, while the camera turned.

The Little Prince was pleased to answer a few bland questions with bland answers. Yes, he was very happy to be going home. Yes, he had liked America very much. Yes, he hoped, one day, to return. The camera held on his handsome face, his charming smile.

("He's just adorable!" "Isn't he cute!" "Bless his heart!")

Meanwhile, the ambulance driver had taken out a wheel-chair. Inga folded herself around the Prince like a mother hen with protective wingspread, and then he was seated in the wheelchair where the camera couldn't get much of him, through the surrounding throng, thick with guards and uniformed police. The newsmen trotted at the edges as a path was swept before the Prince, and he was moved within the throng, and pushed to where his mother was waiting.

"We must get you aboard," his mother said, smiling at him.

"I do not wish to be carried."

"Of course not. Inga, you go beside him, I'll come just after."

Saiph said to Tamsen a gay, "So long. See you later," which was only in fun. Their real farewells, equally gay, had been said in the hospital suite. They were very fond of each other; they would never meet again. No use to fuss about it.

On television, it was the King's turn.

Al Asad was looking stern in the morning light, tall, presumably lean, and all business, whatever a king's business may be. A man in white stood at either side of his striking figure.

"The King of Alalaf—who speaks no English, by the way—"

27

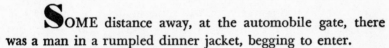

SOME distance away, at the automobile gate, there was a man in a rumpled dinner jacket, begging to enter.

"You can't go through here, sir."

"You don't understand. I am Rufus Tyler. Tyler." The man's voice was shrill with strain.

"I can't help—"

"Beg pardon," said the other guard. "Tyler?"

"Yes, Tyler. I am Rufus Tyler. Look," Rufus held out his identification. "I have to speak to the King. There's something I have to tell. It has to be told. Don't you hear me? It has to be told. It will have to . . ." He looked exhausted and he sagged.

"Are you related to Dr. Tyler, sir?"

"Yes. Yes. I am the Doctor's brother." Rufus braced up. "Both of my brothers are out there. Let me through, before it's too late. This is important. It has to be told. I tried. Please. Call somebody, then. My father is Judge Tyler. My mother is Maggie Mitchel. Tell somebody, will you please?"

The guards were wavering. Then, Rufus was through. He began to run. The guards at the gate gazed after him dubiously. Then they had to jump to let the ambulance out. Now that its passenger was delivered, it had business elsewhere.

Tamsen and Duncan, Mitch and Phillida, were drifting slowly behind the progress of the Prince and his entourage toward the plane. Duncan was the first to stiffen. "No," he said sharply, and pushed through the people and away.

Then Tamsen saw the running figure. She bit her own finger violently, not to scream. (Oh, no, not now!)

Mitch turned and saw it. All heads began to turn. But Mitch pushed, decisively, the other way. "Get him up there, quickly," he said. "Saiph, walk. Quickly."

Inga turned her head. She whirled her body around and took something from her pocket.

Mitch said quietly, "None of that." He grabbed her hand, and wrenched the gun out of it in so swift and brutal a movement that he was scarcely seen to have made it. Everyone else was now looking back toward the gate and the lone man, running in that exhausted stagger. Several guards were now running and converging on him.

Mitch said, "Wait. Better *not* go up those steps. Some idiot might shoot. Stand tight around Saiph. You two, and you and you." The bodyguards, the nurse, and the mother closed to a human square around the boy. Inga held her right hand in her left; her eyes blazed but she said nothing.

Mitch took three strides to Phillida. "Open your purse." She did so at once, and he dropped the gun therein. He pressed his car keys into her hand.

Phillida said, "What must I do?"

"Go to the car. Take Tamsen. *Now*. We'll see."

Then Mitch began to run in an easy lope.

Duncan was running hard. He saw that one of the guards was getting there first. He saw Rufus dodge and duck. But Rufus was inept. He was clumsy. He didn't make it. The guard hit him a hard blow to his middle and Rufus doubled over, toppled, and went down.

"Just a minute," Duncan bellowed. Rufus was on the ground and the guard was pulling his arm to a lock. Others were swarming. But Duncan could now be fairly sure that Rufus was unconscious. So he shouted, "Hold it. That's my brother."

Unconscious. (Silent!) Thank God, thought Duncan. Yet he couldn't help noting that Rufus had failed again. Whatever he had intended to do, he had muffed it, as usual.

"Let him go," said Duncan, with moderate indignation. "That's my brother."

Mitch now came trotting to enter the circle. "Yes, that's my brother." He crouched to examine Rufus once again. (Once again.) All three brothers were now locked within a circle of legs, uniformed and otherwise, and over their heads hung a cloud of babble. The camera couldn't see in.

"What happened?" Maggie was saying. "William, what happened?"

"I don't know, Maggie darling. Trust the boys. Trust the girls."

Duncan was saying into the Doctor's ear, "Get him out of here. Get him *away*."

"I'm working on it," Mitch said.

"Throw your weight around," Duncan said fiercely. "I'll be the decoy."

When the Doctor rose to his feet, everybody became quiet to listen. "Wind's out of him. Bumped his head, maybe. He's not hurt," the Doctor said, dourly.

One of the guards from the gate was there. "He told us he had something to tell the King. He had his I.D. So we let him . . . He was in a rush . . ."

"I'm sorry as hell, Doctor," said the man who had hit Rufus. "But how could I know?"

"Too bad the ambulance went," said a man. "Look, we'll call the Airport Hospital."

"Don't do that," said Mitch.

217   *

"Listen, Doctor, that's what it's there for."

"He's my brother," said Mitch, "and my patient. I want him where *I* want him. Do you mind?"

The men fell back from his anger. "Honest to John, Doctor," said the one, "I sure hope he's not bad. I didn't know."

It was Duncan who said, "All right. You made a mistake. But that happens to be our brother." He turned to the gate guard. "He told you he had something to say to the King?"

"Yes, Mr. Tyler, that's what he said. He said 'before it's too late.' He said it was important."

"Well, he may not be hurt, but he's not talking, is he?" said Duncan ferociously. "Let me through, please. I'm going to find out what this is about."

He walked rapidly away with the air of purpose that goes with decisive motion. It was attractive. He could tell that a large part of the pack, the news people (who also wanted to find out what this was about) were being drawn after him. Duncan did not know what he was going to do or say. But he appeared to know.

There was still a tight knot around the Prince. But the old King stood apart, his robes fluttering in the breeze. On either side of him, his cohorts were fluttering like twin white hawks. All three faces were hot-and-cold with outrage and suspicion. They looked as if they each had only a toe on the ground. Duncan strode toward them, wishing he could say "Shoo! Fly away! Fly away!"

Phillida was in the driver's seat of Mitch's car and Tamsen was beside her. "What are we going to do?" Tamsen's eyes were bright with excitement.

"We don't know. We're ready, that's all."

"It's another ballet? An improvisation?"

"It's a mess," said Phillida. "How *can* he be gotten away from here?"

Tamsen seemed to know how. "I suppose we are going to

take him," she said, gazing back toward the excitement. Phillida chewed her lip.

The television men were having a fit. "Close up, can't you?" "Damn white thing, on his head." "Get Tyler, then." "Guy's in the way." "Come on, buddy." "I'm trying. I'm trying."

Duncan said to Al Asad, "Your Majesty, the man on the gate says that my brother wanted to tell you something."
The King said "Ah" in a condescending manner, as if he didn't believe a word of it.

"Damn," said a television man. "Go, tell some of those birds to move, will ya?"
But new guards were circling with locked arms, and against them the swarm pressed, making a wall.

Duncan Tyler, for a man speaking to a monarch, was not being very humble. "The guard who hit him had no way of knowing who he was, or what he wanted. But the point is, what important message did my brother have for you? He has been knocked out. He is unconscious. He can't tell you, now."
Al Asad's eye was piercing, yet opaque.
"Boy, is he ever out," muttered a newsman helpfully.
Duncan looked around him and said imperiously, "If you people can't keep quiet, you will have to move away. This is important."
So they became quiet, but naturally, they pressed in ever closer.

On camera, it looked not unlike a football huddle, in plain clothes.

Off camera, two policemen, under the Doctor's direction, were lifting a limp Rufus as gently as they could. They then began to carry him across the field. A half dozen men tagged along.

"*We* get him," said Phillida.

"So I thought," said Tamsen. She was smiling.

Mitch had the men place Rufus tenderly on the back seat of the car. Rufus seemed to know nothing of what was happening. The Doctor squeezed in to bend over him, while the other men pressed to stare through the glass.

"Can you drive, Phillida?" Mitch wasn't looking at her nor she at him. "Of course," she said.

"Maggie's. If there's a chance. Just cool it. But take the first chance."

"Yes, Doctor."

Mitch backed out of the narrowness. An argument began at once. "Doctor, you've got to understand that we may be held responsible." "We have our own facilities . . ." "If he's not hurt, why not take him into the Lounge?" "After all, he is a witness." "Insurance . . ." "No negligence, on our part . . ." "Must insist . . ."

Mitch contrived to draw the arguing group slowly away.

Three newsmen, including the very young one, had stuck to Rufus. They were not attending to the argument, but peering into the car with noses flat.

Phillida said, "Will you gentlemen move, please? I must turn the car." She had the motor on, the car was powerful. The men backed a wary few feet away. Tamsen was trying to think of something she could do to help.

One of the King's cohorts, the one named Colonel Hafsah (or something like that) was translating what Duncan had said. The King replied to it, then, coldly. The interpreter said, "His Majesty asks if you know what the message was?"

"No, I do not," said Duncan. He knew, by the tail of his eye, where Rufus was. He knew he *had* made a diversion, temporarily, but where did he go from here? He said, "I would like to ask if there wasn't another member of your party? I don't see Colonel Gorob. Where is he?"

"Who he?" mumbled a newsman.

"Hey! Hey! Hey!" said another. "They're loading the Little Prince!"

So the swarm trembled, being drawn two ways. The Doctor had shaken off his group and was standing at the bottom of the steps, superintending the embarkation of the Prince. Beside him stood the steward, all smiles.

Duncan decided to surrender to the rival attraction. He said, "Excuse me," not very humbly, and walked rapidly toward his brother Mitchel.

The King said a sharp word. He and his cohorts began to move in a stately pace toward the plane. The guards kept guarding; the swarm was strung out, on both sides of the procession.

On camera, the Little Prince was halfway up the steps.

Duncan Tyler, remaining in his part, that of the puzzled, the indignant, the probing, said to the steward, "Is Colonel Gorob aboard?"

"No, sir," said the steward. He was going to swing up the steps himself, soon. The Prince was aboard. So was the Princess. The King was approaching.

Duncan could now feel the white hawks at his back.

"Where is this man?" said Duncan loudly.

The steward said, "Colonel Gorob came aboard early to inspect, sir. I have not seen him since."

Duncan swung around and looked at Al Asad. The King's eyes flickered. Al Asad said (In English! Sensation!), "Let the airplane be searched."

The camera had zoomed in and it was getting that face. "Wow!" The TV people were exultant. "Have we got a picture!"

The guards began to surge and heave. The crowd was

pushed and it milled; it divided. The guards were ruthlessly in control, now. Almost immediately the Little Prince reappeared and began to come down the steps. Behind him, people began to pour out of the plane.

Tamsen cried, "Oh! Oh, *look!* Something is happening! Oh, what is *happening?*"

Their contingent of newsmen began to run toward whatever was happening, this being their duty.

So Phillida caused the car to move softly, softly, toward the gate.

The guard there said, "Mrs. Tyler?" respectfully.

"Doctor's orders," she said, in her bright casual way.

"Not hurt too bad, is he?" The guard was looking in. "I probably should have got hold of your husband, Mrs. Tyler, before we let him through."

"But the Doctor was so busy with the Little Prince," said Tamsen, with an air of warm understanding. "How *could* you have?"

"I guess that's right, too," the guard said, not without gratitude. "Taking him over to the hospital? Want an escort?"

The guard looked around. But all the motorcycles had long ago departed.

"We'll be fine," said Phillida. "I've been told exactly what to do."

"O.K., then. Good luck, Mrs. Tyler." He let them through. The ordinary people, just outside the gate, stood aside to let the car pass. They didn't seem to realize that the two women ("Hey, that's Phillida." "The other one is Tamsen." "Tyler." "Tyler.") had an unconscious man lying helplessly low, behind them.

Then they were free and rolling. Phillida drove with grim care. Nobody seemed to be following them.

"What if he comes to?" Tamsen whispered.

"You may have to shoot him," Phillida said. "Mitch put a gun in my purse. See if it's loaded."

"I couldn't. I simply couldn't do that." It was as if they were discussing some new and scandalous style.

"Then hope for the best because if he comes to, we'll have to handle it ourselves."

Tamsen was turned to look over at the limp man, lying on his back with long legs trailing to the floor at an uncomfortable-seeming angle. His face was flaccid. He looked as if he had been so tired that he had fallen asleep in his tracks and cared for nothing anymore.

"It's a whole damn hour to Maggie's," Phillida said. "Not much less."

"Never mind," said Tamsen. "And don't worry. He isn't going to rise up and clobber you. Just drive. I'll watch him."

What will I do, though? she wondered. She had not hunted Phillida's purse for a gun. That was ridiculous! Impossible! You did not, you could not shoot a bullet at a living person for just being confused, for being not really responsible, even for being (in so mad and helpless a way) such a dangerous nuisance. No. Anyway, *she* couldn't.

Tamsen reflected that she had never even seen a gun except in some movie or play. She didn't believe in guns. But what must she do, if Rufus became mobile? Understand him? The fact was, Tamsen did *not* understand him. That was impossible, too.

She kept a sharp watch on his face, feeling her wound crack and sting with the pull of her shoulders, as Phillida swooped up to the Freeway and began to drive as fast as Mitch drove a car.

It occurred to Tamsen that Rufus might be shamming again, as Mitch had once suspected. If so, that was pitiful. But had she the time to pity him, now? She must watch, and if his eyelids so much as fluttered . . .

We could be killed, thought Tamsen. Very easily, all three of us, if Rufus rises up and does something violent in this speeding car. What must I *do?* Well, I'd better search my soul another time, she thought grimly. I know what I'm *not* going to do. I am not going to *allow* him to kill us by some blundering, mindless lurching. He must not, in whatever misery or distress, kill us all. And I won't let him. She began to grope for Phillida's purse.

Neither she nor Phillida spoke another word. They seemed to know that they had better not chatter. It was as if time might go by unmeasured as in a dream, providing that no word, no exchange of idea, nothing broke into its passage and betrayed that it was passing.

28

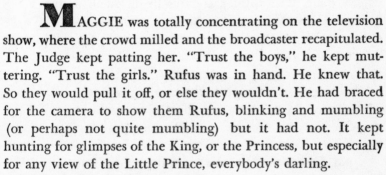

MAGGIE was totally concentrating on the television show, where the crowd milled and the broadcaster recapitulated. The Judge kept patting her. "Trust the boys," he kept muttering. "Trust the girls." Rufus was in hand. He knew that. So they would pull it off, or else they wouldn't. He had braced for the camera to show them Rufus, blinking and mumbling (or perhaps not quite mumbling) but it had not. It kept hunting for glimpses of the King, or the Princess, but especially for any view of the Little Prince, everybody's darling.

Suddenly the broadcaster said, in a perfectly human and personal surprise, "What?"

The camera began to steady on the door of the plane where a policeman had appeared.

The broadcaster said, with caution, "There seems to have been a device of some kind. . . ." His voice gained confidence. "Ladies and gentlemen, there seems to have been an explosive device on the King's jet. A bomb has been found!" Now he could not help an exultant excitement, "Ladies and gentlemen, you are getting this *live!*"

But the Judge was already up, and at his desk, reaching for his telephone.

Maggie rose and walked toward him. "William, who?"

"It was never Rufus," the Judge said, loudly enough to seem joyous, "who planted any bomb on the King's plane. He couldn't have managed that, Maggie darling. He simply isn't, and never was, clever enough."

Lurlene just sat there, watching the confusing swirl of the crowd on the screen while the voice said, over and over again that, in a "most dramatic incident," a bomb had just been found on the private plane of the King of Alalaf, "on which the Little Prince" . . . and so on, and so on. It seemed, now, that the plane would be searched, inch by inch. The Little Prince would not depart . . . no, no . . . until this had been thoroughly done. The royal party was being taken to the V.I.P. Lounge, in the building. "Ladies and gentlemen—" The camera showed a phalanx of people moving away from it. But it didn't show Rufus.

The Judge was saying into the phone, "Is there a good guess where he might be? Very fine thing if he could be picked up, quickly. No, this Colonel Gorob could pass for almost any Westerner. Reddish hair. Very freckled-faced. Medium tall. . . . No, I don't think he can get at them now. But we had better be concerned that the blame for this is put where it belongs. And fast. . . . There are some people, including Colonel Gorob, who would like nothing better than the news going out of an American attack on the Prince. Oh, it would spread in ten minutes. The world's too small. Even a rumor . . . Yes, of course, it is a big city. Well . . ."

The Judge had no sooner hung up than his phone rang again.

Duncan said, "Dad? The girls have got Rufus. They'll bring him there."

"Good. What about Gorob?" Maggie was hanging over the Judge's shoulder.

"It was Gorob, all right," said Duncan. "He showed up early this morning, the only one except the crew to enter that plane. That's pretty clear."

"Good," said the Judge. "But it had better be very clear, and clear right away. It had better get on the air and into the papers. The foreign press, for instance. Authoritatively."

"Yes, sir," said Duncan cheerfully. "So all I have to do is go tell the King of Alalaf exactly what *he* must do and say in the next five minutes."

"That's all," said the Judge fondly.

Maggie said, "*We* had better brace ourselves, William, for the press."

"Oh, yes, they'll be on us."

"We have no guards anymore."

"I may be able to rustle up one or two. I have other calls to make, quickly."

"I must warn Sam, at least."

Lurlene thought, Yah, look at them! Here they saw their own son knocked down and out, and lying on the ground. And all they got to say is 'he wasn't clever?' Um boy! And the TV, it don't show one sign of him and he could be dead and who gives a damn? Who cares? Lurlene put her handkerchief to her eyes. "Excuse me," she sobbed. "Excuse me."

She ran out of the study and sobbed her way upstairs.

But once there, she stopped sobbing abruptly. She went into the east guest room and picked up her evening purse. Then she went along the passage to Maggie's room. Maggie's purse was lying on her dressing table. Lurlene opened it and took the money. She then walked downstairs.

The Judge was on the phone again. His study door was open. He could see her perfectly well, so she walked back toward the garden side. Maggie was not in the lanai. If she was in the kitchen, the angles of the house were a protection. Lurlene kept on going. She went out through the glass doors and turned to her left, and began to walk along the west terrace, past where the musicians had been last night, and the nook where she and that Mrs-Somebody had sat and frittered time away while all kinds of stuff was going on. All kinds of secret things. But they hadn't told Lurlene. Not *they!*

She crept around the west wing of the house. The Judge could see the driveway from his windows but he probably wasn't looking out his windows. Lurlene tripped along close to the shrubbery. She made it to the end of the drive and put thick shrubs between her and the house. She was scurrying along the street, a hundred feet away, when a fast car swooped into the driveway. Mitch's car. Hah, and Phillida driving, and a woman next to her. Tamsen, yah!

Well, Lurlene certainly didn't want to be around when *they* got there.

She had *had* it. She had absolutely *had* it from those Tylers. She didn't know where to go, or what to do, or even whether her own husband was alive or dead. The truth was she had to have a drink. And if Lurlene needed a drink, she was going to get a drink. *She* was alive, wasn't she? Not in San Marino, a drink. Not in this stupid town. Culture, yah! O.K., she'd call a taxi and she'd go where there was a bar. She had sixty bucks. She'd blow it if she felt like it. Maggie would never say a word. All in the family, Lurlene thought bitterly.

She had come to Huntington Drive and she saw a phone booth. So she'd call a cab. Get farther away from them, go some place and think. Think what to do. And find her husband. Listen, she had a right to find her husband. She had a right to say what she thought, and also, tell what she knew. Because it shouldn't have been for nothing, she was thinking. So what was he doing at the airport, I don't know, but if they *killed* him, if they just *killed* him, and don't even mention it on TV! It shouldn't have been for *nothing* that he died!

The thought of Rufus dead was not shocking because she had known, for a long time, that Rufus had *had* it. He'd not been figuring to live, exactly.

Sam was a strong man and Hilde a stout woman. Phillida had her own physical strength. Yet Rufus, once pulled from the car, stood up and walked into the house. He did not seem to be conscious, but he walked.

Maggie followed them up the stairs to the west guest room, where they were going to put him down. Tamsen, who couldn't help in this way, went into the study. The television was still on, but the Judge wasn't paying it any attention. He came to her and took her hands and then he said, "What's this?"

There was a small gun in Tamsen's right hand. She didn't quite know how, through several hands, it had come there. The Judge took it away gently. He looked it over. It was in no state to be fired. He didn't tell her so. He put the gun away. He placed a cushion so that her upper back would be held away from the back of the couch. He sat her down. He mixed her a therapeutic drink.

He would not go upstairs, to where Maggie would be mourning. (Although only he could know how deeply. He knew it, where he was.)

The familiar sound of Duncan's voice made them both turn to the screen.

"His Majesty," Duncan was saying, "may have a statement. I don't know. In the meantime . . . ."

The background was a wall. Duncan looked (his wife thought) handsome, young, strong, intelligent.

"Mr. Tyler?"

"Mr. Tyler?"

He was interrupted.

"What happened to your brother Rufus?"

"The doctors are probably finding that out right now," said Duncan evasively.

"Hey, Mr. Tyler, your brother *knew* about this bomb, do you think?"

"Your brother knew it, did he?"

Duncan's face filled the screen. He looked handsome (and

all the rest) but also wise, his wife thought. "Somehow, and we do not know how—during the night he must have learned something. He came here with what he said was an urgent message for the King. Now, this Colonel Gorob—"

"But *will* he talk, your brother?"

"When, Mr. Tyler?"

"Is he going to be O.K., Mr. Tyler?"

"Where is he? Is he in the hospital?"

Duncan did not answer. It seemed that the King of Alalaf was just now coming outside to make a statement.

In the V.I.P. lounge the boy, the servants, and the women had been sitting quietly, sipping refreshment. In that haven also, Al Asad and his cohorts had been standing—and two Americans (quiet men who had drifted in) and Mitch leaning watchfully nearby, besides. All of them had been listening to Duncan Tyler.

"In the event that you may not understand the American newsmen as well as I do," he had said into the King's teeth, "they jump *fast*." The King's eyes had been opaque.

Duncan had turned to this Colonel Hafsah (or whatever his name was). "Tell His Majesty that if he does not wish the first advices to confuse your people dangerously, it must be made very clear, very quickly, that no *American* planted that bomb."

Both of the King's white hawks had fluttered a little. But no one had replied to this impertinence. (Who was *this* young person to advise a king?)

"If you like," Duncan had said, because time was wasting, "*I'll* go, and do it myself."

The King's eye had then glittered. The one called Hafsah (or something like that) had said, "You have no authority, Mr. Tyler."

Duncan had said, "I have a tongue."

Al Asad had said, in English, "My people would not believe

a statement from you." His thin lips had curved contemptuously.

Duncan had turned and said, "Will you tell His Majesty that *mine will?*" Then he had walked away, sensing that the two eagles (in business suits and horn-rimmed glasses) were stirring, softly.

The King had looked murderous.

But now, here he came.

He spoke in the other language. The camera was on his very lips. His interpreter then translated. The statement made it very clear, to the whole world, that the bomb on the royal plane had, beyond a doubt, been planted there by an enemy of the regime, a man formerly trusted in Alalaf, but now turned traitor and would-be assassin. This Colonel Heinz Gorob had gone into hiding, but American authorities (it had been agreed) would hunt him out for quick extradition. American vigilance had prevented a terrible tragedy. The King and Al Saiph were pleased to be most grateful. His Majesty wished to say that he was arranging for some twenty-eight American professors (whom he had been keeping under his protection for some time) to be flown safely to their homes as soon as the King himself was at his home safely. However, His Majesty hoped that they would return to their positions when certain discordant and dangerous elements had been eliminated from the campus.

In a very short while, the royal party would board the plane. His Majesty wished to say, for himself and for the Prince, his grandson, a gracious farewell to the American people, and to convey his gratitude to Dr. Mitchel Tyler, and, indeed, to the entire Tyler family.

His Majesty was sanguine that, in the future, bonds between the two countries would be strengthened by other such profitable friendships. The Prince was well.

The broadcaster took over. "That, ladies and gentlemen, was the King of Alalaf." But he did not say the whole thing all over again. He took another tack. "Ladies and gentlemen, it was *Rufus* Tyler, son of Judge William Rufus Tyler, and the incomparable Maggie Mitchel, a brother of Dr. Tyler's—it was *Rufus* Tyler who . . ." and so on and so on.

Tamsen said wonderingly, "Rufus is a hero?"

Phillida was standing in the door.

"How is he?" said the Judge quickly.

"Delirious," said Phillida, "or as good as. Sam's there. By the way, where is Lurlene?"

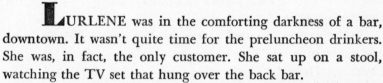

29

LURLENE was in the comforting darkness of a bar, downtown. It wasn't quite time for the preluncheon drinkers. She was, in fact, the only customer. She sat up on a stool, watching the TV set that hung over the back bar.

The local channel was still doing a "live" broadcast from the airport. They had preempted yet another half hour, and this sponsor had given them the go-ahead. So would the next, they hoped. Or, even if not, they weren't going to surrender their luck, to be exclusively on-the-spot and "live." They would stay to see the royal plane off.

But meanwhile, there was nothing much to show on camera. The plane stood there lumpishly, and what feverish activities might be within were not visible. All the interesting V.I.P.'s were now hidden away within the lounge.

So the truck had wheeled around and a newscaster had become the M.C., doing a man-in-the-street kind of interview with the crowd of ordinary people. It was only to mark time, and as uninspired as such things normally were.

There was the wiggly girl who thought everything was real thrilling. But *she* didn't want to be a princess. She was going to be a dental assistant. "Good for you," the M.C. said.

There was the middle-aged housewife who knew exactly how world peace could be achieved. Let everybody, at all times, behave exactly as *she* behaved. This would solve most earthly problems.

There was the humanitarian, infuriated by man's inhumanity. This Colonel Gorob ought to be lynched; the speaker would be glad to tie the hangman's knot himself, in person.

Lurlene sipped up these ideas with her liquor, on the whole, approvingly. But they weren't saying one word about Lurlene's husband. (The people who were being interviewed, not being at home, had not heard the King's statement nor the present legend of Rufus. Neither had Lurlene, who had been in the taxicab.) She was beginning to think that probably he wasn't dead, but probably the family had him, and probably they had tied him up again. A fine thing. . . .

On the screen appeared a man, an ordinary citizen in jeans and plaid shirt, with dark-rimmed eyeglasses, and a gleaming bald head. He said, "I know where this Colonel Gorob is."

"Is that so, sir?" said the man with the mike, politely.

"I sure do. I happened to see him go in there last night."

"I see. You know this Colonel Gorob by sight, do you, sir?"

"Yah," said the interviewee, with a sudden furious snarl, "*I* know him by sight. You don't want to believe that, do you? So I know him by sight because I seen him on TV. How do you like that?"

"I see." The M.C. moved the mike toward somebody else.

But the bald-headed man pushed himself, and his mouth close, again. "You don't want to believe that, right? O.K. But I'm telling you, I see this Gorob go into this old Spanish house—"

"Oh, you did?" smirked the M.C. The crowd was giggling.

"On Mynard Street. Listen, I live down that way. It was kinda late—"

"You saw him in the dark, did you?"

"*Naw*, I didn't see him in the dark. It so happens, he's right under the streetlight, which is right where this house happens—"

"I see. If you know the address—"

"*I* don't know the address."

"I see."

"Whole street is only two blocks long."

"Excuse me. Miss? How do *you* feel . . ."

"You don't want to believe me?" Baldy pushed in again. "When I'm only trying to tell the Goddest truth. But *you're* not going to believe me, are you?"

"I think, sir, that if you have any important information, you ought to take it to the police," the M.C. said, against the warning noises in his earphone.

"Hah! *They're* going to believe me?"

"I'm sorry. Madame? Or is it Miss? How do *you* feel about . . ."

"Listen," howled the bald-headed man. "Look at this fellow Rufus Tyler. *He* was only trying to tell the Goddest truth, and look what they done to *him*. The po-lice!" He spat on the ground.

The M.C. turned all the way around as the picture went back to the studio. Troublemakers in sidewalk interviews had to be handled.

"Hey, that's *right!*" Lurlene burst aloud. "Look at that! *They're* not going to believe him. *They* don't want to listen to somebody trying to tell them the truth. That's *right.*"

"Yeah, maybe he don't know what he's talking," said the bartender. "This Colonel what's-his-name is from this foreign country. How come this character knows what he looks like?"

Lurlene held her forehead in her hand. "Um, boy," she said. "How dumb can you get? He just *said* he saw him on TV. You don't believe him either, do you? Who listens to the truth? Who?"

"You want to believe him, go ahead, be my guest." The bartender smiled placatingly and polished glass.

"I happen to know what this colonel looks like myself," she said. "You believe that? Naw."

"If you say so, I certainly do, ma'am."

"Yah! What do I owe?"

So he told her. He was just as glad she was leaving. Never did like seeing a lone dame up at his bar. Couldn't get used to it; that was a fact.

Lurlene went out and found another taxi. "Listen, you know Mynard Street? Only about two blocks long, right?"

"That's right, lady."

"So take me down them two blocks," Lurlene said, "and maybe I'll tell you where I get off. And maybe I won't."

She was fuming. It shouldn't be for nothing, she was think-ing. No, it shouldn't. They never let him have one chance. They keep him down, all the time. Well, Rufus isn't any liar; that I know. Oh, *they* can lie. But here's this thing and he done it for me. (Lurlene was swimming in her dream.) Here's Ru-fus, he actually tries to shoot the kid. Well, it's the truth, and they got no right to cover it up and Rufus don't want them to cover it up, but they think they can do anything, they think they're so smart. And I don't care what you say, it's not right to tell lies and this colonel, he ought to be glad to know that *he* was right. Sure he was right. He had a hunch, you bet, last night. He was the one said about a woman and a knife. And he was right, because that was Tamsen-baby. But, oh no . . . Well, that's what *they* think. Somebody's got to listen. This colonel should be glad. And spread it around, in ten min-utes! (Lurlene remembered.)

On Mynard Street, the old Spanish house was easy to find. There was only one old Spanish house. Its number was painted on a stone. The stone was under the streetlight. Everything seemed to fit.

Lurlene was feeling frightened as she went up the leaf-arched path. But she summoned up enough righteous indignation to be able to ring. After a few exchanges at the door, somebody spoke from deep inside. Then they let her in.

At the airport the royal party, ceremoniously and at last, boarded the royal plane. The door was closed, the steps were drawn away, the big bug began to crawl. "Ladies and gentlemen, the Little Prince of Alalaf has just . . ."

Duncan said to his brother Mitchel, "Come on. I'll drive you."

The newsmen swarmed after them to Duncan's car.

"You going to the hospital, Doctor?"

"He's there, is he?"

Duncan said, "Look, friends, it's been a rough morning. How about giving us some breathing time?"

"Yes, but where's Rufus?"

"We want Rufus."

"He talking yet?"

"What?" "Why?" "Where?"

Mitch said, "Rufus is at my father's house. We are going there now."

Mitch said to Duncan's eyebrow as they moved away and the pack raced for transportation, "You dreaming they wouldn't find out where he is?"

Duncan said, "I *hope* he's there."

Rufus was there. But Lurlene was not.

Almost as soon as they had entered the house to receive this blow, the house was besieged. The Judge finally went outside and said a few words.

His son Rufus was here, yes, but in collapse. Not physically injured, no, but in a state of emotional collapse. He was not yet coherent. The family did not know his story. They might not know it for some time to come. Would the press please have the goodness to allow a very ill man and his worried family some respite?

"Listen, Judge Tyler?"

"Judge Tyler?"

"Why did Rufus show up at this police station, sir?"

"Why was he talking to the cops around midnight?"

"Judge? What did he mean, a big important crime?"

"I am very sorry," said the Judge. "I cannot tell you anything. I don't know what to tell you."

This, at least, was the bare truth, he thought, as, amid protests, he went back into his house having done (he feared) no particular good.

The family was gathered in the lanai. Except for Rufus, who was upstairs with the burly male nurse Mitch had called in to attend to him. Except for Lurlene, who was God knew where, saying God knew what to whom.

When the Judge came in, feeling futile, Maggie said at once, "Never mind, William."

Tamsen said, "Saiph is all right. They'll get him home safe, won't they?"

Duncan said gloomily, "There *is* that."

The Judge had heard this said before. When he had told the right people the right things, one of them had said, "There *is* that." And so there was. The Judge sat down.

Mitchel said, "Well, the hell with them out there. I'm running the gantlet and going back to work."

Phillida said, "Work, for the night is coming." Her eyes shone, as if with tears.

But Mitch shrugged, saying you never knew. He kissed his wife, and then his mother, and left to push ruthlessly through and escape.

The Judge said, to encourage the others, "With the King's statement and Saiph coming home, I suppose all is well enough in Alalaf. There *is* that."

"It's just us Tylers, then?" said Tamsen.

"That's who it is, honey," Duncan said. "If we try to say that Lurlene is *also* off her nut, that won't wash, I'm afraid."

"What could she do?"

"She can tell the truth," the Judge said.

"She can tell it," said Maggie dreamily.

The Judge gave her a very suspicious look. Maggie, who had come downstairs as from a bier, had sat among them, the most detached and calm. Maggie, who mourned Rufus as if he had died (and properly so, the Judge agreed), had seemed held in the peace of that finality. But now she had a sphinx-look on.

Colonel Gorob was in conference with two of his new masters. They had all listened to what this Mrs. Lurlene Tyler had to say. They had all thanked her courteously. Now she was being given refreshment in another room.

"Do you believe her story, Gorob?" said the thin one.

"It may very well be true," the Colonel said stiffly, noticing the absence of his title and rank.

"Really of no moment whether it is true," said the fat one. "We can't afford to have it told."

"No?" The Colonel was somewhat surprised. "It seems to be the very story I had wind of last night. With an improvement. An American attempt to assassinate the Prince. Surely, this is useful."

"It will not be believed."

"No?"

"Rufus Tyler is, at present, a great man in the eyes of the populace. He is supposed to have known about the explosive and come in time to 'save' the 'Little Prince.'" The fat one's voice put in the sneering quotation marks. "Now, how can Rufus Tyler be held up as one who tried to assassinate the same child he so nobly saved?"

"He knew nothing," said the Colonel irritably. "It was a freakish misunderstanding."

Failure, however, was failure, whether freakish or no.

"Our people would be accused of inventing a completely silly falsehood," said the fat one. "Not clever at all. Against a Tyler?

That respected family? No, no. It could weaken our propaganda machine. We would look like fools. Wiser to keep her quiet."

"I agree," said the thin one. "I saw that at once. But she obviously came here for the very purpose of getting publicity for her story. How can she be convinced to keep quiet? Now that she has been here, and met us, in the bargain?"

"The safe way, then," said the fat one. "No use arousing any more inquiry than is unavoidable."

"It has been laid on, just in case," the thin one said smugly. "Speaking of inquiry, Gorob, are you aware that we must abandon this house because of you?"

"No. No."

"You were seen entering last night. You were recognized."

"I doubt that." The Colonel bridled.

"You know that. The woman heard it stated to the public. That is how she came here."

"Why did we not hear it?" But the Colonel knew the answer to this. Those sidewalk interviews had seemed useless, boring, time-wasting and unimportant. His masters had turned the broadcast off, to discuss and assimilate the news of failure.

"Quite enough, of course, that it was stated," the fat one said. "The Americans will be around to 'check it out,' as they like to say." (Gorob began to feel time pressing.) "We shall be leaving within the quarter hour."

"I see." The Colonel did not ask his next question aloud. He wondered it. "Am I?" he wondered.

They did not say whether *he* was. He didn't trust them.

Lurlene, in another room, thought they were certainly being very nice to *her*, around here, for a change. The woman had respectfully brought her a cup of tea and some little cakes. And now the woman said to her, "If you would care to come and wash, madame?"

"Say, thank you very much," said Lurlene archly, getting out of her chair. The cakes *had* been a little sticky. In any event, Lurlene wanted to do what was proper and expected of a great tragic figure. Say, maybe they knew she was going to be on TV pretty soon. She thought these people were certainly thoughtful. The woman actually bowed before she turned to lead the way.

The bathroom looked pretty fancy, for an old place like this. Then Lurlene noticed that the tub was half full of water. Was she supposed to take a *bath*, for heaven's sakes? She looked a second time. "That water don't look clean to me," she said. It certainly looked kind of funny, kind of brownish-greenish, and there was stuff floating in it, too. Lurlene bent and put her fingers into the water. "Hey," she said, "this is ice cold! Listen, *I* don't get the big—"

The woman had a hard hand at the back of her neck. Two men were there, suddenly. Lurlene got the big idea in a few seconds, as her face went into the sea water. For all her threshing, it stayed there, long enough.

Therefore, at eight o'clock that evening, the Tyler house was besieged more violently than ever.

Just at dusk, Lurlene Tyler's fully clad body had been fished out of the ocean. Mitch had rushed to where she had been taken. The cause of death was drowning. In sea water. No sign of foul play. Suicide?

But why? Why? Why?

30

THE whole house had recoiled upon itself. All draperies had been drawn. Sam, having snipped the wires to the doorbells, was stationed in the front hall. Hilde was near the back door. The family was in the lanai.

Duncan was pacing. "We've got to give them a story. There has to be at least a theory. The one thing the human race can't stand is an absolute mystery. They'll hunt and they'll pry and they'll guess. Consider how many mysteries we have, here. Nobody knows what got into Lurlene. Nobody knows what Rufus intended to do at the airport."

"Except that he didn't go there to tell about a bomb," said Phillida, "although they have that theory."

"All right." Duncan stood corrected and went on. "But we can't go out there with the true story, and even if we thought we should, the fact is, we don't know it. Nobody knows where Rufus was all night. Not a one of us knows whatever got into him, that he tried to shoot the Prince of Alalaf in the first place. There *was* no reasonable reason. Which is pretty intolerable."

"He had an unreasonable reason, I suppose," said Tamsen, in pain.

But Duncan kept thinking of that piece of paper, on which Lieutenant Dennison had made his "rough" notes. "We'll have to incorporate what *is* known," he said, "into some kind of story. They're human. They've got television cameras out there."

The Judge, who had done his private duty long ago, and told all of the truth he knew—to people who needed to know it, but who would not, for reasons, tell it everywhere—was feeling the peace of the acceptance of the finality of death. He couldn't, in the moment, rouse himself to Duncan's anxiety. To life's fitful fever, he thought dreamily.

He said, "I don't think I can cope, Duncan. I don't think I am the one to go out there and tell them a story."

Phillida said, "I don't think I am, either. I would be willing, but I'm not the kind who could."

Tamsen chirped up. "If somebody would help me, with what to say . . ."

"No, no," said Duncan, but with appreciation. "You haven't the gift, honey. Or the authority. I suppose, after all, this is up to Maggie."

"Yes," said Maggie. "Yes, I know." She said to the Judge, as if he had asked her, "I'm all right." Then she looked at Duncan. "You did very well. You may come, too."

"We can share it off, maybe?" said Duncan. "*I* can wind in and out of what's known about Rufus."

"I'll speak of Lurlene, then." Maggie nodded sharply. "All right? It is a mistake to rehearse too much when you are basically going to wing it."

"Is there a theme?" Duncan asked keenly.

"The theme is tragedy," said Maggie in a low voice. "For this family." She turned up her plain face. "God knows, but there may be more than one kind of truth."

"Amen," said the Judge, rousing himself after all. "And I'll come too. No, I won't speak. I may need to know what you say." The Judge had realized that the peaceful contemplation of finality was not for him—not for a while yet.

Duncan went out alone to make the arrangements. They wanted a television interview. It would be on the portico. Duncan bore himself soberly, waiting out the preparations, the lights, camera, the set made ready. The decision was that all questions would come from off camera. For their picture, they had a star.

But all the theatricality seemed to have been knocked out of the incomparable Maggie Mitchel by what had happened, in real life, to her own children. She was just a woman, a sad and stricken woman, trying not to let her bewildered sorrow be a nuisance, the way any decent woman would try. Bearing up, not going to make a big scene, speaking somewhat monotonously, and faltering sometimes.

Lurlene had not been feeling well at all last night, she told the world through the relentless lens and sound track. "So we put her to bed and kept her overnight. Then, this morning, we were all . . . well . . . upset by all that was happening. Lurlene seemed to be feeling better . . . I mean . . . in her health. She did cry. I recall that, now. I thought it was nerves."

"When did she leave, Miss Mitchel? I mean, Mrs. Tyler?" Tragedy deserved hushed questions.

"About the middle of the morning, I think it was. She said she wanted to go home. I didn't understand at all. I thought she just wanted to go home, that's all. It might have been something to do with my son's leaving here last night—and not coming back at all."

"How is *he*, Mrs. Tyler?"

"He is not well at all."

(The Judge thought, Bad lines! No playwright on earth would have written this dreadful sequence of repetitive "all" sounds! Well, she is still incomparable.)

Duncan cleared his throat, touched his mother's arm, and took over. "The fact is, my brother . . ."

Maggie didn't use her handkerchief. She didn't smile. She didn't cry. She just stood numbly, in the shelter of her husband's concern for her, as any stricken woman would.

"I'm afraid my brother is having a serious breakdown," Duncan said.

"Has he told anything yet?"

"What happened last night, Mr. Tyler?"

"How did he find out about the bomb?"

"We have been trying, of course, to piece it together." Duncan was using a lecturer's manner, sounding a little wordy and stuffy. "We do know that when he left here last evening, this Colonel Gorob also left, at the very same time. Now, I had better say that this is theory, at best. However, we do get the impression that my brother was . . . or may have been . . . picked up by those people. It is possible that he may have been given drugs of some kind. They may have been trying to find out, from him, some things they wanted to know. Such as the security arrangements for Prince Saiph. But we believe that if anything of this kind did happen, he must have got away from them at some time during the night."

At this point, the flow of his much qualified "statement" was broken by a question.

"What about your brother's arrival at a police station, around twelve o'clock?"

"Yes. Yes, that is what I mean." Duncan congratulated the bright pupil. "He did go to that police station, as you know. Now, I myself went there as soon as Lieutenant Dennison called this house, in a very understanding way, I might add."

Duncan was feeding them a wild yarn in as long-winded and boring a manner as he could. "By the time I arrived, he had slipped away, and this, I might add, was no one's fault, really. Why he left there, as he did, we do not know. Whether he feared that those same people were on his . . . er . . . trail again." Duncan apologized for a gaudy word, "Of course, they may have been, for all we know."

Duncan had the stage, although they had kept Maggie in the picture. She was helping by giving him a stillness of attention. But his listeners were becoming restless.

"Yes, but, Mr. Tyler, what *is* your brother's story?"

"He tried at that time, as you may know," said Duncan,

"to give the police his story. Obviously, he knew by then that there was a plan. That a crime was to be committed. A 'big important crime.' He said as much."

Duncan intended to go down the notes that existed on a piece of paper in that police station. The "rough" notes. He was going to rough them up some more. Several of his listeners were taking notes right now.

"That would be the bomb on the plane, you think, Mr. Tyler?"

"That would be it, presumably. My brother seems to have tried to tell them that the boy was to be killed. But he was very difficult to understand. He still is. He does say 'shots.' Lieutenant Dennison was shrewd enough to surmise that he may have been drugged. You see, if they had given him shots of some kind, and perhaps had overdone the dosage, that would possibly account for his having been so rambling and incoherent."

Duncan stopped and bit his lip. "There has evidently been damage," he said flatly, "to his speech centers."

"You mean he can't talk *yet?*"

"He tries very hard," said Duncan, looking suddenly younger. "Oh, yes, he does keep saying that someone 'wouldn't let him go.' So that seems to indicate that he was imprisoned somewhere for some period of time."

(Duncan thought he was sounding like a perfect ass. All right.)

"Where did he go, though, when he left the police station?"

"We do not know, in full detail. The police were looking out for his car during the night, but they had no luck. It is our theory that since he must have known what was planned for the royal plane, when he realized that he could not speak clearly enough, he could not put his words together in such a way as to make himself understood, he felt he simply had to stop the thing anyway. So he must have gone as directly as he could to the airport. His car *was* found there, finally."

"That's right." Another piece clicked in.

"He must have known the time for departure. After all, it was on the air. We hear that he was seen—or was thought to have been the man who was seen—in the coffee shop there, very early this morning. We suppose that he was trying to pull himself into condition, into some shape to be able to talk, to tell somebody 'before it was too late.' In fact, he said *that* to the gate man."

Duncan was speaking more vigorously now. He put on a proud look. "As a matter of fact, he *had* pulled himself together, to the point that when he came to that gate he *did* speak rather clearly."

"So then they had to go and knock him out, right?"

"Yes, they did. However, you must see their point of view. Those men—the man who hit my brother, for instance—can't be blamed for doing what was done. My brother looked . . . well . . . very much disheveled after the kind of night he must have had, and he *was* running, as you know, toward the royal party. It was the duty of those men not to let anyone near the Little Prince." Duncan was being terribly "fair."

"Too damn bad, though," somebody said.

"Well, it worked out," Duncan said, "for Al Saiph. I think that's all, really, that we can possibly say until we know more."

"I'd like to ask you . . ." said one of the interviewers. "Mrs. Tyler?"

"Minute," said somebody. The camera wanted more of Maggie, and closer up, if there was going to be any more of her.

"Mrs. Tyler?"

"Yes?"

"Do you think there is a connection between what happened to your son Rufus, and what happened to his wife?"

"There may be," said Maggie sadly.

"Mother," said Duncan (who never called her "mother" in real life). "Don't you think that's enough?"

247   *

"No," said Maggie. "No, it isn't. *I* want to say"—Maggie had drawn herself up—"that I have tried, as hard as I can, to understand how poor Lurlene could have taken her own life. But I knew her." Maggie began to shine with the look of reckless honesty. "And I don't believe she did that! I knew her *very* well, and I don't believe it was in her character. I don't think it's possible that Lurlene could have done such a thing. I don't believe it!"

Duncan stepped quickly between her and the camera's eye. "Take her inside, Dad?"

So the Judge took Maggie gently inside, while behind Duncan there was some protest, much murmuring, and a few cries of "Thanks." "Thanks very much."

When he turned around they had stopped taking pictures. They had had their "dramatic highlight." Duncan, alone, waited out the brief final barrage.

"Lurlene didn't leave any note, did she, Mr. Tyler?"

"Said she was going home, eh?"

"Same clothing as when she was found?"

"Didn't live too near the beach, did they?"

"No, they did not," said Duncan, answering the last one. "Will you excuse me now, please? At least the Little Prince is safe, and we can all be very glad of that." He put on a pained smile, but they hadn't waited for his final asininity. They were leaving him.

He left them, and went in.

Within the shrouded house, the Judge was already on his telephone. Duncan went back to the lanai, feeling so deep a depression that he could hardly wade through an account of his part of the interview. Phillida said she wouldn't bother to remember the ins-and-outs of it all; she intended to take up the position of refusing, as usual, to discuss her husband's patients.

"Do, dear," said Maggie wearily.

Tamsen said, "What you told them was only supposed to be

guessing." She was weary and in pain, but she wanted to be helpful to somebody. "So it wasn't really—"

"Lying?" Duncan pounced. "Oh, yes, it was. Even the guesses were lies. They left Rufus our hero, didn't you notice?"

Then he was ashamed to have indulged himself. He said to his mother, "Mitch will take care . . . of taking care of Rufus now, won't he, Maggie?"

The Judge came hurrying. He had news.

The dead body of Colonel Gorob had just been found in an otherwise deserted old Spanish house on Mynard Street. The informant said that the house had been under surveillance all afternoon, until the time had come when it had seemed . . . well . . . rather dead. There were indications that the Colonel, who may even have been the aggressor, had fought hard for his life. Some vanished tenants were suspect and wanted, and furthermore, guessed to be of a dubious political character.

"I guess that takes *us* off the hook for a while anyhow," said Duncan, rubbing his head with hard hands, because it had been a rough day and he couldn't shake off his depression, "Gorob won't be talking. You realize? Now that 'they' have killed Gorob, there is going to be a big fat theory, marching with my lovely guesses, that 'they' also murdered Lurlene. You wait and see."

The Judge said, "I wonder how they ever got hold of her, poor girl." His lips were shaking.

Duncan found himself much startled. "Do you mean . . . ? Maggie really did guess . . . ?"

His mother said tartly, "I wasn't guessing. And for once, I wasn't acting, either. Did you think I was putting on some sentimental loyal vote of confidence because Lurlene had been a member of this sacred family? No, no, no. To drown oneself . . . that takes some resolute despair. It wasn't in her character to do any such thing. One minute's honest thought and all of you—" She broke away from her nervous anger. "I'm sorry. I'm sorry. I'm sorry. For both, and all, and everything."

249　　✳

The Judge sat down beside her with a sigh. What amount of honest thought, he wondered, can explain the absolute mystery of Rufus?

Duncan said it, heavily: "Will we ever understand? Will we ever guess what got into Rufus?"

Phillida said brittlely, "Maybe we ought to run people through an every-six-months checkup for emotional health. They check out automobiles for public safety." She seemed on the verge of tears.

Tamsen said, "But *he* had . . . He was the one who must have had some kind of resolute despair." (Yes, she thought, he did try to destroy himself—within that act of senseless destruction. He tried.) "But he failed?" she asked, wonderingly.

The Judge didn't want this kind of talk.

"We didn't understand, we don't now; and I doubt we will, in the course of this evening," he said severely.

"But oh, I wish . . ." Tamsen began.

Duncan found that he didn't want any heart to bleed, out loud. "Come on, Tamsen," he said. "Let's go home."

Phillida said, in her normal fashion, "With quite a load of secrets, eh? Don't worry. We'll manage. I'm going, too. I've got a few kids to look in on."

"Do, dear," said Maggie.

So Phillida went away.

But Tamsen said, "I don't want to leave them alone. If there's anything . . ."

"Show a little respect," said Duncan grimly.

When they were gone, Maggie said, "Secrets?"

"Hush, Maggie darling."

31

ON the royal plane, as it sped homeward, the boy was
huddled to his secret pain, and Inga, who shared this secret,
fetched him some water for the taking of pills. No thought of
the U. S. A., behind them, was present in either of their minds.
They had a performance coming up. The pilot had just informed his passengers that the home airport was already swarming with people in a mood for turbulent welcome and rejoicing.

The pilot had also relayed a message from Alice Foster to
the Princess. "Love and cheers, from all."

The Princess, sitting alone, knew that "all" meant Dhanab,
who was with her mother because that male creature had
needed to be within the aura of Jaylia. This was a secret. She
thought she would marry Dhanab soon, now. It wouldn't be
a bad match. Aljedi had been the dashing one, the one with the
verve and the charm. But two people with verve and charm, in
one marriage, had been a bit much. Dhanab was a man of less
force, but not stupid, reasonably attractive. He was the natural
regent (religiously sound) if the old King should die. Jaylia,
who had once expected to be a queen, saw no reason why she
should not be one, at least in fact, until her son grew up. Dhanab could be ruled. The Princess smiled to herself. She had her
methods.

The old King, riding in his private compartment, looked

down at clouds. He had lived a long time. His secret may have been that he knew all these secrets, and many more besides. If so, such was his destiny.

Duncan Tyler, driving Tamsen home, was thinking about secrets. Individual human dignity, he decided, required the keeping of some. He had, for instance, told one of his own, and now wished he had not. Times change, and the truth now was that he felt enormously relieved to be rid of the Princess—as well as of the Prince, the King and the whole shebang. Why should a human, competent to learn, put obstacles in his own path by bleating forth his current foolishness? Let him, from time to time, suspect himself of unwisdom.

"Were we wrong?" said Tamsen, who was sitting in a forward lean, looking very tense and miserable. "Because Rufus needed what he thought was prominence, should we have just let ourselves be destroyed?"

"Well, we didn't." Duncan had been thinking of something else, in order not to think of this. But it cost us, he thought, now. And something is wrong, somewhere. (Oh, my brother.)

Tamsen looked at him. She had reminded him of his sorrow and she was sorry. Now, must she make him sorry for her sorrow to have . . . No, no, no. There she went, into foxiness, a spiral of guilt and part-time vanity, not necessarily kind. Tamsen had a new secret. She would have shot a man to death. She wasn't going to discuss this not-in-the-least theoretical limit to her code of ever-be-kind. She was going to have to think the whole thing over.

Phillida Tyler did not take a freeway but crept home through surface streets, driving hesitantly and rather ineptly. She made it to the garage, went up in the elevator with trembling thanksgiving. When she came into her own place, she sat down to sigh, alone. She had been living in the weakness of near-panic for some time. But she had *behaved* well. So, not having been turned aside from anything she had been required to do, she could keep her humiliating secret.

Dr. Mitchel Tyler sat in the hospital canteen. He was in the business of keeping secrets, all day long.

A Dr. Boyer now sat down beside him. "Say, you've certainly hit the headlines, Doctor."

Mitch grunted.

"Sorry to hear about your sister-in-law."

"Yes."

"Despondent for long, was she?" This seemed sly.

Mitch shrugged. The other doctor seemed to be a rumor or two behind.

"There's always the good old ethical question, isn't there? Should the family be told?"

Mitch looked sideways at him. Told what? Lurlene had been drowned. That was the verdict and it was correct.

"You know, I dreamed up this . . . well, pretty convincing motive for suicide the other day," said Dr. Boyer. "Hypothetically, that is."

"That so?"

"Suppose there is some poor dumb woman. Childless, let's say for a lot of years. Suppose one day she says to her husband, 'Hooray, I'm pregnant!' But she happens to say this just about the time he's been trotting to some fella, like me, for tests, at last. And he's just found out that he is sterile, always was, and always will be. Terrible timing, wouldn't it be? Poor woman."

"Poor man," said Mitch calmly. "Hypothetically, that is."

"Right," said the other doctor amiably. "Say, what does the word 'ironical' mean?"

Mitch let out a short laugh. "Look it up," he advised, and he left.

So Rufus had a secret? Had had. God knew what he had left, now. The Doctor, trained to cut his losses, cut them (with a pang). Lurlene hadn't been pregnant. She had been, no doubt, virtuous, although probably murdered. Still, poor man. Poor brother.

In the west guest room, upstairs, the male nurse was feeding his charge. "Open. Open. That's the boy."

But Rufus kept letting the soft food dribble out of his mouth. He was gazing up at the nurse with melting eyes, begging for pity. "Can't."

"Sure, you can. Sure, you can," the nurse said in a comforting croon. "Come on, just a couple more swallows. Then we'll tuck you in. O.K.?"

The nurse was thinking, Oh, oh, this one's sure regressed, and how! Still, he felt sorry for the poor fellow. "That's a good boy," he said, out of the kindness of his heart.

The swimming eyes shot a second's worth of life. Don't kid me, they said. But then they began to beg again. Am I a good boy? Tell me again. I will stay here, just like this, if you will tell me again. *I am? I?*

Down in the lanai, Maggie had put her head over against the Judge. "I act. That's what I was born to do. But oh, William, I am so . . ."

"Hush. Hush."

"No. Let me spit the taste out of my mouth, for now. Just now."

The Judge waited helplessly.

"Oh, William, we said that we would be fair." She was not weeping aloud, but her voice keened, as might have been effective in a theatre. He understood. She couldn't help that. "We said that we would tell them all, all three, that they were adopted children. Chosen Ones."

"We were as fair as we knew how to be," he said, "and they were all legally adopted children."

"And we said that they were, nevertheless, truly our children, and we would not say different to the world." The melody rose and fell.

"Yes, and we have not." The Judge could only stay beside her, wherever she was going.

"But Mitchel," said Maggie, "and oh, let me speak these truths, for now. Just now. Mitchel was not born my son, although he is yours, flesh and bone."

The Judge winced a little. Mitch's mother had been . . . well . . . a girl. (Oh, young days, white with joy, black with agony! Very little compromise. But one grows gray.) This excursion of his mind suddenly amused him and thus restored him.

"And Duncan, God bless him," Maggie was continuing, "was neither of ours. The only Chosen One."

"Yes, darling. Humanly speaking." The Judge was on balance, now.

"And Rufus," she mourned, "never yours, was truly born of my body, in secret, before we ever met."

(And some things are told without telling, and although Rufus had not known that he knew, if he had nevertheless known. . . . But this, the Judge thought, is, or may be, simply nonsense. What shall a little animal care, except that he is loved and fed? And it was *all three of them* we "chose," and took to love and feed—a little late. Still, he sought to turn his mind, lest she read it.)

"They were all ours," he said stoutly, "and are now."

The somewhat elderly woman lifted her plain face. "More kinds of truth than one? Truly?"

"God knows, as I dare imagine," said the Judge in his calm way, "that all children are our children. None alike, God knows that. But all ours, just the same."

"Just the same," she wailed softly. "All ours. In sickness or in health."

"Yes, Maggie darling." The Judge still heard the mourning

music, but he could tell that she was steadying to turn forward again, and that was as good as could be. All that was possible.

Yet what it is to be fair "just the same" (he thought in his private mind) to all these children—who are none alike—we must soon apply our human wits to discover.